WALKING DEAD

'Do none of these windows open, Doctor?' called the Prime Minister. 'I want to shout at that idle ruffian.'

'They're all sealed, sir. The nearest one which opens is out in the corridor.'

'Stir him up for me, please, Captain.'

Foxe, going towards the group in the logic-room, passed Captain Angiah going in the other direction. The Captain's face had a look like the death-mask of a saint, stiff and drained of all emotion, but still somehow bearing the print of ecstasy. He must have been moving fast, for by the time Foxe was standing beside Dreiser and gazing down at the sleeping gardener, the corridor window was swinging open. Its glass hid the shape behind it, then a fine-boned hand steadied a big pistol on the sill. The snap of the shot was sharp and deep . . .

Also in Arrow by Peter Dickinson

WALKING DEAD

Peter Dickinson

Gainsborough Press

This edition published in 1996
by Gainsborough Press
An imprint of Leopard
20 Vauxhall Bridge Road, London SW1V 2SA

Random Century Group

London Melbourne Sydney Auckland
Johannesburg and agencies throughout
the world

First published in Great Britain in 1977 by
Hodder & Stoughton Ltd
Arrow edition 1990

Printed and bound in Great Britain by
Cox & Wyman Ltd, Reading, Berkshire

ISBN 0 752 90370 5

Prologue

'A very serious piece of work, David,' said the Director. 'Top notch, as you would say.'

'My grandfather might have, sir,' said Foxe.

The Director reached across his desk for a little pad of pink paper with deckled edges and made a note. He spoke eight languages and behaved as though the main function of his staff was to keep his idioms up to date.

'Yes, a remarkable match,' he said, tapping the page of Foxe's report where a blue and a red line wriggled across the graph-paper in rough parallel. 'I needn't ask *you* whether you have, hum, improved your figures to achieve this narrow spread.'

'Well, sir, I've cheated a bit. On my first batch of figures the match was too good to be true. I mean it *was* true, but it just looked too good, so I popped a couple of nutters back in to roughen it up a bit.'

'Nutters?' said the Director, reaching for the pink pad again.

'Eccentrics, sir. Statistical outliers. You always get at least one, even if you've bred the animals yourself, and monkeys are particularly dicey. This lot weren't lab-bred, and I had three. I kept them in the experiment, but normally I'd have left them out of the figuring. It's just that this time they came in handy for making the figures look a little hairier.'

'So in your opinion – your personal opinion – the result is even more clear-cut than it appears in your report?'

'Yes, sir.'

'First rate, David. And all in four months! I'd budgeted for it taking at least until March.'

Foxe shrugged. A little lab time saved, for somebody else to waste. But there was no harm in your personal file containing a note that you weren't extravagant with Company money. Some day when you needed to be extravagant . . .

'You look tired, David.'

Four months trying to keep sixty monkeys under exactly equal conditions of stress. Your girl formally giving you the push and going off to sing *Freischütz* in Copenhagen.

'I do feel a bit beat up, sir.'

'It's because you will do everything for yourself.'

'It's the only way I can work. At least it's the only way I know of getting results as clear as that, sir.'

'I know. I know. Still you've won two months from nowhere. Would you like a few weeks' leave?'

Copenhagen? Don't be a stupid child.

'I don't think so, sir. Wrong time of year. But I wouldn't mind moving on to something where I can use rats for a bit.'

Nodding and smiling the Director took a sheet of paper out of a drawer and pretended to read it, though he'd clearly put it there ready to produce. Foxe swivelled his chair and watched the sleet falling on the steep-pitched roof-tops of Vienna. At least the scene was less bleak than the emptiness of his inner landscape.

'I have a very cosy little posting here,' said the Director. 'Would you care to spend the rest of the winter in the Caribbean?'

'I didn't know we had anything there, sir.'

'Hog's Cay. One of the Southward Islands. It's mainly an industrial plant processing local materials – sugar, bitumen, that sort of thing – to a stage where we can use them in Europe, but there's a small lab attached. I believe it was originally set up to investigate alleged properties of certain local flora, but now we use it, hum, for this and that. Galdi's there, and Kaswal – you've met them?'

'No, sir. Galdi's working on this longevity thing, isn't he?'

'How did you know that, David?'

The Director's tone was conversational, but Foxe guessed he had put a foot wrong. There were areas of secrecy in the Company which it was thought somehow disloyal even to be aware of. He'd better shift ground. Something tickled his memory – some newspaper column which Lisa-Anna had insisted on reading aloud to him – very much her sort of thing, not his.

'Lab rumour, I think, sir. I haven't spread it any further. Isn't the Government of the Southward Islands supposed to be pretty rackety?'

'Rackety? Between these four walls, yes. It was a British colony, but for historical reasons it was less well administered than some of your other possessions. Hum. Currently it is a dictatorship with democratic trimmings. There is a ruling dynasty of people called Trotter. But you needn't worry about any of that, David. All the, hum, unpresentable events occur on Main Island, I believe. The other island, Hog's Cay, is being developed as a tourist resort, so there the authorities are anxious to present a smiling face to the world. They are equally anxious for budgetary reasons that the Company should not close down its plant. You might almost say that we have them eating out of our hat.'

'Hand, sir.'

'Of course. Thank you. You'll go?'

'It sounds OK. What will I be working on?'

The Director looked down at the sheet of paper he had taken from the drawer. He seemed to shrink a little, as though he felt his own authority diminished by what he had to say next.

'I can't tell you the details of your briefing, David. It's all Category Two. The Director on Hog's Cay, a man called Dreiser, will give it to you when you arrive. All it says here is that they want a very good man working with rats to evaluate a substance called GN 117.'

In the hollow of Foxe's mind flickered an ember of interest he'd thought dead, dead with Lisa-Anna's going, dead with sixty dead monkeys. GN 117 was learning-enhancement, or so the lab rumour asserted; but this was another area of secrecy, so he did his best to look blank.

Into the Maze

1

To pass the time while he waited for Dreiser's signal, Foxe studied the view from the laboratory window. Main Beach, white as detergent powder, reached away in a long scimitar curve, as if some fairly simple equation was drawing it towards the axis where water met sky. The line of it divided the blue of the sea from the green of the shore, and all would have been too dazzling to stare at but for the double tinted glass of the lab window. The only real interruptions to the curves of colour were the jagged hiccups made by the new hotels of Front Town, each in its own way a sample of tourist architecture at its larkiest and most ebullient. Foxe could never understand how any of them had got built. In the six weeks he had been on Hog's Cay no progress at all seemed to have been made on the newest one, which remained about four-fifths finished a few hundred yards along the beach. The same web of irregular scaffolding mottled one wall, and the same man in a yellow singlet and blue jeans lay sprawled on the planking near the top of it. He'd only been there for three days, to be fair, but he hadn't moved during that time. Perhaps he was dead, or perhaps just a bundle of bright rags, but most probably he was having a snooze, not unusually long by Island standards.

It took a lot to disturb this pervading lethargy, so it was a proof of the day's importance that Foxe could see a man actually working in the foreground of his view. The laboratory buildings stood on the hummocky promontory that closed off this end of Main Beach, and the ground up here was so irregular that the bed of raw, red earth which this man was raking rose half way to Foxe's own level on

11

the upper floor of the buildings. The gardener's black arms were thin and stringy, his singlet ragged, his hat an irregular plate of woven straw. Presumably he was one of Ladyblossom's sons, so he was unlikely to be more than thirty, but the weary strokes of his rake were those of an old man.

Foxe watched the gardener without much interest until he was distracted by his own reflection, faint and doubled by the double glass, standing like a ghost between him and the whole scene. Curiously, it seemed to belong there. You wouldn't have thought of it as the ghost of a scientist who was briefly on Hog's Cay for a working rest: the reddish, choleric face; the pale eyes, slightly pop; the ginger hair, already sparse at thirty-two; the hulking frame, and flesh which it would have taken a lot of exercise to keep trim; it only needed a hand gripping a bull-whip to complete the picture of colonial power. The doubled ghost might have been that of the heir to some plantation, slaughtered in a brief uprising of maddened workers. For a while Foxe postured and pouted, playing with the mask to distract himself from the void behind it.

Suddenly the scene below became more amusing than the Foxe-ghost and its doppelganger. The gardener had stopped raking and was now thwacking a blue-flowered shrub with his rake. Blue petals snowed to red soil. The gardener stopped thwacking, bent to peer into the bush, then reversed his rake and poked with the handle among the stems. An olive-coloured snake nearly three feet long came out of the bush and flowed rapidly away over the raked earth until the gardener, following it with eager, prancing strides, swung his rake and struck it full-strength just behind the head. The rake-handle snapped. The snake continued to move, but not now in any direction, simply wriggling and squirming where it lay. The gardener, hands on hips, stood watching it but occasionally let his feet fidget into dance-like movements, expressive of excitement and happiness. When it was still he picked it up and raised it to his face.

For a moment it looked as if the snake had come to life again, but then the man's hat fell off and Foxe could see that these new convulsions were caused by his trying to gnaw throught the creature's neck, though he had a perfectly good sheath-knife in his belt. The head jutted from one side of his mouth while he clasped the body with both hands on the other side, gnashing away and pausing only to spit out morsels of flesh. When he had bared the spine he took the snake from his mouth and tugged its head off, then tossed the body into the bush before fetching a canvas satchel from the path and tucking the head away in it. As he strolled back to his work he was laughing like a drunkard.

He put his hat on and picked up the shattered rake. For a half a minute he made scraping movements at the ground with the headless shaft, then dropped to his knees and tried raking with the shaftless head, but soon gave that up, fitted the broken parts of the rake together so that they looked like a whole tool, placed it carefully on the ground, stretched his arms and lay down with his hat covering his face.

The phone bleeped twice and stopped. This was the signal, a typical Dreiser arrangement. Dreiser inhabited a world of plots and below-the-surface secrets. Though the Prime Minister's visit to the laboratory had only been announced yesterday, Dreiser claimed to have known for a fortnight that it was coming. He had muttered something about the improved quality of the phone-taps as evidence. He also hinted that the Prime Minister was coming to check on Galdi's work, because he proposed to be first in line for a longevity pill when it was perfected; but since it was more amusing for a layman to inspect rats nosing through mazes than a computer counting deformed leucocytes, Foxe had better lay on a show. Foxe nomally ran his animals on a rigid time-table – injection, feed, weighing, performance and so on all exactly the same time for each rat every day – and it was a measure of the unsatisfactoriness of his present task that he permitted a

13

hiccup in this routine. He had even altered the apparatus, accepting a couple of strips of one-way mirror which Dreiser had dug up so that the great man could actually see the rats doing their thing, but he'd turned down Dreiser's suggestion that the rats be shampooed.

Yesterday Dreiser had done a timed rehearsal of the visit, so in theory the party would reach Foxe's lab four minutes twenty seconds after the signal. Dreiser wanted work to seem to be in progress when they came, rather than obviously starting for their benefit – this was, after all, a surprise visit – so Foxe put on his lab coat, went next door to the animal room and fetched out Keith and Karen. They should be about half way through when the visitors came, and then Lionel and Ladyblossom could put on a complete performance.

(The rats were all males, to avoid the variations in performance caused by the female oestral cycle, but they were named alphabetically like hurricanes, boys' names for the groups on Drug A and girls' for those on B. Ladyblossom's original name had been Lucy, but the human Ladyblossom – who was married to Charley the caretaker and cleaned the laboratories – had been so outraged at the omission of her name from the list that it had seemed simplest to rechristen the rat. Simplest it had not turned out because the human Ladyblossom next determined that her rat must outperform the others and began to smuggle crushed prawn into its feed – no doubt some local witch had told her it was a stimulant to intelligence – Hog's Cay seemed to be riddled with that sort of thing. It was odd how quickly she'd guessed the purpose of the experiment. Foxe could have kept the animal room locked and done the cleaning himself, which he'd have done in any case if the experiment hadn't turned out to be so dull and unnecessary; but he was supposed to be on Hog's Cay for a rest, so he now fed crushed prawn to all the rats. Next the human Ladyblossom demanded a more normal sex-life for the rat – 'A man ain't a man when he ain't got a woman,' she would say almost every

14

day, peering so intently at Foxe that he sometimes thought she was getting at him about Lisa-Anna, whom she couldn't possibly have heard of. There was an uncanny facet to Ladyblossom – the human Ladyblossom, that is; the rat of that name had been bred for normality, reared for normality, and finally selected from nearly a hundred normal rats because it was more normal than average. Though even that process didn't stop you getting the occasional nutter – Foxe had one this time.)

Of course the visiting party messed up Dreiser's timing; Foxe, irritated enough by the intrusion to mess it up still further, already had Lionel and Ladyblossom in the runs by the time they arrived. The main door opened and a woman's voice, deep and emphatic and unceasing, flowed through the glass-panelled compartments like a wave washing into a peaceful inlet. Dreiser's harsh voice had to rise above it.

'Now, this is Doctor Foxe's zoo.'

Foxe made an unnecessary note, a man too busy to look up even for Prime Ministers.

'Carry on, carry on,' said a third voice, bass and genial. 'You can tell me what you are doing when you reach a suitable point.'

Foxe felt a presence beside him, saw a large reflected mass appear in the plain glass panel between him and the maze-room, but still didn't turn. All the while the woman's voice, thick and guttural, flowed on.

'. . .got to be a Catholic graveyard. You try a Prodesdant graveyard and you get nothing, not if she been the virginest virgin in the Islands. A Catholic virgin best but a Catholic whore better than a Prodesdant virgin. And so you plant your melon pips, only five pips, on this grave you found, and then . . .'

Foxe would have liked to stay watching the rats. Because of the enclosed construction of the mazes he hadn't actually seen them performing until Dreiser had come up with the strips of one-way mirror, and he was finding their behaviour – those unmeasurable tiny changes of move-

15

ment, indecisions, starts and stoppings, twitches and still-nesses – not quite what he'd have guessed; perhaps it was the new mirror above their heads that distracted them; even in the near-dark of the maze it'd be different from the old matt black lid. But the presence compelled him and he turned.

It is always a slight shock for a large man to encounter somebody much bigger than himself; for the moment he becomes a small man, with a small man's feelings.

Doctor Onesiphorus Trotter smiled at Foxe as though posing for one of the thousand posters that ornamented the walls of both Front Town and Back Town – in parts of the latter the shanties seemed papered together with that smile. From them Foxe already knew the yellowish face, the big-muscled cheeks, the sleepy-lidded eyes with their delta of crinkles at the corners, the close-cropped hair and beard, grizzling slightly. He'd heard too that Doctor Trotter was big, but had failed to take in that the man was such a slab. He was not much taller than Foxe, a couple of inches perhaps, but he seemed half again as broad. He was wearing a bright green silk shirt, open at the neck, to display a slice of hairy chest and emphasise a torso that had the massive fitness of a weight-lifter's.

Foxe had winced in preparation for his handshake but the huge grasp turned out to be soft and dry and, quite mysteriously, humorous, as though the hand had a semi-independent life of its own, knew what Foxe's hand had expected and was teasing it, not in a contemptuous fashion but out of the hand's own natural quirk of fun. The Prime Minister smiled his public smile as though unaware of his hand's private doings. Another man stood just beyond him, and over their shoulders Dreiser's scrawny head poked up at a straining angle, as if aware that he ought to be making the introductions but couldn't because he was trapped in the mesh of the woman's monologue. She was still invisible to Foxe.

'Now, this is what I like to see,' said Doctor Trotter, gazing round the five glass compartments and letting his

16

eyes linger on the neat rank of rat-cages in the animal room. 'Order, cleanliness, modern equipment, all functioning. What do you do with your computer during our power failures, Doctor Foxe?'

'The Company installed a back-up system, sir.'

'So I suppose you use it as your main system, with my state electricity as your back-up. Or – no, don't tell me – you have a back-up to your back-up and you don't use my electricity at all.'

He chuckled. Foxe saw Dreiser's face take on a look of a silent movie comic – one of the earnest, deadpan sort – whose trousers have fallen down at a public function. Indecent exposure of intimate Company secrets. Doctor Trotter's voice was like his presence – one was conscious by the very quality of its softness and deepness that it was capable of those famous four-hour harangues to ecstatic, swaying crowds of half-starved Islanders. The woman's voice had something of that staying-power, it seemed; she was now telling Dreiser to water his melon pips with water containing nine drops of the blood of a tree-toad. Doctor Trotter seemed to be able to treat her stream of talk as a sort of thickened silence.

'This rat's taking his time,' he said.

Foxe turned with relief to the runs. Ladyblossom had finished his food and was quietly grooming. Lionel had found his way to the fourth gate and was trying to trigger it as though it were the second.

'Yes, he's out of time,' said Foxe. 'Would you like to see a complete run?'

'Please.'

Foxe went into the maze-room, removed the mirror panels, lifted out Lionel and Ladyblossom and took them to their cages in the animal room. He came back and sprayed the runs, then fetched Michael and Marion and dropped them into the starting boxes, replaced the mirror and came out to the observation area.

'This is the learning-enhancement project, I believe,'

said Doctor Trotter, who had been chatting quietly with the man beside him.

'That's right,' said Foxe, startled.

'How's it going?'

Foxe mumbled. There was no way of catching Dreiser's eye, to see how much he might be expected to reveal. But if the Prime Minister knew about Galdi's work . . .

'Well?' said Doctor Trotter.

'The trouble is I don't yet know how I'm getting on, sir,' said Foxe. 'The Company has supplied me with two substances to compare. I imagine one of them's inert, and the other one may or may not have some effect on learning ability. At a later stage in the experiment I'll send a telex to my co-ordinator who will tell me which is which. The Company likes to play this sort of project very close to its chest. I mean there may be up to thirty people working on aspects of it round the world, none of them having much idea what the rest are up to.'

'Yes, I know your Company is neurotic about security.'

'It isn't just that, sir. You actually get more reliable results this way. For instance, perhaps what I'm doing is a re-run of someone else's work, to check it over. If I know how he's set about it and what his results are, then I may be influenced to produce similar results, consciously or unconsciously. But if I don't know, and I get comparable results, then that's a much better indication of their validity. Of course my briefing from the co-ordinator is carefully framed so that I don't start doing a quite different set of experiments.'

'I see,' said Doctor Trotter a little less genially. 'So what are you doing?'

'Well, sir, you'll see those are identical mazes. We start by letting the rats simply find their way through. We always race the same pairs of rats against each other. This is the M pair, Michael and Marion – that's what the letters on their backs mean. When they've learnt the maze we block it off with gates which they have to find, and when they've learnt that we put simple triggers on the gates so that the rats have to learn to open them. The gates are all connected electrically to the logic room, where there are machines which time every run, so we can compare all the learning-speeds, both for the different drugs and for different doses of each drug. In effect we put in three layers of learning and then test whether the drug has any effect on the ability to retain the earlier layers.'

'And unlearning? That is most important, you know.'

'We're into that, sir. At a later stage I will alter sections of the maze and study the effect.'

Doctor Trotter watched the rest of the run in silence, broken by a few chuckles. The only other sound was the woman's voice chanting what seemed to be some kind of spell, dreary and repetitive, but Foxe found it difficult to concentrate on the rats. Marion seemed to get through the maze pretty fast, but Michael was off form and barely triggered the last gate when the timing-light winked on. Foxe went into the maze-room and fetched them out.

'I expected them to be white,' said Doctor Trotter.

Foxe slid Marion into his pocket and held Michael up for inspection, a handsome hundred-day rat, glossy with well-being, white but patched black over his head and along one haunch and the opposite foreleg. The nude tail dangled, looking vulnerable and ridiculous, like an attempted obscenity which has somehow got misdirected and become an absurdity instead. Foxe enjoyed the excuse to handle a rat more than he should. It was a nonsense experiment anyway.

'Some people do work with albinos,' he said. 'But the Company has its own strain of these hooded rats – they're a little less biddable than albinos, but a lot hardier. You weren't in very good form this morning, were you, mate?'

'I see you let him have his reward,' said Doctor Trotter. 'He barely deserves it after taking so long.'

'You have to reward them, sir. They need the stimulus to learn.'

'Stimulus is not only by reward, doctor. Will you race us another pair? Mother, come and look at this.'

Foxe would have liked to refuse. He could have said, with perfect truth, that he only injected three pairs of rats in a batch so that he could be sure of running them a precise time after their injections, thus eliminating one minor variable. Nor could he run uninjected rats, because each run was a learning process and a pair that had had an extra run would cease to be comparable with the rest. Foxe's reputation, his value to the Company, was built on considerations such as these, but the Prime Minister's presence was a variable of a different order. As he sprayed the runs he was aware of the woman's voice drifting nearer.

'. . . and long as that melon-flower stay in that woman's maddress,' she was croaking, 'her man got nothing to give her. He try all night, but no fun for that woman. What that stink?'

'I have to spray the runs, ma'am,' said Foxe without looking up. 'Rats have a very keen sense of smell, and I need to be sure that they aren't finding their way through the run by following a trail of scent left by other rats. This stuff does the trick.'

'How can you be sure?' said Doctor Trotter. 'You are not a rat.'

Still spraying, Foxe explained how the tests had been done.

'Good,' said the woman. 'I take that can when we go.'

'Now, mother,' said Doctor Trotter. 'You can't possibly need . . .'

'Visitors do come to this earth,' she said in a sombre voice. 'Hunting with their noses. Smelling for a man in the no-moon dark.'

Doctor Trotter laughed indulgently.

'If you've got a spare can, Doctor Foxe . . .'

'Of course, sir.'

Foxe put the can down and fetched Quentin and Queenie. It didn't really matter giving them an extra run, because even this early he knew he'd be leaving Quentin out of his final figuring. Bred from the same small gene-pool as every other rat in the cages, showing no sign of aberrance during Foxe's selection tests, Quentin had quickly developed into a classic nutter. Foxe put him and Queenie into the starting boxes and walked up to the other end of the run to refill the reward dishes.

'What you give them?' called Mrs Trotter through the door. 'I tell you what. You want indelligent kids, what you give them? I want a boy get to be Prime Minister one day, what I give him? I give him crushed prawns!'

She had abandoned Dreiser to shout at Foxe, who as he came out of the maze-room looked at her properly for the first time. She was a short woman, but proportionately even broader than her son, and wore a pink satin jacket and yellow satin trousers. Her hair was dyed deep amber and stood out in a crimped fuzz all round her flat, grey-yellowish face. Her eyes were hidden behind polarised dark glasses in which Foxe could see his reflection, double, tiny.

'Yes, they all get crushed prawn, ma'am,' he said.

Doctor Trotter's laugh was like gunfire.

'Don't I keep telling you that all science is one, Mother?' he said.

Mrs Trotter was watching Foxe, her head cocked a little to one side. Dreiser too was staring at him, in plain bewilderment which cleared to a small smile – presumably he'd decided that Foxe had told a politic fib. Doctor Trotter continued to chuckle while Foxe gave the rats a few seconds to settle before he opened the starting gates. They came out of the traps with that characteristic and strangely pleasing scuttle which makes it look as if their motive power were a blob of mercury, ears half-pricked, noses inquisitive and eager.

'What that mark?' snapped Mrs Trotter. 'Why he got the mark?'

'You're seeing it the wrong way up, Mother,' said Doctor Trotter in an odd voice, both soothing and teasing. 'It's only a big Q, upside down. Look, the other one's got a small q.'

21

She grunted, unsatisfied. The rats made no mistake in the first section, Quentin reaching the gate a couple of seconds before Queenie. But Quentin made a muddle over the trigger and Queenie was half way along the second section before he got it right.

'This section's the mirror image of the previous one,' said Foxe. 'They've got to take the left fork this time. Look, Queenie's got it wrong. No . . . he's remembered. Now he'll back out. Quentin's got it wrong too . . .'

Foxe was mildly interested in Quentin's behaviour, apart from the rat's status in the experiment. Normally he was careful not to get even distantly involved with any particular animal, partly because his own attention might marginally affect the rat's behaviour, and partly because he preferred not to finish an experiment mashing up the brains of an animal he had, so to speak, known personally. But sometimes the relationship grew, unwilled.

Quentin paused, his nose twitching at the blank side-wall of the run as though he expected to find a gate there. He lost interest and leaned against the wall like a bum on a street corner. Foxe knew quite well that Quentin was only making room to scratch an ear with a hind leg, but the effect was exactly as if he had yawned, shrugged and lit a battered fag-end.

'You have a subversive there,' said Doctor Trotter.

He was joking, of course, but from his tone it was a joke on a serious subject, like a priest's mild blasphemies. Foxe's eye was caught by a movement from beyond Mrs Trotter – the brown, long-fingered hand of the man who had so far been no more than a vague presence, sliding up a khaki-trousered thigh to caress the butt of a big pistol that dangled there in a leather holster. Foxe looked back at the runs. Queenie had reached and passed the second gate and was well on his way to the third, but somehow Quentin occupied the attention as he backed lethargically to a turning-space.

'No-good rad,' said Mrs Trotter.

'You feel like a God?' said Doctor Trotter. 'I do not

speak of the Lord Almighty, just in literary terms. A God above Troy, watching the heroes scuttle round the walls. What if we are only rats, and somewhere above us there is a scientist, timing us and taking notes?'

'If there's a God like that he's running a very messy experiment,' said Foxe.

'You think you could teach him something, Doctor? No, it's in the nature of the experiment. Man is a messy animal. And you know what that God is looking for? Not intelligence, my friend – oh, no. He is looking for virtue. Have you considered developing a drug which would make men good?'

'Good?'

'Good.'

Foxe decided to back-out.

'I'm not on the development side, sir. My job is controlling and interpreting the behaviour of animals.'

'So is mine. Let us consider this problem.'

'Besides, how are you going to measure goodness?'

Again the Prime Minister's big laugh blanketed the laboratory, but this time not in pure good humour. There was an undertone of roaring.

'How would *you* measure goodness, Captain Angiah?' he said.

The man with the gun moved so that he could look directly at Foxe. He was as tall as Doctor Trotter, but no more than ordinarily broad. He might have been almost startlingly handsome – his face was narrow and fine-boned, his skin a very clear brown, but his nose ended at a curious angle, displaying large black nostrils.

'I begin with crime statistics,' he said. 'We have enough of those.'

'Well, Doctor Foxe?'

'I don't know . . .'

Foxe found it difficult not to show that he found the whole question boring. They waited for him, all staring, ignoring the rat-runs. He remembered an incident that might inject a bit of practicality into all this muzzy guff.

23

·'I mean, what makes a good rat?' he said. 'For instance, a couple of years ago I was evaluating a stuff called SG 19. I'd pretty well finished the experimental part when I got called away for a fortnight. I don't normally use assistants, but I left my rats in charge of an experienced girl, but she got hurt in a road accident and somebody quite inexperienced took over. It was just a matter of feeding and cleaning, but for some reason he put my rats, which I'd left in separate boxes like these, into two larger communal cages. It was quite a normal thing to do, as a matter of fact. Unfortunately the cages he chose weren't big enough. Now, rats are semi-social animals in the wild state. They don't live in organised packs, but they like a bit of company and get on pretty well – just the odd nip to establish the hierarchy. But at a certain point of over-crowding – there's a lot of work been done on this, and the sequence is well known – they suddenly manifest stress symptoms of an extreme form, including murder and cannibalism. Well, I got back to the lab at this point, and I found that the control group, which hadn't been having SG 19, were already well into their stress behaviour. Their cage was a real mess, blood and fur and excreta everywhere, and a third of them dead. But the other group – well, they were quite a mess too, but they hadn't been going for each other in the same way. They were mostly still alive, and the dead ones seemed to have suffocated or had heart-failures . . .'

'Your SG 19 made those rats good?'

'No, sir. I mean it was one possible cause of their behaviour, but this wasn't a controlled experiment. I can think of half a dozen other possible causes. But suppose it had been the SG 19, was the failure to demonstrate the normal range of stress symptoms an indication of what you call "goodness"?'

'Certainly. Certainly.'

'But it was unnatural behaviour, surely.'

'My dear Doctor, all virtue, I say all virtue, consists in the suppression of some natural instinct. It is the nature of man to lie, to steal, to murder. Virtue consists in the

24

suppression of such instincts, as Captain Angiah will tell you.'

The Captain's long, puritanical face nodded, unsmiling. Foxe guessed that the Prime Minister had chosen his bodyguard partly for his look of refined self-denial. They made a good contrast, at least.

'But presumably, sir,' Foxe said, 'stress behaviour has a function. It's a reaction to circumstances in which the population can't survive without reducing itself drastically. So in evolutionary terms the rats in the SG 19 group were behaving badly, by not killing each other off.'

'Doctor, to be good is to obey the will of God. In your laboratory you are God. If you wished your rats to kill each other off, then they were being good. If not . . . what is it, mother?'

Foxe had been vaguely aware that Mrs Trotter, though amused for a while by the rat-runs, had been as bored as he was by the argument about virtue. She had wandered into the logic-room and was trying to open the window.

'Look there at that no-good man,' she snapped.

Doctor Trotter strolled over. Foxe returned to the runs and saw that Queenie had made very good time and was now nosing at the final gate – it was almost as if he was better off without his injection. Quentin on the other hand had found the second gate at last and got through it, but was now staring at its other side with twitching whiskers, just like a householder who has gone out, closed his front door and then realised that he has left all his keys on the hall table.

'Do none of these windows open, Doctor?' called the Prime Minister. 'I want to shout at that idle ruffian.'

'They're all sealed, sir. The nearest one which opens is out in the corridor.'

'Stir him up for me, please, Captain.'

Foxe, going towards the group in the logic-room, passed Captain Angiah going in the other direction. The Captain's face had a look like the death-mask of a saint, stiff and drained of all emotion, but still somehow bearing the print of ecstasy. He must have been moving fast, for by the time Foxe was standing beside Dreiser and gazing down at the sleeping gardener, the corridor window was swinging open. Its glass hid the shape behind it, then a fine-boned hand steadied a big pistol on the sill. The snap of the shot was sharp and deep. The gardener's hat leaped like a large springing beetle. For a moment Foxe thought that Captain Angiah's idea of stirring a man up was to shoot him dead, but at last the gardener blinked. His head craned, blearily. Still supine he reached for his hat, stared at it and poked a dark finger through the bullet-hole in its brim, then peered, with all the whites of his eyes showing, at the stillness around him. The corridor window was shut by now. Doctor Trotter was grinning, watching the scene with narrowed eyes, but the group in the laboratory must have been invisible behind the tinted glass.

The gardener convulsed to his feet and ran a few steps, stopped, scuttled back for his rake.

'The rake will come apart in his hands,' said Foxe.

It did, of course. The man stared for a dazed instant at its fallen head, tossed the handle down, ran to his satchel, grabbed a small object out and hurled it into the trees like a grenade. Before it had fallen he was scampering, head ducked, round the corner of the building.

'How you know that?' said Mrs Trotter. 'The rake break when you say. How you know that? Whad that thing he throw away, Foxy?'

Nobody had called Foxe that since his schooldays. Ancient miseries, long thought dead, twitched. Unthinkingly he responded in the old way, with the schoolboy's shield of casual apathy.

'A snake's head, I shouldn't be surprised,' he said.

She became rigid. Her arm began to rise stiffly towards her spectacles, as though she were about to unveil her own counter-armaments.

'Didn't I tell you all science is one, Mother?' said the Prime Minister, laying his hand on the rising arm and stilling it. 'Doctor Foxe, you never told me the end of your story.'

'Which story, sir?'

'The drug which made your rats virtuous. What became of it?'

'SG 19? I don't know, sir. I don't even know what it was supposed to do, but I expect it was a dead end. We get a lot of them, I'm afraid.'

2

Foxe's bike was a lady's model, ancient, black and absurdly heavy. It looked as though it had been engineered to carry the gaunt governesses of the children of English colonial administrators, forty years back. Its bearings were far from frictionless, and even with seat and handles raised to their limits it was a couple of sizes too small for Foxe. But it had a single invaluable asset, which was that it wasn't worth stealing. The machine he'd bought on arrival in Hog's Cay had vanished in twenty-four hours, and so had its smartish replacement, but this old beast remained faithful. Besides, as Foxe told Galdi (who drove the mile and a half to work each day in a 140 mph Alfa), if anybody did nick it he'd have a fair chance of tracking them by sound; its characteristic squeaks and rattles were audible a block away. He didn't tell Galdi that he cycled because Lisa-Anna had persuaded him to take at least that amount of exercise in Vienna.

Foxe coasted, clanking, down the twisty tree-shadowed road from the promontory where the lab buildings stood and out into the blazing flats below. The shortest way home lay along the handsome new beach road, past the absurd hotels, but at noon there always seemed to be a steady wind from the south, just strong enough to whip bitter little sprays of white sand into his face as he pedalled; so over the weeks he'd explored and perfected his own route through the sordid maze of Back Town. Now he branched off the main road, crossed the screening dunes and dipped in among the tangle of shanties.

Poverty without picturesqueness, colourful with the hues of rust and tar and scum, rich smelling with much-used cooking oil and rotting fruit and open drains. Foxe had seen tourists being politely turned away from this end of Back Town by two of the Island police, and pointed in the direction of the gaudier and more presentable sections near the harbour, but till to-day nobody had tried to stop him. He was about half way home, already savouring the beer and fish-salad which he'd left in his refrigerator, when it happened. The alley he was in twisted round the back of one of the few large buildings among the shanties – a sort of dance-hall tavern – and reached a larger road. At this point Foxe's path was blocked by a crowd, mostly with their backs to him.

'Scuse me,' he said, 'scuse me,' and began to nose his way through with his front wheel. A few of them looked at him, but mostly they gave way without interrupting their chatter. He reached the front of the crowd and saw that the road itself was empty but a similar mass of people lined the far side, all evidently waiting for someone to pass. As he eased his bike into the space a policeman – khaki shirt and trousers, black cap, white whistle-cord round neck, gun at hip – stalked in front of him and held up a hand.

'Can't cross here, mister. Prime Minister coming.'

'Oh. How soon?'

The policeman's black brow furrowed as he peered up the road.

'Can't hear no cheering. Bit of time, yet.'

'In that case . . .'

The policeman stared at Foxe, both startled and angry.

'Prime Minister coming, I tell you, man,' he said.

'Got the Ol' Woman with him,' said someone in the crowd.

An area of chatter stilled into quiet sighs. Foxe hesitated.

'Better go back, man,' said someone. 'You don' want to cross where the Ol' Woman coming.'

'OK,' said Foxe. 'Thanks.'

They made way to let him back his bike into the alley

and then paid no more attention to him. He noticed another policeman close by, a smaller, scruffier figure than the one in the main road. This man was standing by the foot of a ladder which leaned against the tavern wall. Foxe approached him.

'How long will he be?' he asked.

'Get it done by time the Prime Minister come long,' said the policeman.

Foxe blinked and looked up. A man on the ladder was frantically white-washing a section of wall, trying to obliterate a large symbol which Foxe had noticed in several places in Back Town, a circle with a vertical bar projecting at the top. Hitherto it had meant nothing to him, but now he suddenly caught the policeman's warning gaze and guessed that this was something which the Prime Minister would prefer not to see – the symbol of some underground opposition movement, perhaps. Indeed, it looked vaguely like the old cartoonist's convention for an anarchist's bomb, so it might be just that. More important at the moment, the painter was going to take at least another twenty minutes to obliterate it, and that meant that Foxe wasn't going to be able to get back to his flat for lunch.

'Thanks,' he said, then turned and cycled back along the alley, only now noticing how much quieter and less populous the shanties were than normal. What now? The Prime Minister's visit had already spoilt half a morning's figures, making timings less precise and the rats' behaviour – because of the shift in routine – less comparable with other days. Foxe was determined to get the afternoon back on keel, starting precisely at 2.15. That meant eating somewhere close by. With a shrug of distaste he turned towards the beach.

He came out behind a hotel whose architecture had often caught his eye. It had clearly been designed by an admirer of the Sydney Opera House and had the same look of being unlikely to stand on its own feet, but then somebody had become bored with all that scalloped whiteness and ordered the outer shell to be painted in great swoops of pink and orange and green. Inside this gaudy carapace, like a hermit crab in an exotic shell, lurked the mean-proportioned slab of the hotel proper. Foxe pedalled round to the front and found a wide terrace where tables were laid for a formal meal and white-jacketed waiters moved beneath a trellis of scarlet-trumpeted creeper. Foxe didn't feel like that at all, and by now knew that it was inconceivable that a waiter on Hog's Cay would bring him a meal in thirty-five minutes flat. He was just about to cycle on when his eye was caught by a neon sign saying 'Igloo Bar'.

The phrase had a weird appeal. It seemed to incorporate the coolness he longed for after the frustration and heat of his ride, and the stillness and isolation he preferred for his meals. He locked his bike to the trellis and followed the pointing arrow.

The bar was a small, white-domed room with settees upholstered in polar-bear skins. It was empty except for a handsome black barmaid wearing an Eskimo parka.

'Morning,' said Foxe. 'Got anything to eat in here?'

'Nuts,' she said.

Foxe sighed. The air-conditioning was actually working. There are more forms of food than the merely solid.

'Can you do me a bloody mary?' he said.

'Bring it to you, sir,' she said.

Foxe sat on one of the bear-skin settees. The table in front of him was a plastic rock, flat-topped. The ash-tray was a trepanned seal-head. When the girl brought his drink it came in a walrus tusk. Her parka stopped at hip-level and below that her uniform was fish-net tights and immensely high platform shoes.

'You don' mention snow-shoes to me, sir, please,' she said, gritting the teeth behind her smile. As she moved away the door swung open and a tall thin man came in. He was black, and wore a pale blue suit, white hat, pink tie and shirt of the most intense iridescent violet Foxe had ever seen. Though his clothes were new and smart and clean, he was still somehow a little dishevelled and moved with the stooping, fretted look of the native Islander.

'Rub noses, honey?' he said.

The girl didn't look up but poured some green goo into a tall glass, added soda and then something which instantly sprang into a ball of fluffy foam on top of the concoction, which she pushed towards the newcomer. He craned towards her, wrinkling his nose invitingly. She whispered swearwords through her compulsory smile. He took his hat off and put it over her face, then picked up his drink and carried it across to join Foxe.

'Like it, sir?' he said.

'It's a change,' said Foxe, guessing he might be talking about the bar.

'American?'

'English.'

'You poor old imperialist wash-out. Didn't think you'd have the dough for a place like Hog's Cay.'

Foxe realised that the man was fairly drunk.

'I'm not a tourist,' he answered. 'I work here.'

'Uh? You the new feller at the Dorchester? Feller they've hired to teach that accent to the waiters?'

The Dorchester was a gabled, half-timbered, diamond-paned-windowed, twisty-chimneyed fantasy a mile along the beach.

'No,' said Foxe. 'I work up in those buildings on the headland.'

'That right?' said the man, not at all interested.

'Yes. What do you do?'

'I keep this hut. I'm the boss round here. My name's Trotter.'

'Uh?'

'No need to be surprised, man. How else you think I come to run a joint like this. What do I know 'bout hotels? All my life I tell them I going to be a herbalist, and they push me into this job. Honey, you can take that fur coat off if you want – the boss ain't looking, and 'bout every-one else gone watching my cousin ride through the streets.'

Foxe was a fairly reticent person with strangers, but there was something oddly appealing about this drunk young man that made him want to keep the conversation going.

'I was talking to your cousin this morning, then,' he said. 'He brought his mother to look at my rats.'

Mr Trotter's eyes widened.

'You hear this, honey?' he called softly. 'This gentleman been talking with the Old Woman this morning.'

The girl stopped smiling, put a finger to her tongue and drew a little cross on her forehead.

'She struck me as a pretty formidable figure,' said Foxe.

'Formidable! You got the word for her. Formidable! Sure. She try anything. She try anything. She don' know nothing, but she got the power, and she try anything!'

His voice was losing its clipped, neutral accent and becoming closer to that of the poorer Islanders, deep and a little slurred, with a rhythm that brought some sentences to the verge of song.

'She tried to tell my boss a spell about planting melon-pips on a virgin's grave,' said Foxe.

Mr Trotter gave a sour laugh.

'This one everybody know,' he said. 'Sure, sure, all the little girls. I take you up the cemetery, show you graves with twenty, thirty melon-plants growing there!'

'Does it work?' asked Foxe.

Mr Trotter reverted to more learned tones.

'Course not,' he said. 'Wrong kind of melon, wrong grave, wrong phase of Venus, wrong words to say on the grave . . . Oh, it work with the Old Woman if she try it. It work for her with a plastic tulip from a Datsun showroom. She got the power!'

'Haven't you?'

'A little bit. Just a little bit. I ain't so interested in that. I'm after the *knowledge*. Listen here. There's a little tree grows on Main Island – *Ferdinandusa hirsuta* – glittery long leaf, hairy stem, red flower like a bunch of little ball-point pens – we call it the sorry-bush. Reason why, it's a little poisonous, not enough to kill you, but you try smelling one of those flowers and you cry all morning. Sorry you smelt it. Sorry-bush, see?'

Foxe nodded. He realised now why he felt at home with Mr Trotter – he was a creature of the same kind as himself, who knew his subject well and liked to talk about it.

'OK,' said Mr Trotter. 'All the little girls know that. Hide a piece of sorry-bush in a bunch of flowers and send it to the girl who steals your boy, make her sorry, see? That ain't *knowledge*. But listen. Every sorry bush got one little leaf on it – 'nother drink for the gentleman, honey – just one leaf. Now, suppose there's a feller wants to kill you. You find a sorry bush, find this leaf, take it to the priest, give him a dash of money, tell him "Here's this enemy wants to kill me." OK, the priest takes your leaf and gives it a blessing. Saturday night he wraps it round one holy wafer. Sunday morning your enemy comes to Mass, and priest takes care to give him that one wafer. After Mass he gives you back the leaf. OK? Now, long as you keep that leaf, your enemy stops wishing to kill you. Still your enemy, sure, but not your murderer.'

'I see. And what you mean by knowledge is not knowing the story, but knowing which leaf to pick.'

'Right. And that I ain't got yet. Too busy bossing this bloody hotel.'

The barmaid came swaying over with another bloody mary for Foxe and a green horror for Mr Trotter.

'Think I ought to change the decor?' asked Mr Trotter.

'It's a bit rough on the girl,' said Foxe, 'and I don't suppose any visiting eskimos would care for it much. But it's nice and cool.'

'While the air conditioner keeps working. What you doing to-night, honey?'

'Staying far as I can get away from you,' said the girl over her shoulder.

'That's a compensation,' said Mr Trotter to Foxe. 'For herbalising I got to stay chaste – no good less I do. But it don' apply for hotel-keeping.'

'Are the Trotters a chaste lot?' asked Foxe. 'I mean, there's so many of you about . . .'

'Don' you know the story?'

'No.'

'Uh. Hundred and fifty years ago there was this little runt of a man called Trotter. Now *he* must have had the power. First, he persuaded all the men in three villages that just over there, beyond the horizon, there's this island where you only got to put a leaf in the soil and a cane jump up, you only got to dig a hole for water and you find pirate gold. Only no women allowed on this Island. So all the men get in their boats, and Trotter leads them away. Month later, all the women down on the shore, looking for their men to come home with the boat full of rubies, when they see Trotter coming back all alone. I tell you he must have had the power, cause of he tells them their men ain't coming back no more and now they're all going to be Mrs Trotter. And the women agree.'

'What had happened to the other men?'

'He poisoned them. Bought a barrel of rat-poison from England, my Granmammy told me. That shows he never got the knowledge, cause of there's bushes and bushes all growing on the Islands he might have used. Root, leaf, flower, seed.'

'So that's how the Trotters came to be the ruling dynasty?'

'Sure. I tell you, man, the top Khandhar, he's my cousin.'

'What's a Khandhar?'

Mr Trotter paused and took a swig from his drink. The froth gave him a snowy moustache which he licked pensively away, watching the barmaid while he did so.

'You don' hear any of this, honey,' he said.

'You be the stupid one, I be the deaf one,' she answered.

'Surprising you never hear about the Khandhars,' he muttered. 'Nobody won't talk about them on the Islands, less they're drunk, like me. But when I was in New York, learning about hotels, people keep asking me are they really Marxists? Are they going to go Castro?'

'Oh, yes,' said Foxe. 'The revolutionaries. They told me about them in Vienna – at least they told me not to talk about them. Are they Marxists as a matter of fact?'

'They better be. Long as Doctor O's fighting Marxists, the State Department's going to stay happy with Doctor O. Only he's done a pretty stupid thing – he's wiped them out. Shot most of them, put the rest in the Pit. So least until next time there's a cane failure, and Doctor O needs somebody to blame it on . . .'

Foxe's eye caught the barmaid's and she instantly glanced away. She looked far from deaf. Two bloody maries weren't enough to make him incautious, as far as Company briefings were concerned.

'I've got to go pretty soon,' he said. 'Perhaps you could explain something else to me – something quite different.'

'Sure,' said Mr Trotter, obviously relieved at the change of subject. He listened attentively while Foxe described the episode involving the gardener, the snake, the rake, Captain Angiah's revolver and Mrs Trotter. At the end he shook his head, smiling sadly.

'Stupid ignorant peasant,' he said. 'I got a little knowledge, I got a little power, but sure I'm not going to try a trick like till I got a lot more of both of them. Listen. Asimbulu, Lord of Thunder, when he takes a body he becomes a snake, wide across as a rum barrel. He's a joker, too. You want to find treasure, perhaps Asimbulu will help you, providing you bind him right. First, you got to bite the head off of a living snake, that olive kind we call the brassa. After that you got a lot more to do – prayers, plants, dances, blood, water – I don't know it all. When you finish you tell Asimbulu you won' loose him from your binding less he leads you to a treasure, OK? But you get one little bit wrong and you don' bind Asimbulu. He binds you. He's a joker, I tell you; so your rake breaks in your hand; your hat flies off with a bullet when there ain't nobody there to shoot. All that. OK?'

'I see. Yes. Mrs Trotter seemed to think I had something to do with it – it was my fault – she'd irritated me, and I didn't tell her how I knew about the rake and the snake's head . . .'

'Ho! Man, you begun something there. Ho! Listen to this. You come here but you don' belong here, like these bloody tourists don' belong. We're two worlds. You got your own knowledge and your own power and we got ours. Your science, our science. A piece of our science, in your world it's a ghost – you walk right through it, you don' even see it's there. You walk even through Asimbulu. Maybe he changes you, but you don' know you been changed. OK, two worlds. I can go a bit in both of them. I know the science name of the sorry-bush – your world – and I know the power in it – our world. You, man, you live all in your world. What I tell you about the sorry-bush, that makes you laugh inside. You tell yourself, How can the leaf of a plant stop a man from doing a murder? How can it make him a good man? Show me. Find me two hundred murderers and let me test them with my shining instruments. That's what you say, right?'

'I suppose so. Something like that.'

'But listen, man. This morning, when you talk like that to the Old Woman – you best stop calling her by her name, best talk about her way I do, the Old Woman – OK, she's a stupid peasant. She never says to herself, How come that rake broken? How come that snake-head in that bag? But she got the power. You talk to her like you belong to that world this morning. You put one foot inside it.'

'I'd better take it out again, then,' said Foxe rising.

Mr Trotter shook his head, staring down into the froth-rimmed crater of his empty glass.

'Will she let you?' he whispered. 'Remember, man, she's the one got the power!'

3

Later that week Foxe had another show-down with Lady-blossom, and with the help of new-found weapons won the encounter. This small and silly victory cheered him at a moment when he had become thoroughly depressed about the experiment.

Foxe was good at his job, and therefore valuable to the Company. Both they and he knew that he lacked the intellectual metal which produces the sort of work that reshapes theory; he had good degrees behind his doctorate and an adequate knowledge of biochemistry and neurophysiology, but in his heart he thought of himself as a very good laboratory technician, and was quite content if the Company thought so too. Now he had been posted to Hog's Cay to do a very ordinary piece of hack-work; fair enough, but by his lights he wasn't being allowed to do it properly.

The times when Foxe felt most fully alive came when he was setting up a new experiment. Then his two complementary skills – the flair for understanding animal capabilities and tolerances, and the rigorous intellectual discipline needed to ensure that the piece of animal behaviour he was measuring could be interpreted to mean one thing and one thing only – these two skills seemed as it were to breed together and for several weeks fill the whole envelope of his skin with excited happiness. Lisa-Anna had called him an empty man, but it wasn't true at these times.

The trouble with the set-up on Hog's Cay was that this part of the experiment simply didn't occur. It had been eliminated in his briefing. He had been supplied with his apparatus – the mazes – and with a wiring diagram detailing their connections to the logic room. His briefing told him the numbers of rats to use, and the dosage levels for each group – in fact it left so little scope for his own abilities that when he had read it he had almost decided to go home. Then he had told himself that he was in Hog's Cay for a rest, and a few weeks' extremely undemanding work with rats would be almost soporifically restful, so he'd decided to stick it out. Unfortunately Dreiser's production of the strips of one-way mirror so that Doctor Trotter could see the rats in action had also allowed Foxe to see them; dissatisfaction with his part in the experiment had become dissatisfaction with the experiment itself. He came early to the lab that morning, determined to do something about it, but was sidetracked by finding Lady-blossom still there.

Foxe's speciality, once he'd set the experiment up, was the elimination of variables, and his technique was very simple. While the tests were running he did everything himself, in a precise way, at a precise time of day, seven days a week. It could be very tiring – during the last experiment in Vienna for four months no one except Foxe had entered the room where the monkeys were. He had even cleaned the floor himself, every day, because anything that he did any day had to be done every day – but that had been a highly refined experiment to compare two variants of the same drug, one much cheaper to manufacture than the other.

But a healthy, lab-bred rat learning its way through a maze is a more tolerant creature than a wild imported monkey under a constant stress-load, and besides Foxe was supposed to be resting, so he'd decided to allow the normal room-cleaning arrangements to go ahead. If he'd known that on Hog's Cay the normal room-cleaning arrangements consisted of Ladyblossom, he'd have kept her out, but it was too late now. She was an uncontrollable variable, if ever.

As he came into the lab that morning he saw her at

once. She was standing in the animal section in front of the cages, in what looked like an attitude of prayer. The glass screens between the sections were almost sound-proof, so he was able to watch her as he approached. She was moving her arms about like a priest at an altar, but as soon as his hand touched the section door she gave a mountainous start and backed away.

'What are you doing in here, Ladyblossom?'

'Just the cleaning, sir.'

Foxe looked at the cages and saw a small red duster on top of Beryl's one. Beryl was craning up to it, nose twitchy with excitement at new smells. Foxe picked it up and found that it was not a duster but a white rag, damp with a reddy-brown stuff that seemed to be blood. Under it he found an H-shaped structure of twigs. A bead-covered thread lashed the joins, and also lashed to the cross-piece a twisted scrap of the dried skin of some animal.

'What's this, Ladyblossom?'

'That thing, sir? Nothing. I never see it. Pupupupu.'

She darted forward, snatched the rag and twigs and swept them into her rubbish sack, then fell ponderously to her knees and began to rub the floor with a tattered piece of pyjama. Foxe stood watching her. It was curious and a bit disturbing that she had chosen Beryl. In order to prove to himself that Quentin was a nutter he'd collated the figures for all the rats in the experiment, and had found one other who might perhaps need to be eliminated from the final calculations. Beryl was in the lowest dose-group, but was outperforming most of the other rats in the experiment, and his own group by a fair margin. The case was not so clear-cut as Quentin's, but it would need watching: a genius is just as much of a nuisance as a thickhead, and both are worse than a nutter whose eccentricities may in the end cancel themselves out. But Foxe had done the calculations only for his own satisfaction, and then thrown them away. Apart from him no one but the computer knew about Beryl.

'Would you come with me, please, Ladyblossom?'

She followed him into the office section and stood watching him, remote and untouchable, a creature of a different world.

'I see you've got the knowledge,' he said.

The remoteness dwindled. Her eyes widened.

'A little of the knowledge,' he said. 'Like the girls who know how to use the sorry-bush, or perhaps a bit more. Your son is stupid enough to try to bind Asimbulu, when he hasn't got the knowledge and he hasn't got the power. Are you stupid like him, Ladyblossom? Or have you got the power?'

She opened her lips to speak, then shook her head.

'There are two worlds, aren't there?' he said.

'For sure,' she whispered.

'You think, because I'm not an Islander, I live only in one world. You think you can bring the powers of the other world in here and I'll walk through them, as if they were ghosts.'

'I just don' think this, sir. No. No.'

'You remember that day the Prime Minister was here? He brought the Old Woman with him?'

To his astonishment Foxe actually saw her almost black skin go paler.

'I talked to her,' said Foxe. 'I showed her I had the knowledge and the power.'

Ladyblossom's mouth began to work so that for a moment Foxe thought she was having a stroke. Her duster dropped from her hand.

'You got the power,' she croaked.

Embarrassed and ashamed Foxe turned from her hypnotised stare. Her reaction was far stronger than he'd calculated for, but if it meant stopping her from mucking around any more with the rats . . .

'It's all right,' he said. 'I'm not going to hurt you. That sort of thing doesn't work in here. This place belongs to my world, so it's a waste of time trying to put spells on the animals. It's a waste of your knowledge and your power. You won't go trying it again, will you?'

41

'Just sure I won', sir. Truly just sure.'

'Good. Why did you choose Beryl, as matter of interest?'

'Damn clever rat.'

'Yes, but how did you know?'

Ladyblossom watched him with her broad face half turned away. He felt her withdrawing again into remoteness, but wasn't prepared to use his new terror-weapon to satisfy silly curiosity.

'I just see it,' she said, and padded away to her cleaning.

Foxe started the day's routine, injecting the low-dose group. Then came a small 'window', which he normally used for paper-work, then the injections for the second group, then running the first group, then injecting the third, then running the second, and so on, an unstoppable treadmill, each rat receiving its injection at a precise time and running a precise time after that until the mid-morning 'window'. To-day there was no urgent paper-work, so he used the first 'window' to stroll into the logic section and remind himself of its circuitry. If he wanted to install an error-counter he'd have to do it himself, so it couldn't be anything too fancy. The tricky part would be in the runs themselves, attaching equipment which wouldn't alter a rat's perception of the run, but before he spent too much time thinking about that he wanted to be sure that he had the outlets and counter-boxes spare on the logic frames. He was still there when Ladyblossom tapped on the door.

'Going now, sir.'

'Right. Thanks. Don't worry too much about what I said this morning. It's just that I can't have my animals mucked around with, or there's no point in my being here.'

'I won' touch them no more, sir. That Beryl . . .'

'Yes?'

'She got the knowledge, but does she got the power?'

Her fat chuckle wobbled her flesh. Relieved that the episode could now be treated as a joke, Foxe replied in kind.

'No. In fact I should think Quentin's the one for that.'

Her eyebrows rose and the wobbling stilled for several seconds, until he winked at her. She chuckled all the way out of the lab.

Just as the 'window' was ending the telephone bleeped in the office. Foxe finished putting his lab-coat on and picked it up.

'OK, OK,' said Dreiser's voice. 'Your next free time is when? Eleven, I think.'

The American accent didn't quite obscure the German, and this, allied with his liking to show how much he knew about everything his colleagues were up to, made him sound like the cartoon image of a psychoanalyst.

'That's right,' said Foxe. 'But please don't bring any more warlocks round. The dust's still settling.'

'I will spare you. All it is, I have this telex from Head Office I'd better talk to you about. Can you come down?'

'See you then.'

Foxe hung up, sighed, and settled into the first sequence of runs. His own time had been as precisely allotted as the rats, but he managed to clear a ninety-second period in the middle of each sequence during which he could himself count errors, visually with his own eyes, manually with a ball-point on a scrap of paper. It made him feel like a sort of cave-scientist, and the resulting figures were hairy as a donkey, full of subjective decisions about what constitutes an error, but even so it didn't need a computer to tell him that they meant something. Very odd. Very odd indeed. At least he'd be able to talk to Dreiser about it.

From Dreiser's windows you saw a different world. Only the sea was the same. The beach was gone, and the impudent hotels, and the sense of distances reaching away; instead there were black crags plunging down to the waves, and there becoming foam-fringed reefs. Dreiser's office had a subdued and casual aura, a smell of tweed and pipe-tobacco; the desk was small and battered, and the arm-chairs looked as though they had not been born comfortable, but had had comfort thrust upon them by many, many sittings. The only thing at odds with this ambience was the huge oil painting on the wall behind the desk, dribbles and splodges of hot colours which might have come in useful, Foxe thought, for adding to the stress-load of a roomful of monkeys. This garish horror was more surprising because the tone of the rest of the room was so carefully calculated. Indeed, Galdi said that Liz (Dreiser's half-Japanese secretary), had instructions to delay all visitors in her office long enough for Dreiser to spray his room with a tweed-and-tobacco aerosol and adopt a pose of leisure at the window.

'Ah, David,' Dreiser said, swinging slowly round, as if reluctantly tearing his soul away from high intercourse with nature. 'I seem hardly to have seen you since the great man's visit. That went off quite well, I thought. Your rats were a star turn.'

'Not such a star turn as the gardener.'

'True, true. Unplanned but fortunate. He needs opportunities to demonstrate his power, that type. While he is seeking power the search satisfies him, but once he has attained it he has no outlet but caprice. By its nature caprice is hard to anticipate, but sometimes it is worth trying. The sixth finger syndrome.'

Foxe grunted the expected interrogative.

'You don't know about that? A professional cartoonist once told me that it's often possible to anticipate the need of editors to exercise their editorial power by submitting a drawing containing some deliberate error – a sixth finger on someone's hand, for example – and the editor will be content with telling the artist to put that right instead of making him alter essential elements in the drawing.'

'I see. You got a telex?'

'Yes, indeed, and you have only twenty minutes. There is never enough time for talk, is there. One day you must come fishing with me . . . Now, this is a typical bit of head-office security-mania, to do with the safe-keeping of your report . . .'

'I haven't begun on that yet. The figures are all still in the computer.'

'Good. What is your timing? You have a reputation for quick work.'

'Not this time.'

'Uh? David, my instructions were that this was to be a very straightforward exercise. And from what I saw when Doctor Trotter was there you seemed to be establishing a clear difference in performance . . .'

'Exactly. I thought at first that it was a bit odd to ask *me* to take on something like this. I mean, I wasn't given much latitude – I was even supplied with the mazes, ready made. Maze-work is a slightly old-fashioned technique, but . . . well that didn't bother me, much. I wasn't actually told not to alter the mazes – in fact I didn't care for some of the gate-release mechanisms and I did change them. On the other hand the mazes made no provision for error-counting and my briefing said nothing about it, so I didn't bother with that. I came to the conclusion that somebody in one of the other research labs had come up with a set of figures which the Company weren't happy about. They wanted them checked, and they didn't want this first chap to know, so they arranged for the work to be done out here. Anybody could have done it, almost, but I happened to be free and my Director at Vienna thought I needed a holiday . . . That all made sense of a sort, though I wasn't exactly pleased . . .'

'One moment, David. My watch has been losing. Do you mind if I get a time-check.'

Foxe was too astonished to be outraged as Dreiser, who had half-settled onto the arm of one of the chairs, rose, crossed to a side-table and turned on a large transistor radio at high volume. He twiddled knobs till Caribbean pop filled the room with its tinny thumps and twangles, then returned and pulled his chair closer to Foxe's.

'Time check in about six minutes,' he muttered, looking at his watch. 'I'll have to turn it off then for plausibility.'

Foxe restrained a shrug. In his experience most

Directors had obsessions, and it was less inconvenient if these were directed at the external world than inward at the laboratory staff.

'OK,' he said. 'Now, you remember that you dug up a couple of sheets of one-way mirror for me, so that Doctor Trotter could actually see the rats running? Before that the maze-covers had been wood, so that day was the first time I myself saw the animals perform too. Of course all the counting and timing is done electronically in the logic room. Now, about five years ago there was some publicity about a learning-enhancement drug which all blew up when somebody pointed out that the rats which were doing their tasks so much more quickly than the control rats were still making just as many mistakes, if not more. You see what that means?'

'It's not my field, David.'

'Well, put it this way. They then installed counting devices in the rats' cages, and discovered that the dosed rats were moving around on average twice as much as their controls.'

'Ah. I see. The drug simply enhanced activity. The rats were going through their mazes, or whatever, faster simply because they were moving faster.'

'Yes. And being more inquisitive and so on. But they were making just as many mistakes while they did so. They weren't *learning* anything.'

'I see. And you are beginning to think that this substance you have been asked to test is of the same kind?'

'I've only been counting errors by eye, but I'm pretty sure of it. The next thing is to rig up some error-counting gadgets, though the design of the mazes is going to make that pretty difficult, which is really why I didn't bother with it in the first place. That'll all take time. Then . . .'

'One moment, David. Whoever wrote your briefing, would he have known about this earlier work?'

'Yes. Pretty certainly.'

'Then I suggest that you carry on with the experiment strictly according to your briefing. You had better start using the wooden tops on the runs again, and let me have that one-way glass back.'

'But . . .'

'We must be quick, David,' said Dreiser, glancing warningly at the radio. 'You were sent here to do a job which you felt was not worth your while. You then discover that it is worse than that – it is not worth doing at all. You also tell me that the people who sent you must have known that. We must therefore assume that the Company thinks the job worth doing, but not for scientific reasons. And yes, they have thought it worth sending *you* out. Your considerable reputation in your field is part of this charade. Therefore . . .'

The music quietened to a nervy buzz, over which the DJ told his listeners, as though that were the most exciting thing in the world, that the time was 11.15. Dreiser rose and turned the radio off.

'Sorry about that,' he said. 'Now, to continue with this telex. I'm instructed to take steps to see that your report is kept under the best security conditions we can achieve here. Your office safe isn't much better than a tin box, so we'll keep it in here. Help me down with this, will you?'

Foxe felt stupid. The Dreiser hypothesis . . . if it had been anybody but Dreiser he would have felt worse than stupid – sick, used, cheated – because the hypothesis fitted the facts better than anything Foxe could think of at the moment. But Dreiser was one of those facts. The hypothesis was exactly his sort of fantasy . . . Foxe saw that Dreiser had gone to the far end of the awful picture and was waiting for help in lifting it from the wall. He rose and took the near end. It was far lighter than he'd expected.

'I thought this only happened in comic strips,' he said as they lifted the staring canvas down to reveal not one but three large safes set into the wall. Their combination locks looked as complex as any that Foxe had seen.

'In my last job I had just one safe in my office,' said Dreiser, 'with a charming Dutch sea-scape to hide it. Here I must endure this bestial invention. I believe it was painted to hang in a New York fashion house, which then went bankrupt; some idiot in the Company decided it would make a long-term hedge, but I'm glad to say it's still a tax-loss.'

'I must go in a couple of minutes.'

'Right. All I've got to show you is that there are two locks, with eight-figure combinations. We can set them afresh whenever we want. So if you set one combination and I set the other, the safe can't be opened without both of us being there. It's very straightforward. Look . . .'

Dreiser's manner had changed while he was talking about the safes, become sharper and more eager, even a touch fanatical. His fingers reached for the dial of the combination as though he were going to caress it, but at the first click he sprang back snatched a handkerchief from his pocket and pressed it to the front of the safe. Slowly the fierce hiss that had followed the click dwindled. A smell of surgical spirit prickled through the room. Foxe saw Dreiser's handkerchief had turned bright purple, and there was a splash of the same colour on the breast of his linen jacket.

Foxe tore the top sheet of blotting paper from the pad on the desk and took it to Dreiser, who was muttering angrily to himself in German.

'Does that happen every time we get my report in and out?' asked Foxe.

Dreiser shook his head.

'Forgot it was loaded,' he whispered. 'Still thinking about what you'd told me. There's a hidden catch to disarm it before we use the combinations. I had it put in so I'd know if any of the staff fancied themselves as cracksmen. I think that's the lot. Right, David, I can get this picture back by myself. Don't wait.'

'Sure you can manage?'

'I've done it before. But listen, I mean what I said about that fishing trip. You get this experiment of yours wrapped up quickly as you can, and we'll go out in my boat for a day.'

'That sounds fun,' said Foxe. 'I've never done any serious fishing.'

'Ah, you have a world of pleasure to explore. A new world.'

4

Foxe arrived for work next day thinking that the only cheerful aspect of the whole charade was that he now had Ladyblossom taped. Apart from that he didn't know what to do. Suppose the Dreiser hypothesis was wrong, and the omission of error-counting from his briefing was a mistake, then the natural thing would be to query it by telex. But suppose Dreiser was right; then the mistake was deliberate. Would Head Office want him to draw attention to it? It was even conceivable that it wasn't a mistake after all, and that what Foxe was re-running was somebody's work on tolerance – did the rats under test show a diminishing improvement in performance as their bodies became accustomed to the drug? In that case errors might possibly be irrelevant – or at least be thought irrelevant by whoever had prepared the briefing.

Fox had re-read the briefing several times since he'd talked to Dreiser, and had come to the conclusion that it had been deliberately framed to exclude error-counting, without actually saying so. In any case, to install counters at this stage of the experiment would mean taking the runs out of commission for at least three days, which would play havoc with the rest of the figures; and to start again from scratch with fresh rats would mean over-running his lab time by at least two months. On the other hand, continuing with this obvious hole in the logic, spending weeks on work which he knew to be meaningless, was an appalling prospect. But at least he had Ladyblossom taped.

And even that turned out to be a delusion, or if true Foxe had somehow managed to tape himself into the bundle. As he opened the door he knew at once that no

50

cleaning had been done; the rooms lacked the vaguely pleasing smell of whatever it was Ladyblossom smeared her mop with. The waste-paper baskets were unemptied. Perhaps, Foxe thought, he'd scared her away with his show of mumbo-jumbo, and he was going to have to clean the rooms himself, after all.

Just then there was a rattle and a thump and Ladyblossom came barging in, backwards, dragging her cleaning trolley behind her. She beamed at Foxe.

'Changing all the rooms round so I come to you last,' she said. 'Just so you see I try nothing on your rats, uh?'

'If you like,' said Foxe uneasily. 'I didn't mean . . . Oh, I suppose it's all right. I may have to ask you to keep quiet while I'm actually working with the rats – I don't want them distracted.'

'Be just as quiet as a dead man,' she said.

And she was. Almost for the first time Foxe found himself noticing her, as a person rather than a phenomenon. She manoeuvred her implements and her own bulk without a sound. Previously if you'd asked him to describe her walk he'd have said it was a waddle, but he now saw that it was in its own way so efficient as to be almost graceful – stumpy, cushioned legs taking tiny quick steps which made no sound at all. Having seen this he then noticed how the motions of dusting and sweeping were done with a thoughtful, slow rhythm, as though she were responding to the rubrics of a ritual. Out of the oblivion-shrouded plains of childhood a memory flickered – a musty, near empty church, a few embarrassed voices straining to follow the wheedling organ *A servant with this cause* (one two) *Makes drudgery divine* (one two) *Who sweeps a room as for Thy laws* () *Makes that and the action fine*. Only whatever music underlay Ladyblossom's movements was something different from those prissy rhythms.

When he'd finished injecting the first group of rats he came back to his office and found her on hands and knees, brushing under the desk.

'Be good an' quiet?' she whispered.

51

'Fine,' he said. 'But you don't have to keep it up all the time. It's only when I'm doing anything with the rats, and these partitions are supposed to be sound-proof.'

'I be going to the dances last night,' she said. 'The singing be all still in my mind. This quiet, help me remember the singing.'

'I was just thinking you moved like a dancer.'

'Oh, I don' dancing no more now. I be sitting in the circle to sing and to clap. Long time pas', when I be young and strong to take the spirits, then I be doing the dances. But nowadays I be jus' an old sack, all full of patching, and the spirits tearing me apart if so I try to bring them in me. So . . .'

She paused, cocking her million-wrinkled smiling face to one side while she considered whether to go on.

'I tell you,' she said, almost in a whisper. 'This last night Queen Bridget com' first, then we know it going be friendly time, happy and singing. And Good Saint Paul, he show up and bless us poor people. So nobody ain't scared when the Sunday Dwarf appear, he be full of jokes, just happy and friendly. Bit of time the three of them go dancing together, but then Queen Bridget want dance all alone. So Good Saint Paul go up into the roof, but the Sunday Dwarf come and sit in the circle, with us poor people, close next me. And cause of for Queen Bridget there and Good Saint Paul I ain't scared and I give the Sunday Dwarf my rum bottle and he pull a long drink. Then if I ask him what I want to know, he got to answer, cause of for taking my rum. I ain't scared. I tell him I clean these rooms for this white feller, who got the knowledge, who got the power. Mister Sunday, I say, is this feller my friend, or is he my enemy? And the Sunday Dwarf pull more of my rum, and then he sing out, all loud, how you be his very good friend, and he know all about you, and how you gonna be my saviour when I be needing it. That's nice, just nice, huh?'

'Lovely,' said Foxe, overwhelmed by the smiling charm of the old lady but wishing he'd never begun this. Saviour?

52

In what unpredictable ways was Ladyblossom going to exploit this obligation? Perhaps he'd better get her to ask this Sunday Dwarf figure what Head Office really wanted him to do about the error-counting. Now that'd make a good telex . . .

'Since my Sonny go an' join the army,' she sighed, 'nobody don' take care for me.'

'Yes, um, well,' said Foxe, 'I've got to be in the animal room and the test room for a bit. You can do the logic-room if you want, and finish in here . . .'

'Fine,' she said, gracefully accepting this rather clumsy close to the conversation. 'I be coming back for those others.'

She bent back to her cleaning.

The only decision Foxe made that morning was to put off any decision, and to keep the strips of two-way mirror until he had a whole week's errors logged. Counting these was the only part of the experiment that now had any interest for him. He began to refine the process – perhaps the figures needn't be as hairy as he'd feared . . .

When the mid-morning 'window' came Ladyblossom reappeared.

'I be doing the animal's room now?' she said.

'Fine. I don't think it needs much. If you can do it in twenty minutes.'

'That Quentin am my very good friend too?'

'Oh yes, he's a friendly little devil all round. He'll keep an eye on you.'

Foxe spoke carelessly, almost impatiently, but regretted it as he saw the cheerfulness wiped from Ladyblossom's face. She turned away, then looked pleadingly up at him.

'I won' be telling the boy no more,' she said. 'Truly sure I won'.'

'That's all right,' said Foxe, smiling. He had no idea what she was talking about. There were no more interruptions till lunch-time.

*

As Foxe was easing his bike through the automatic doors of the lobby (something of a knack, if you didn't want them crunching back onto your rear wheel before the machine was clear) Dreiser appeared on the tarmac outside. He seemed to see what was up and strode gawkily forward to stand on the outer mat and thus keep the doors open.

'Thanks,' said Foxe, wheeling clear.

'You're welcome,' said Dreiser, turning and striding beside him up the steep stretch to the gateway. 'OK if I send Charley up for those bits of mirror soon as you're back?'

'I'd rather keep them for a couple of days, if that's all right.'

Dreiser shook his head, a strange, stiff movement which looked as though there should have been audible clicks to accompany it.

'Better not, David.'

'Now, listen . . .'

'No. You listen to me,' said Dreiser in a low voice. 'I don't imagine this area is bugged, but I don't want this to look like more than a bit of casual conversation . . .'

'Oh, for heaven's sake!'

'I called head office this morning. We've a code – I don't think it's been cracked yet – it sounds like we were talking about financial details. I asked whether they wanted you to add any frills to your experiment. Guy I talked to didn't know, but he called back almost at once and said you were to lay off.'

'You're not making this up?'

'See here, David, I'm aware you and Galdi and the others think I've got a case of neurosis, but I've been living on Hog's Cay four years now, and I know how things are run here. Why do you think Head Office think it worth while to set up a special code for my use?'

'I don't know . . . but even supposing the place is crawling with spies, I bet you none of the mikes work, or

54

anything. I mean the people here can't even run a one-route bus service.'

'Their heart is not in running bus services efficiently. It is in other things. So I'll send Charley up for the mirrors.'

'Oh, I suppose so. At least it'll simplify things.'

'Good. How many more days will you need to run the rats, in that case?'

Foxe shrugged. There was no point in running them at all, really..

'If I stick exactly to the briefing, ten.'

'Fine. And on the eleventh day we'll celebrate by going fishing, uh?'

'If you like.'

'You are here for a rest, remember.'

'So it appears. See you.'

Lisa-Anna used to complain that Foxe never got angry about anything except his own work. He would shrug or laugh and put up with all the horrors of the outside world, from the treatment of Soviet dissidents to cafés which charged for instant coffee as though it were the real Viennese brew, whereas interference with his work brought on a slow, churning anger that made him an unspeakable companion. Now, as he pushed his bike to the top of the slope and let it freewheel into the green and shadowy tunnel under the tree, he felt this state coming on, like the onset of flu. He fought against it. I'm here for a rest, he thought. I'm a tourist. What does a tourist do? Forget the bloody rats. Go and photograph something. Go and have a tourist lunch.

At the bottom of the hill he didn't turn off along the back way between the shanties but pedalled into the hot and gritty wind, along the sea-front, past the unfinished hotel, past another one which consisted of an eruption of concrete bubbles, to the one where he'd met Mr Trotter the herbalist. As he propped his bike against the trellis he noticed that the sign directing drinkers to the Igloo Bar was unlit, but this didn't surprise him. There were very few neon signs on Hog's Cay which spelt out their whole message; the night sky was full of gibberish, floating between the palm-tops and the stars, announcing things like EAFOO and OPLESS BARM and AL-NITE RAGE. In his first week Foxe had made a special trip half way along the beach to see what was blazing HA HO HO into the tropic dark, and had found a half-built wilderness of bungalows on the edge of a marsh, owned by something called The Happy Holiday Home Company.

But when he reached the bar itself he found it closed; the vestibule outside was half-blocked with a litter of polar bear skins and seal heads and harpoons. From beyond the door came the thuds of dust-smell of demolition. Foxe threaded his way through the hotel to the main entrance, where he found that the two black girls at the reception desk were wearing the national costumes of Japan and Wales, the latter modified for extra sexiness. A sign directed visitors to the Safari Lounge, and another to the Bierkeller, proving that the Igloo Bar had been an aberration only in absolute terms; in the context of the hotel it was another nation accommodated.

'Can I help you?' said the Welsh-costumed girl, not attempting the accent.

'Is Mr Trotter about? He's the manager, isn't he? My name is David Foxe.'

She nodded and worked the switchboard.

'Be a minute,' she said.

Foxe wandered across the lobby and found an illuminated scroll, lush with reverberant adjectives, extolling this hotel in which the tourist could effectively visit the whole world without setting foot outside the building. A voice at his elbow said, 'Mr Foxe, sir?'

He turned and saw a chubby little brown man, very sharply dressed in a dark pin-stripe suit with a yellow shirt and orange tie. The man was smiling anxiously up, as though Foxe's slightest frown or sneer would cause him to break into sobs.

'That's right. I wanted to see Mr Trotter.'

'You do see him, sir. At your very good service. Gibson Trotter, managing the finest hotel in the West Indies.'

He held up tiny pink-palmed hands in a priestly gesture, as though he were offering up the inner fineness of the hotel for Foxe's own especial use. His soft, brown gaze was happy and candid, but the blink was a mistake; it was somehow willed, a deliberate addition to the general impression of softness and innocence, but it was one detail too much.

'I'm looking for the Mr Trotter I met here last week,' said Foxe. 'Tall and thin. He didn't tell me his first name . . .'

Foxe felt the watching intelligence behind the eyes relax a little.

'There are many, many Trotters,' said Mr Gibson Trotter. 'And many others use that name because they hope it is good for business.'

'This one told me that the Minister of Tourism was his uncle.'

'Could be. My uncle has so many nephews – a hundred perhaps. But I think this man is lying to you, sir. He tells you that he is managing this fine hotel, but I am managing it. So perhaps when he tells you his name is Trotter . . .'

'He behaved like a manager, you know. The girl in the Igloo Bar heard him say that, and she must have known. And he didn't pay for his drinks . . .'

'These girls!' sighed Mr Gibson Trotter, frowning with his forehead but still smiling with his lips and eyes. 'I don't know what to do with them. I pay them a wage and they say it is too little and they strike. I pay them more, and at once they take a lover and buy him smart clothes and give him free drinks in my hotel. But, sir, you were not wanting to see this actor man. You were wanting to see the manager of this fine hotel. That is me. Now, how can I help you?'

Foxe couldn't lose his temper – he didn't know how. His anger at what Dreiser had told him was still there, stirred to fresh churnings but unable to find an outlet. Mr

Gibson Trotter's version of events was perfectly possible, except that it was all lies.

'I don't know,' Foxe found himself mumbling. 'I wasn't looking for him because he was manager here – it was something else. He told me he was a herbalist.'

'Tsk, tsk, tsk, tsk,' said Mr Trotter.

'. . . and I thought he might be able to tell me how to attend one of these dances I've heard about.'

'In this very hotel,' cooed Mr Trotter. 'Friday, Tuesday, in the ball-room. Tuxedos optional.'

'No, not that sort. I mean the ones the Islanders go to.'

'Oh yes, yes. I tell you. Saturday night, in the big dance hall on the road to Liberation Bay. Very colourful, very funny, very good lights for the tourists to film . . .'

Foxe still felt that he was being somehow defrauded. It didn't sound quite what Ladyblossom had described. He was anxious to pin the little squirmer down.

'This is the sort of dance the spirits come to?' he insisted. 'Queen Bridget and Good Saint Paul and the Sunday Dwarf?'

Mr Trotter's smile lessened at each name and blanked out on the last. For a moment the wary watcher stared at Foxe, undisguised.

'Who has been telling you these things?' he whispered. 'All that is over. All that is finish with the slave days. You are breaking our laws to talk about such stuff. Next time you hear this talk, you must tell at once the police. Was this actor, this herbalist, telling you all this?'

'No. It was just something I heard.'

'Where? Where?'

Ah well, thought Foxe, two can lie as cheaply as one.

'Outside my bedroom window, as a matter of fact,' he said. 'I've got a flat in Freedom Street, and I was woken up one night by two men arguing about it. They were drunk, but I thought it sounded interesting. I didn't know it was illegal, so thanks for telling me. What are you going to put instead of the Igloo?'

Mr Trotter's eager innocence magicked back to life.

58

'My idea for rich Arabs – you know Arabs are not allowed to drink, but . . . oh, I could tell you stories. We will have a great tent, with a stuffed camel, and drinks which do not seem to be drinks. Will you try a whisky sherbert? On the house, of course.'

'No thanks. I suppose that poor girl will have to wear a veil now, instead of her parka.'

'New girl,' said Mr Trotter. 'But you will have a bloody mary, yes? And tell me if there is a stuffed camel in your laboratories, perhaps.'

'No thanks, really. I doubt if there's a camel, but I'll keep my eyes open. Do you really think I ought to go to the police about that other thing?'

'What is the use?' said Mr Trotter, half turning away. 'Two voices in the dark? You waste a little police time, perhaps they waste a lot of yours.'

'That's what I thought,' said Foxe to his back. 'Thanks.'

Foxe had his tourist lunch at a shack which had sprung up from nowhere in the last three weeks, a little further down the beach. He drank two cans of the fizzy, thin, quinine-flavoured Island beer, which he rather liked, and ate fresh-caught mullet with hot green-pepper sauce. A fat American at a nearby table leaned across and remarked that at least the Islanders knew how to cook fish, and Foxe agreed with him – it was one of those mysterious pockets of competence which the Islanders managed to maintain, like jungle clearings, amid their general chaos.

Another such pocket, Dreiser said, was spying. Curiously, Foxe's anger had been a little appeased by his success in lying to lying Mr Trotter, and he could now consider the incident almost objectively. Talking about the spirits was illegal, and Mr herbalising Trotter had talked about Asimbulu. He had told the girl not to listen, but she'd listened – and, presumably reported to the police. Mr herbalising Trotter was in jail now, most likely, it must have been the girl who reported that Foxe drank bloody marys and worked at the lab, though it was a little

59

curious that Mr Gibson Trotter had bothered to brief himself on these facts – unless he was the sort of born hotelier who automatically registers people's likes and habits. At any rate, it didn't seem to add up to a spy network on the Dreiser scale. Foxe decided to forget about it – though at least Lisa-Anna would have been delighted that he'd managed to get angry over something outside his work.

Lisa-Anna. That was over. He decided to forget about her too. In ten days, he thought, I shall have some spare time again. I'll get a new girl.

5

'In a few years they will have a hotel here,' said Dreiser, pitching his voice above the rattle of tumbling water.

'No beach,' said Foxe.

'They'll build one. With forty-five miles of perfect natural beaches round the Cay, they'll still decide to build an artificial one.'

'Why on earth?'

'Because they've only got one waterfall. That makes it necessary to spoil it with a hotel, and people won't come to the hotel without it's got a beach.'

'It might be cheaper to build an artificial waterfall where one of the beaches is.'

'Excellent thinking, David. Send in a report to the Minister of Tourism.'

Dreiser finished paying out the anchor cable, made it fast and came aft to sort through the fishing tackle. His sea personality was markedly different from his shore personality. In the hour's journey up the coast Foxe had noticed none of what Galdi called 'typical Dreiserisms', those almost deliberately self-induced accidents of phrasing or behaviour, a sort of creative clumsiness, which invariably on shore destroyed Dreiser's image of the brisk but reliable administrator. The time when he'd squirted dye all over himself from his safe had been a fair example. But at sea he seemed to relax. Here there was no need to put on a show of competence, because he was already competent. Even the jerky, inhuman movements of his limbs became somehow functional and controlled. Foxe found it difficult to get used to. It was like a trick with perspective, where the object drawn on the paper seems at moments to recede and at others to protrude towards one; in the same way, though it was natural for Foxe to think that he was now seeing the real Dreiser, and the other one – the Dreiser of the Dreiserisms – was a sort of mask or carapace, he kept going through moments when things seemed the other way round; this Dreiser, this efficient seaman, was the mask and the spy-bedevilled gawk was the real thing.

The same uncertainty affected the bay where they had come to fish. Here Nature was at her most artificial, carelessly achieving a series of symmetries and contrasts which a human landscape architect would have rejected as excessive. The boat bobbled gently at the edge of the marbled turbulence below the fall, an area of ceaselessly repatterned eddies which set off the stillness and clarity of the rest of the bay's surface. The cliffs were blackish, and the volcanic upthrust which had created them had flowed into columns of smooth rock, sombre and massive pillars supporting a frivolous frieze of palm-fronds and garlands of blue-flowered creeper among which small parakeets flashed like fishes among seaweed. These cliffs ran through three-quarters of a circle, enclosing a space which would have been unspeakably hot under the vertical noon sun but for the mitigating spray from the fall; the fall itself was only about thirty feet high and three or four feet wide, and poured its lacy ribbon down with strange apparent slowness, as though the laws of gravity had been relaxed to conform to bye-laws more in keeping with local inertia.

The final artificiality was negative. There were no hoardings, no neon signs, no tin shacks selling varnished cowries, not even another tourist. An artificial beach, with basting bodies and gaudy umbrellas, would have been more natural than this solitude.

Dreiser handed Foxe a stubby rod.

'You'll have to show me what to do,' said Foxe.

'You'll soon learn. I'll start you off. If we fish over the stern I can cast for you and give you a hand if you're in trouble, but we're unlikely to get into anything very big in here. The best ones are round the fall.'

'Not what I'd choose if I were a fish,' said Foxe.

'No? In that case you'd stay a little fish, David. Fish go where the food is, and never mind the racket – they are like commuters in a city. The stream that feeds the fall is the sewer for three villages. It is strange, David, that you can think like a monkey or a rat, but not like a fish.'

Foxe shrugged. His skill, such as it was, lay in thinking like a laboratory animal, not like a rat in a burrow under somebody's warehouse. But at the moment he was more concerned to think like a tourist. His rats were on holiday too. No more needles prodding into their bellies, no more gates and levers – just a few days of lounging around in their cages, while Foxe reorganised the computer data, then a quick painless death and a deep-freeze shipment back to Europe for dissection. So Foxe deliberately studied the scenery, or thought about the new girl – a tourist she'd better be, not too pretty or amusing so she'd be easy to say goodbye to when her plane was due. Or his.

'Yes,' said Dreiser, fiddling with bait. 'If you look at it you'll see that the bay is really the bowl of a gigantic lavatory pan.'

'Let's hope nobody comes and sits on it while we're here – you might keep that sort of fantasy to yourself, Fred. Wasn't there anywhere else where we could have gone to catch fish?'

'The fish here eat pretty good. Now I'll cast for you . . .'

Dreiser reached across with an arm almost as hairy and angular as a spider's leg. He was wearing a short-sleeved shirt patterned in swirls of orange and cerise. His dark and corvine face was shadowed beneath a floppy linen hat, and his sun-glasses were very black. The rod became an extension of his arm, whipping the line to and fro above the boat and then letting it curl forward, lazy as the falls, to mate with the tumbling foam.

'Easier than it looks,' he said, handing Foxe the rod. 'Wind it in very slowly. If you feel a bite, snatch the tip up to make the hook bite.'

Foxe obeyed, his mind elsewhere. The odds were about

fifty-fifty, he thought – a German girl, perhaps, but an American for preference, easy-going and insensitive . . . empty starlit beaches and the silky warm sea . . . half the world away from the fug of the cluttered room on the sixth floor in the Kemperer Strasse . . .

'But it's not only the fish,' said Dreiser. 'I don't see how they can get a microphone on us here. The fall makes too much noise.'

'Now, look, Fred . . .'

'I got a telex yesterday with your next posting. You're on two-month loan to the State laboratories on Main Island. Got something?'

'No. Of course not. I just jerked the thing because you startled me. What on earth . . .'

'When you get a bite, try and do that again . . . uh, David, it's the first I've heard of any State laboratories on Main Island.'

'Why didn't you tell me yesterday when you got the telex? Bringing me out here to break the news! Honestly, Fred, I've got to say this – I go along with your spy neurosis because it keeps you happy, but mucking about with my life . . .!'

'Look at the mouth of the bay. Try to do it naturally.'

Foxe shrugged and swung round. A little beyond the reefs an orange cruiser had anchored, and a man in a wet suit was preparing to go overboard, while another man was adjusting what looked like a fancy camera on a tripod.

'Couple of amateur Cousteaus,' he said.

'That's a directional mike, David. But I doubt if they'll be able to tune the falls out.'

'Oh, come off it. OK, you've lived here for years, you know the form, I can't argue with any of that. But I also know that if the Company's being mucked about the way you say it is, we'd have pulled out of Hog's Cay ages ago.'

'A very good point, David. That's the key to the whole problem – it even explains why you are here, working on an experiment you know to be valueless. Have you ever asked yourself why the Company is on Hog's Cay in the first place?'

'I imagine there are tax advantages. And it makes sense to have the plant here, processing raw materials with cheap labour, rather than shipping them out in bulk. And the labs were set up to look at substances in some of the local flora, I was told.'

'Yes, that's all true – but laboratories on our scale, David? We're a cover, but like any good cover we have to function in our own right.'

'What are we covering?'

'Nothing. We were bust three years ago.'

'You'll have to explain.'

'The company came in here, as you say, to exploit a few raw materials. But . . . have you ever thought about the nature of a big multinational organisation, David? It can be very interesting. Among other things it has so many secrets, secret formulae, secret activities, secret bargains. Where can it hide them all?'

'Switzerland, I thought.'

'Yes, that is one solution. Centralise into a secure country. But if that country isn't as secure as you thought . . . Even Roche has been called to account by client governments, you know. Our solution was to spread the danger, to give as few hostages as possible to any one government, to take advantage of a tangle of different legal systems, and so on. A few years back the Southward Islands looked an ideal refuge – that was under President Afenziah – a little country, poor and backward so that a small investment from the Company had a major effect on the economy, and apparently stable. The plant was already in existence, the laboratory only planned. It was enlarged to undertake work of considerable complexity, well away from the rest of the world scientific community. Large-scale computer storage facilities were installed, and complex safes. A Director was chosen who had experience of security matters . . .'

'You?'

'Correct, but don't tell Galdi. You see it suits me to have this thought of as a neurosis – my colleagues are then security conscious to keep me happy, without believing that there are really any secrets to guard.'

'Ingenious,' said Foxe. He thought so, too. He hadn't realised that Dreiser's neurosis had reached that stage of tortuousness where it became one of its own defences against reality.

'I've wound tight in now,' he added. 'Shall I try and cast?'

'Better let me do it once more. Put your hands on mine and see if you can get the feel of it.'

Dreiser laid his own rod down and took Foxe's while Foxe leaned and twisted across his body. Along the inside of his right forearm he could feel the hard sinews that controlled Dreiser's wrist sliding with silky precision under the hairy skin. The trick clearly lay in timing the movement of the wrist in relation to the swinging arm, and at the same time feeding the right amount of loose line into the rod. No real problem he thought as he took the rod back – after a bit of practice arm and wrist would learn to move almost by reflex.

'And then President Afenziah died?' he said, thinking at least to get the story back to verifiable facts. 'Assassinated, wasn't he?'

'Correct,' said Dreiser calmly. 'A good man – in my opinion a great man. Forty-three when he died. He was working in a clove plantation, helping to dig a drainage ditch, on Main Island. That was his style. He had all the cabinet working alongside him. A man came up the road with a mattock, looking like he wanted to help – when the President was working that way you got this crowd of volunteers showing up always. But this man when he came near enough swung his mattock and smashed in Afenziah's skull. Doctor Trotter – he was Minister of Tourism then – was working nearest to the President. The story is he saw what the man was at a second too late, and then he cut him in two with one swing of his shovel.'

'Was that true?'

'Hold it. I'm into something.'

Dreiser jerked the tip of his rod back, bending it to a straining curve. He flexed it to and fro consideringly then went on talking while his arms played his catch automatically.

'True, David? I think so. There was a security blackout at once, a very thorough one. Under Afenziah the secret police were not a big organisation, and certainly not an efficient one, but straight off after he died there was this solid clamp-down, and next thing anyone knew the Trotters had the Islands in their pocket.'

'You mean they knew it was going to happen before. Who was the man with the mattock?'

'Officially a Khandhar. You've heard of them?'

Foxe nodded.

'Well, don't talk about them on the Island unless you're covered by a waterfall. They've got spokesmen in New York, who've always denied the assassination. Their line is that Afenziah had been trying to come to terms with them, and that part of the bargain was he should break the power of the Trotters, and in particular that the money from Hog's Cay – it was just starting to be opened up for tourism then – shold be re-invested in the Islands ... which is not how Doctor Trotter played it.'

He paused to grope for the net in the bottom of the boat. Foxe, who had been paying no attention to his own rod, discovered that the feel of it had changed in his hands and looked down to see that he had wound the weight clean out of the water. He pulled a length of slack line off the reel and started to twitch the tip to and fro, feeding in line as the weight pulled it out. Yes, it was easier than it looked, but not that easy – at one moment the wicked little hooks came whistling past a couple of inches above his head. The final cast snaked out and plopped into the water a bit to the right of the fall.

'Not bad,' said Dreiser. 'Might be something there. Look what I got.'

67

He held up by its tail a tubby, poutmouthed fish, ten inches long, banded olive and orange.

'Mother will be pleased,' he said. 'That's one of her favourites – grills a treat. Now it's your turn.'

'I imagine the Company weren't as happy with Doctor Trotter as they'd been with President Afenziah,' said Foxe.

'It wasn't only the good Doctor. He was Prime Minister, his half-wit brother was President, five more of his cousins were in the cabinet, and his mother was Life Chairman of the League of Island Women. D'you think they'd have opened a drugstall on the Islands, even, if there'd been a set-up like that?'

'But they didn't decide to cut their losses?'

'No. There was quite an investment here, and there wasn't anywhere quite right to go with some of the more sensitive stuff. They decided to give it a year and see how it panned out. At the end of that time I flew back to Europe to report, and it seemed pretty clear that we'd better start getting ready to pull out. They told me to come back here and take care of closing down this end. I arrived to find that my mother had disappeared. I was frantic. Everybody was friendly, very helpful and sympathetic. That was the first time I met up with the Prime Minister, when he paid a call to tell me that Mother had been kidnapped by the Khandhars (they exist when there is a need for them, you understand?). He'd just had a law passed making it a criminal offence to pay ransoms, but he said this would be relaxed for Mother. The Company gave me the money, and a few days later Mother was found tied up in the porch of a church. She hadn't had too rough a time, thank God.'

'And you let her go on living here!'

'She loves it here, David. It's going to take a lot more than a kidnapping to shift her. We have fourteen senile donkeys in our corrall right now – do you think she'd abandon them because of a few mountain thugs? I never told her who really snatched her, of course.'

'Anyway, I'd have thought that an incident like that would only encourage the Company to pull out.'

'Me too. I got another call to Head Office. The PM put a special guard on Mother while I was away. I flew to Europe sure that the nightmare would soon be over – but you see, David, it's still going on.'

'What happened?'

'Taking my mother was only a warning shot. We'd underestimated Doctor Trotter, underestimated him very badly. I think I told you that he had his own ideas about the development of Hog's Cay as a tourist centre? He'd been Minister of Tourism, remember, and he'd used his time making contacts. There are a lot of big American interests who would like a piece of a new Caribbean holiday centre, and some of them aren't too careful to keep their hands clean . . .'

Oh no, thought Foxe, not the Mafia. The kidnapping of Dreiser's mother had a certain solidity about it – had probably actually happened – so that for a couple of minutes Dreiser's rigmarole seemed to deal with creatures solider than mere mist. The introduction of this antique bogeyman dragged the story back to dream.

'The Mafia?' Foxe asked politely.

'I don't know. But somebody had supplied a few very sophisticated technicians from the American underworld. I found Head Office very shaken indeed, and looking for a scape-goat, but Doctor Trotter wouldn't let them touch me. He had the whip hand now. All he had to do was to threaten to release a few documents . . .'

'What sort of thing?'

'David, you aren't that naïve. For instance, you can't believe that the aerospace industry is the only one that had been handing out bribes in countries where the politicians have itchy palms. Or that there aren't areas where the big drug companies have done a carve-up – surface competition, but never at the cost of thousand per cent profits all round. Or even in your own field, bits of inconvenient research which had better not get known about in case half a million people find they've got a lawsuit against us.'

'It's not the sort of thing I think about much,' said Foxe. He managed to keep the amusement out of his voice, but had to hide his expression by concentrating on his rod.

'You are in too much of a hurry,' said Dreiser. 'Wind in half that fast. Give the fish a chance . . . hi! I'm into something fat.'

The excitement and life in his voice confirmed Foxe's belief that his story of the Company's dealings with Doctor Trotter was mostly fantasy. He'd recounted it all in a harsh, flat drone, hypnotic – or rather self-hypnotic. But now he was wide awake, concentrating, teasing at the frothy water where the invisible fish bent his rod almost double with its weight. Foxe watched him for a while, then looked round the bay. The orange cruiser still lay outside the reefs, but only one of its crew was visible, crouched at the camera on the deck. It looked as though he was waiting to take a picture of Dreiser catching his fish.

'It's not the sort of thing you think much about?' said Dreiser suddenly. 'I think you should, David, because now it affects you. You may ask why Doctor Trotter didn't simply blackmail the Company, why he was so anxious for us to stay. The answer is, I don't know. His is a difficult mind to read. The economy of the Islands needs us, of course – but he wouldn't bother too much about that. We're prestige, and that he likes. And we're power. He likes to make a world-wide company wriggle when he tickles it. You know, he always sends Mother a bunch of flowers on the anniversary of her kidnap. Not the day she got free, the day she got taken. That's his style.'

'And the Company just sit still and let this happen?'

'No. They're getting ready to go. It hasn't been easy. You see Doctor Trotter's a smart man, mad but smart, and he saw that his hold on the Company would grow stale. A bribe paid last year is much more of a scandal than a bribe paid five years back. So part of his deal was that he should continue to know what was doing. He wanted fresh leverage. We've had to feed him secrets all the time.'

'Not real secrets, presumably.'

'He's not an easy man to cheat. First we moved away from what you might call political secrets to industrial ones, which have a shorter life-span. You're not often much more than a year ahead of your competitors in the research field. Naturally that didn't interest him so much, but he's been selling some of the stuff to outfits like . . .'

'Is that worth his while?' said Foxe. 'Financially, I mean?'

Dreiser paused, seeming to consider what he should do next about his fish. All the time he had been talking his arms had continued to wrestle with the bucking rod, but now, though the rod itself was still sharply curved, the line reached straight down to the side of the boat and the weight at the end of it seemed inert. Dreiser picked up a short pole with a wire noose at the end, and manoeuvred it over the thwart. The fish that he eventually hauled out was almost three feet long, blunt-headed, silver below and blue-black above.

'Now, that's quite something with this tackle,' he said. 'What were you saying, Dave?'

'I was surprised that Doctor Trotter would get paid enough for selling industrial secrets. I mean, it might be useful money for somebody like you or me . . .'

'Right. Perhaps for him it's an exercise of power. He likes to show he can do it. Perhaps . . . Anyway, stuff has been getting out, and it must have gone through him. So the next stage . . .'

'Was to give him a lot of stuff which wasn't worth knowing,' snapped Foxe. 'To send poor sods like me here to waste a couple of months on meaningless work! Why *me*?'

'Because learning enhancement would be a big thing if ever it came,' said Dreiser calmly. 'Commercially big – biggest thing since DDT, perhaps. Have you thought of that? No? But it's the kind of thing Doctor Trotter thinks about, and it's the kind of thing he understands. It's got to be somebody of your calibre, so he thinks we think it's important. Only I guess they should have told you – anything to do with Hog's Cay and they screw themselves rigid with security.'

'What's wrong with Galdi's work? He seems to believe in it all right.'

'Carcinogenous. Yeah, he believes in it – he's the only one who does. Him and Doctor Trotter.'

'And now they're asking me – telling me – to go and work for this maniac on Main Island! Do they say what he wants me to do? Experiment with the effect of nine drops of tree-toad blood on melon seedlings?'

'No, David, they don't say. But I got a consignment note about a batch of stuff which I was to ship on to Main Island. Old Mrs Trotter has a regular order for a few things – sulphur's one of them. But this batch included a kilo of a stuff called SG 19. Mean anything to you?'

'Yes,' said Foxe flatly. 'It's a very mild sedative which never reached commercial production. I told the Prime Minister that it affected the stress behaviour of some of my rats. I never said it made them virtuous, for God's sake! I only used it as an example!'

Furious, but unable to express his fury, he wound his line in, waggled the rod to and fro and cast again. The timing was all wrong. The line looped soggily through the air, flicking just clear of Dreiser's rapidly ducked head, and finally as if with a will of its own plopping down into the water behind him, only a few yards from the bows of the boat.

'Wind in and try again,' said Dreiser. 'You were too . . . strike, man! You've got a bite!'

Foxe whipped the tip of his rod towards the falls. The wood bowed as the hidden hook bit flesh, and at the same time what had been a yielding resistance became a savage pull. The rod almost sprang from his hands. Dreiser reached across and flicked the catch of the reel, letting the line whistle out.

'What's happening?' said Foxe, caught, despite his anger, in the rush of action.

'Little fish took your bait, then big fish took little fish. David, you're into the stomach of a shark!'

There was a moment when nothing happened. The line slacked and the rod stood straight. Foxe began to turn gingerly at the reel, still without meeting any resistance, twisting stiffly round to watch his line. Just below the smooth surface a dark shadow loitered, then rose, black and glistening. Not for one glance was it any kind of fish. Goggles flashed. A wet-suited arm shook a raging fist.

They helped the man aboard and Dreiser removed Foxe's hook from just below his shoulder-blade. Apparently it had caught in the cranny between the air-tank and the wet-suit and Foxe's attempt to strike had then wedged it further in, driving the barb through the rubber into the flesh. The man was too sore and angry to make much pretence at being anything except a policeman, and his fishing equipment seemed to consist of an unmistakable microphone with a lead running to a waterproofed pouch at his belt. It was Dreiser who kept the pretence up, making brief brother-of-the-angler-type remarks as he worked first with his pen-knife and then with antiseptic cream and tape. The man – one of the blacker Islanders – merely grunted in reply and when the job was done flopped overboard without thanks. They watched his shadowy course until the angle became too small and it was hidden in the brilliant reflections of the bay.

'That settles it,' said Foxe. 'I'm not going to Main Island.'

'And I thought you were into a shark,' said Dreiser, chuckling.

6

For a while they fished in silence, Dreiser because fishing was what he'd come to do, and the intrusions of policemen were a nuisance to which he was accustomed, no more of a problem to the serious angler than mosquitoes might be; and Foxe because he wanted to leave Hog's Cay next morning and he guessed that if he started making obvious preparations to go he might be stopped. The sensible thing was to behave as though they'd thought the policeman had only been in the bay to record the bubble and squeak of fish-talk. Beyond that he found it difficult to make plans. Everything had changed. It was like walking from one viewpoint to another, from one world to another, almost. You see the same things, but you see that they are not what you had supposed.

Dreiser had changed for a start. Half comic and half pitiable until ten minutes ago, with his clumsinesses and his persecution neurosis, he was now something almost like a hero, sane in a crazy world, balanced amid turmoil. Foxe didn't quite accept that all Dreiser's imaginings were now real, but those that weren't were at least excusable – necessary, even. If you have a lot in your life to suspect, it saves trouble to suspect everything.

And Hog's Cay had changed.

And the Company had changed.

And Foxe?

His plans had changed, certainly. No silken, star-reflecting waters tonight, no exploration of flesh spiced with salt and prickly with sand, not even the amusement of beginning the hunt, let alone its consummation. Instead he found himself thinking of a conversation with Lisa-Anna

74

– his last, almost. 'You are an empty man, David. You will not allow anything to matter to you, except your work.' 'Your work is just as important to you, darling, and quite right too. I don't want you to go to Copenhagen, but I'd think less of you if you didn't.' 'Yes, you are not selfish, not in that way. But I am not talking about our relationship – that has not been as deep as I had hoped, but it has been good. And I would not want you to give up your rats and your monkeys for me. I will tell you why. If you did not have them, what would you consist of? Nothing. No, don't laugh at me like that. I am serious, and you do not understand what it is to be serious. You are amusing, you are a good companion, a kind lover, but you are somehow empty. Nobody should be like that. If you are not careful, David, you will become one of the walking dead.' 'If you want to know, darling, I feel very much alive. Sad but alive. I don't know what you're talking about really – but perhaps when this Copenhagen job is over we'll meet up again, and then you can be serious for both of us.' 'I will not weep for you, David! I will not! Go away, now at once, before you make me weep!' Foxe had gone, embarrassed as much as sad, but he hadn't understood what she meant and still didn't. The words ran through and through his head, meaningless, like a fever-dream. Perhaps, he thought, he was in mild shock after the appearance of the skin-diver, and his mind was automatically harking back to the last time he'd been really shaken, by Lisa-Anna's outburst. That, after all, is the way the mind works. Like a rat in a maze, confronted with a new experience, it seeks for comparisons among its past experiences, and Foxe hadn't had many shocks in his life, because he'd taken trouble not to let them happen.

Or perhaps he was changing too, and not liking it, and was reaching back to Lisa-Anna, the strongest anchorage in his old world. The way to escape from this new world of altered things was, literally, to fly; back to Europe, back to the Vienna laboratories, back to Lisa-Anna. If she would have him . . . if they would let him . . .

He glanced over his shoulder at the orange cruiser and saw the man in the wet-suit climbing aboard. The two policemen began to gesticulate at each other.

'How much do you think he heard?' said Foxe.

'Nothing,' said Dreiser calmly. 'Judging by the way your hook caught he was still coming towards us.'

'You don't think he heard me saying I wouldn't go to Main Island? Or the other chap? I said it pretty loud, I think. I was angry.'

'I doubt it, David.'

'Well, that's something.'

'You still think that way?'

'Yes. I'm getting out of Hog's Cay first thing tomorrow.'

'I think the Company would prefer you to take the posting.'

'Screw them.'

Dreiser sat silent, twitching meditatively at his rod.

'What about your report, David?' he said at last.

'What's the point?'

'The Company wouldn't have sent you here if they didn't want that report done.'

'To keep that crazy bully happy! Screw him! If he expects me to go to his island and waste my time working with SG 19 he's going to be unhappy anyway.'

'Yes. But I think they would like the report in his hands, and perhaps passed on to other hands.'

'Why on earth?'

'Possibly to mislead them about the value of the drug you are working with.'

'Not a hope. Almost anyone would spot what's wrong with it. They might waste a couple of weeks of one man's time . . .'

'In that case to discredit him as a source of information . . . yes . . . or else . . . No matter. They want the report done, here.'

'Well they won't get it done by me. Look, I'd be going to the labs tonight anyway – check on the rats, and so on. And if I'm off tomorrow I'll have to leave instructions

76

about them. Their food hoppers will last four days, and the Company can bloody well get somebody out to take over by then. While I'm there I'll set the computer up to do a printout of all my stuff and leave it ready. Anybody competent will be able to do the report from that – it's almost self-explanatory.'

'They'll fire you, David.'

'Fine.'

'Do you really mean that?'

Foxe considered. He had once or twice talked to Lisa-Anna about leaving the Company, and had discovered then that he disliked the idea very much, not just because they paid him well and let him do work that interested him, nor because he'd got a lot of good will invested by having been a useful Company servant, but because the Company was a controlled environment, safe from trauma and drama.

He looked round the bay, calm, enclosed, beautiful, a sewer; beyond its sheltering arms the orange cruiser waited for the next move. It seemed an absurd context in which to consider his future, but . . .

The Company had changed. It had deliberately opened a breach in his defences and was pushing him through, out, away. Or at least that was how Dreiser and this strange place and the morning's events made it seem. Perhaps back in Europe all would return to normal.

'No,' he said. 'I'd rather they didn't fire me. But I'd rather be fired than take this other thing on. And if you're right about the way things are run here, the longer I stay the harder it's going to be to get out.'

'All right,' said Dreiser. 'What I suggest is this. You go to the labs tonight and immediately set the computer up for its printout and start it running. How long will it take to finish?'

'Couple of hours.'

'OK. You been going to the labs most evenings?'

'Yes. Every evening. I like to stick to an exact routine.'

'So if they've been watching you they won't think you're

doing anything unusual . . . I guess you can get some notes together at the same time, just to give a few clues to anyone who's not familiar with what you've been doing. Right? Then you get all that stuff together, take it back to your apartment. Don't pack like you were going to be away for more than a few days. I'll send your stuff after you, once you're out.'

'Thanks.'

'Flight out tomorrow's 0820. Get to the airport with plenty of time to spare.'

'Why? I was going to turn up at the last minute and . . .'

'No. You've got to give them time to photocopy your papers. There's a seat booked in the Company's name on every flight out, so you needn't bother about reservations. They'll take your case off you and say they're taking it away to search it for bombs, but if you don't give them time for photocopying they won't let you on the plane. OK?'

'I suppose so. It seems very . . . um . . .'

'Dreiserish? Sure. But it'll work. And you'll have got the report where the Company want it, so the only battle you'll have to fight at Head Office is whether you go to Main Island.'

They fished for another couple of hours. Foxe caught a handsome olive and black creature with a great pale eye, which Dreiser said was good to eat the day it was caught and rotten the next. Towards the middle of the afternoon they stowed their tackle, Dreiser started the engine and they began the hour-long journey down the coast, with the orange cruiser shadowing them all the way. Foxe began to feel very tired, washed out with emotion and dizzy with the endless dazzle off the wavelets. The shore – black volcanic promontories, little beaches, spiky and feathery trees, a few clusters of shacks, and once or twice a spruce new villa – filled him with a sense of otherness, of rejection. He didn't belong here. From tomorrow he was going to cut all that loose and let it drift away, gone, nothing to do with him, not even a callus in his memory.

Dreiser's motor was remarkably quiet and the man on the deck of the cruiser had his microphone constantly trained on them, so they spoke very little until they reached the jagged hulk of the final promontory before Main Beach. The laboratories crowned it with a series of gleaming white planes, elegant and clinical, quite inappropriate to the welter of tropical growth and the shapeless outcroppings of barren rock.

'Looks its best from here,' said Dreiser, glancing up.

Foxe grunted, thinking it would look better still in Paris, or Amsterdam, or even Wigan.

They passed the tourist-swarming beach, the water-skiers, the precarious-looking tiny boats that consisted of one tall sail and a shaped board for a hull. The hotels grimaced along the coastline, one by one. Only as Dreiser began to swing in towards the marine entrance did the orange cruiser sheer away.

'Now, see here,' said Dreiser suddenly. 'I've got to protect my own position. I want it to look like I've tried to persuade you not to go. Would you mind acting pretty stiff with me while we're tying up, like we've had a row?'

'Not at all. It'll be a relief. I'll just say thanks now, though.'

'OK.'

The scene went quite well, Foxe thought. Any watcher – and there were several loungers about – would have found it easy to interpret the tight-lipped mutterings, the brusque farewells. Dreiser refused any help with stowage, so Foxe climbed ashore and walked rapidly along the jetty with his catch dangling from his hand. He was surprised to see that it would soon be dusk, and the ice-cream glow of neon was already beginning to seep its aureole into the sky above Front Town. A small girl came cringeing out of a gap between two stores; her glance, furtive but brilliant, flashed up and down the street before she cupped her hand in the illegal gesture – Hog's Cay brochures always boasted that visitors were not troubled by beggars.

'Got a penny, Mistah?' she whined.

Without hesitation Foxe shoved the fish into her arms and strode on while she was staring at him with mixed horror and astonishment. He hoped the irritation of his own gesture had been as obvious. Probably, because he found it difficult to shake himself free of this itchy skin of anger even when he was in the privacy of his own flat. He showered, changed, made a thick spam-and-onion sandwich and ate it with a stiff scotch-and-soda. Mentally he began to sort out his belongings into things he really valued and which it wouldn't be unreasonable to take on a supposed three-day trip. If he pretended the record-player was out of order, for instance, and he was taking it home for repairs . . .

These stratagems were interrupted by sudden thoughts of Lisa-Anna, not the old randy or wistful fancies – they'd been coming to him less and less during the past few weeks – but fragments of imagined arguings, part angry (as though the mess were somehow her fault) and part self-excusing. Surely she could see . . . But these ghostly conversations all petered out almost before they'd begun. A third party intervened, a silent presence, even more ghostly than the imagined Lisa-Anna. The Company stood there, deaf and silent, a stultifying presence. As Foxe tried to get her to agree that he was right to protest at the way he'd been shoved around like a mindless pawn, her eyes kept wandering to this . . . this . . . it wasn't in Foxe's mind a visible creature. Her image wavered, shadowy as the diver's had been under the glassy water of the bay.

All right, if you began to protest, where did you stop? If it was intolerable to cheat Foxe of a couple of months of useful working life, was it any less intolerable to encourage Galdi in work which everyone knew to be pointless? And what about the larger, vaguer pawn-pushings at which Dreiser had hinted – the bribed governments, the rigged markets, the defrauded litigants? What about the advertisements for liver-tonic which plastered Back Town – a Company product which, under a variety of names, had had its sales banned in the United States, Japan, and most European countries? What about the rats?

Foxe was used to being attacked in casual conversation for using experimental animals at all, and had been forced to think out his position with some care. On the whole he'd decided it was reasonable to use rats for almost anything that had a chance of advancing knowledge or improving the lot of mankind – that was what laboratory rats were for. Foxe liked rats and didn't like monkeys, but he thought one needed stronger reasons for using monkeys – it was hard to say why, perhaps because they were more nearly human. He had not, in fact, been entirely happy about the last experiment in Vienna, but had decided that as well as saving the Company money it provided a small clue about the nature of certain receptor areas in the cortex, because of the similarity of the two drugs being tested. So that had been OK, just.

But breeding, injecting, testing and finally killing animals as a *blind*! Foxe was surprised at the strength of his own repugnance. There was a sort of moral insolence about it . . . Perhaps, he suddenly realised, somebody in the Company had guessed that this might be his reaction and that was why he had not been told the real purpose of the tests.

Of course he'd known for years that the Company operated in ugly ways in some areas, but that knowledge seemed to belong to a different grammar from the awareness which was now forced on him. Once before, years ago, he'd gone through a comparable experience, the disintegration of a heroin-addicted friend. He'd had the theoretical knowledge, had smoked a bit of pot, had seen TV documentaries, had gossiped about friends of friends; but none of that seemed to bear on the actual, visible, tangible falling apart, the vomiting, the dirt, the disappearance of trust, the fury at Toni's stupidity in letting this happen to herself, the horror at his own gladness when she

81

took the necessary step and wiped herself out. I wish I'd told Lisa-Anna about Toni, he thought. It might have helped her understand . . .

As usual the Caribbean nightfall had taken him by surprise, the quick dusk vanishing unnoticed. He went downstairs, took his bike out of the garage and used the operation of fixing its lamps on to inspect the street. A man was leaning against a palm tree twenty yards up the slope; rather further down the other way a large car was parked – unusual, because few cars were left unattended in Front Town after dark, there being a tendency for wheels to disappear from them even when the driver was only away ten minutes. So somebody must be sitting there, waiting.

Foxe pedalled slowly up the slope, trying to behave exactly as he'd done every evening for the past two months. He knew he must be easy to follow as his appeared to be the only properly lit bike on Hog's Cay – in fact he sometimes wondered for what purpose his previous set of bike-lamps had been stolen; certainly the thief would have made himself very conspicuous by attaching them to his own machine. Down the hill the car's engine started. It too climbed slowly. A door slammed in the dark – presumably the second watcher was now aboard – but the engine note didn't change. Foxe threaded himself carefully into the traffic of Independence Square, busy with unpredictable taxis just now as the tourists began to arrive at the big casino for a preprandial flutter – a sort of appetiser for the real money-losing sessions of the evening. Galdi wouldn't be there yet, he had a theory that one's awareness of the flow of chance is keenest when one is exactly two-fifths drunk, so he'd still be in his warm-up procedure. Foxe let the slight slope freewheel him along the far side of the square and into the market, where the last of the fruit-stalls were closing down but the knick-knack and souvenir stalls glittered, as they would till the small hours, under their butane lamps.

The car followed Foxe down over the cobbles. The

clatter of his bike drowned minor noises, but twice he heard its sharp hoot, and once a crash of scraped timber, perhaps where it had knocked over one of the tottering towers of empty fruit-boxes. Several voices shouted angrily at it. The market crossed the border at the bottom of the hill and all of a sudden you were in Back Town, with its ranker smells, and ramshackle houses, and stalls selling cheap pots and garish cloths and patent medicines. By this time of night all these were closed and folded away, leaving the road hummocked with litter through which bold rats – wild rats, alien as Martians from Foxe's charges – rummaged. The road ended in a stagnant pool where some drain surfaced, so Foxe as usual dismounted and portaged his bike across the stepping stones. As he rode out into the wider street beyond he heard the tyres behind him squelch through the muck.

This was the road where he'd been stopped by the Prime Minister's procession. He turned right along it, then almost at once left into the dark alley beside the lightless dance-hall, or pub, or whatever it was. Again, as on that day, there was a ladder leaning against the wall with a man at the top and another watching at the bottom – in fact Foxe, swerving to miss the sudden loom of the ladder in his headlight beam actually crashed into this second man.

'What you doing? Where you going?' shouted the man.

'Sorry,' said Foxe, half-dismounted. He glanced up and saw by the glow from Front Town that the painter at the top had almost completed the symbol which had been obliterated on that other day – the big circle with the fuse-like bar protruding at the top.

'Police car coming,' he muttered, then remounted and pedalled on. The man shouted. Lights shone into the alley. A horn blared, ending in a crash and a scream, another crash and more shouting. Foxe rode on round the corner, following the familiar twisting journey between the shanties. Smells apart, the place was rather attractive at this time of night; flaring light shone through irregular doors and windows, the air was full of music, mostly from several

Caribbean stations but some actually made on the spot by groups sitting in front of their houses, bashing or tootling at improvised instruments; some of these people were so used to Foxe passing that they had familiar jokes about the sex and habits of his bike, which they shouted at him. He answered as usual, but thought as he clattered along that the police car would have trouble following him through this obstructed maze. They must know where he was going. Why didn't they simply drive round to the bottom of the promontory road and wait?

He came out at last on to the shore road and as usual pedalled faster over the good surface, trying with the wind behind him to get up speed for the climb through the wood. Under the trees it was pitch dark apart from the fire-flies, silent apart from the light swish of surf on the headland and the shrilling of night insects. He had seen no sign of his followers, but pumped himself up the slope with all his nerves alert. Perhaps, indeed, they had made the detour and would be waiting for him here, in ambush. But when a huge moth floated out of the blackness and baffed against his headlight, soft and sinister, he was far less startled than he might have been on an ordinary night. Panting slightly he coasted over the hill-top and down to the side door below his own rooms. He had his own key for these night visits. As always, he wheeled the bike into the narrow hallway and locked the door behind him, then climbed the stairs, switching on lights as he went. In his office he dialled the caretaker's number.

'Doctor Foxe, sir?' said Charley's rasping voice.

'That's right. I'll be a bit longer than usual.'

'How are the fishing go, sir?'

'Not bad. I only got one, but the Director caught several. I'll give you another ring when I go, Charley.'

'OK OK. You see that wife of mine, tell her come home give her man his meal uh?'

'Right.'

Rats are nocturnal animals. Human experimenters are not. So rats are normally asked to perform during their

84

natural rest-cycle. Short of installing an expensive reverse-daylight system, one can either keep the rats under constant illumination or make certain that any particular animal is always put through its paces at the same time of day, so that, although they may be performing below their peak because they're in a natural rest-period, their results remain comparable with each other. Because Foxe preferred the latter system, on his night-time visits to the lab he kept all the lights he was using shaded. Most evenings there was nothing special to do, but he made these visits every night, so that when one really was necessary it caused no change in the routine to which the rats were accustomed.

Tonight was a necessary night. He sat down at the computer console, switched on the lamp above the keyboard, and began to tap out the instructions he had mentally prepared during his ride. Almost at once the printout clicked into duet with him. The activity was soothing because it was something he was used to, something where he was in control. When he paused to consider a new section the printout continued, clicking away dosages, timings, averages, spreads. It was a very good machine, much larger than was really needed for a lab of this kind, because (Foxe now guessed) coiled away in its memory-discs in the humming, dust-proof basement were endless details of secret Company activities. Sometimes it too paused, and when these pauses coincided with Foxe's the silence of the lab became a wall, the bastion of Foxe's castle, inside which he was lord of all destinies, including his own. A rat fidgeted in its box – a safe sound, a member of Foxe's garrison, wakeful to his will.

Except that he should not have been able to hear it. The animal room was soundproofed, so that meant that someone had left the door open. Automatically Foxe rose and walked down past the maze-room to close it, though there was no longer any point in this; all the meaningless figures were in and it didn't matter a bean now if the rats were disturbed or excited by the clicking of the computer. Still, habit is habit. The suicide hangs his coat up and puts the change from his pockets into neat piles on the dresser before he lies down to wait for darkness.

Yes, the door of the animal room was wide open. The stainless steel bars of the boxes gleamed in faint rows, reflecting the light from the computer console, but below waist-level everything was in the blackest dark. No. Very faint, down at floor level, two small lights gleamed, nacreous but with a pinkness behind the pearl. Foxe sighed. An escaped rat was the last thing he wanted.

He crouched and moved gently towards the gleaming eyes. They vanished as claws scuttled on cork tiles, then there they were again, a few feet further in. Gently Foxe shut the door and crouched again. Somebody, that stupid old bag Ladyblossom almost certainly, had been in here, trying to work her messy little magics, and had taken at least one rat out of its box. Laboratory rats are not quite tame, in the way that, say, domestic cats are tame. They are used to handling and not afraid of man, but a couple of careless grabs can arouse forgotten layers of wildness, and then a single rat can take all morning to catch. Foxe decided to have one more go in the dark and if that failed to snap the lights on and try and catch the creature while it was still dazed with sudden glare. He crept forward, making the little clicking noise with his tongue which he used to calm young rats while they were becoming used to handling. An old lab assistant had once shown him that it is possible to pick up city pigeons provided that once you are close to them you move in a non-hunting manner and watch them only with your peripheral vision, so now he moved without any of the tenseness of the hunter. The eyes stayed where they were, even as Foxe reached smoothly out for them. This was odd – normally even a tame rat will back to a wall and huddle there before it lets itself be caught, but this one seemed to wait in the middle of the open floor.

No. The back of his fingers touched cloth. It *was* huddled against something, a fabric-covered object like a cushion. When he was handling rats Foxe's movements were too schooled to smoothness and restraint for him not to carry through now until his fingers closed round the soft, quivering but unresisting fur. His tongue stopped clicking. He rose, stiff with sudden tension.

'Who's there?' he whispered.

The rats in the boxes stirred at his voice. Shivering, he backed to the door and snapped the light on.

Ladyblossom lay supine on the cork tiles. Her face was blotched yellow and purple, her teeth bared in a stretched grimace. Drunk, he thought with sudden relief; but her broad chest did not stir, nor the breath gargle in her throat. Without even looking at it Foxe slipped the rat into his jacket pocket and knelt beside the body.

Her flesh was warm but rubbery in texture. Her left arm was pinned beneath her body and her right lay apparently loosely across her stomach, but when he tried to feel for the pulse he found that muscular contraction was dragging the arm so fiercely down that he was unable to push his fingers between it and her body. He tried to feel directly for the beat of her heart, but it turned out that Ladyblossom kept her considerable bust under control with a rigid lattice-work of corsetry. He could detect no sign of breathing.

He let out a long breath, trying to sigh away his fright, and rose. Well, the first thing was to ring Charley. Then it would be his responsibility – poor old Ladyblossom – probably poisoned herself with some potion. But why here? Why in Foxe's lab, goddamit?

He was aware of the door opening before he had finished turning towards it. His heart gave one appalling bang and his whole body went rigid, then he completed the movement much more slowly until he was face to face with Captain Angiah, who stood half-lounging in the doorway with his big pistol dangling from his brown, long-fingered hand.

The Pit

1

As the plane climbed it seemed to create the dawn, rising into whiter and yet whiter light. Itchy with sleeplessness and nervous tension, Foxe undid his safety belt and tried to relax into the soft upholstery, but a wriggling movement at his hip reminded him that he still had responsibilities outside his own skin. He took Quentin out of his pocket, stroked the sleek fur between his shoulder-blades and put him on the table, where he promptly produced a neat little dropping like the black stone of an olive. His touch was strangely restorative. The violet Q on the white fur behind the dark head seemed to glow with its own light. He nosed around the table-top, found Foxe's arm resting on the edge and immediately began to burrow up inside the sleeve of Foxe's jacket.

Spools of talk ran and re-ran themselves in Foxe's mind.

'You are under arrest in connection with suspected homicide.'

'Oh, don't be stupid. I can't have had anything to do with it. I've been out fishing with Doctor Dreiser all day, and your own men were watching us.'

'Nobody was watching you.'

'Come off it. I caught one of them with my own tackle.'

'That is irrelevant. Under our law, in cases of serious crime all witnesses and potential witnesses are automatically taken into custody.'

'What the hell's a potential witness?'

'Anyone the investigating officers believe may have knowledge bearing on the investigation.'

'That means anyone at all.'

No answer.

'May I ring the British Consul?'

'You will see him on Main Island.'

'But there's one here, on Hog's Cay.'

'An Honorary Consul only, and he is on holiday.'

'Anyway, I don't . . .'

Pause. Actually to admit that he wasn't going to Main Island if he could help it . . . Captain Angiah seemed to half-guess his thought.

'You will not really be inconvenienced, Doctor Foxe. Your arrest will be merely technical, and the President has offered you rooms in his palace while you are working on Main Island. Our investigations will certainly be completed by the time you have finished your work there. These magical slayings are straightforward. Are you ready to go now?'

'No. I was half way through getting some figures out of the computer: I can't leave it like that.'

'Then please hurry.'

That was the point at which Foxe should have put the rat back into its cage – or perhaps twenty minutes later when he'd stood up from the computer console, having fixed things so that someone else could extract and use the rest of the figures. But by then there'd been three or four policemen in the animal room, and Charley was standing by the door, his face greyish and covered with sweat-pearls. Besides, if the rat could get out of its cage once it might do so again. And besides . . .

Even now, lolling in the aeroplane, Foxe couldn't analyse why he'd felt it was somehow a small victory to walk out of the laboratory with a rat in his pocket, as if it were a concealed weapon. Of course he didn't then know that he'd got Quentin.

'Coffee, suh?'

A white jacketed steward had appeared, smiling in the nightmare.

'Yes please,' said Foxe. 'And some popcorn or something for my friend.'

The man's eyes widened. Foxe reached up under his

collar, withdrew Quentin and placed him on the table. When he glanced up again the smile had vanished and the black cheeks were blotched with sudden sweat.

'Yes, suh,' whispered the steward then turned shivering to the other passenger.

'Coffee, Captain?'

'Beer,' said Captain Angiah.

'How long is the flight?' said Foxe.

'Twenty minutes,' said the Captain. 'Waste of a jet flight, but Doctor O felt you would like to travel in his own plane. See there – that's just about half way.'

Foxe looked out of the window. All the stars except Venus had vanished, and the iron-coloured sea was rippling with silver-pinks and silver-blues. In a few more minutes, between a blink and a blink, it would take on the peacock colours of day. About a couple of miles away and separated by a mile of sea lay two islands, which might almost have been put there to demonstrate how different it was possible for two islands to be. They were both quite small, the nearer a classic coral horse-shoe, a slim curve of palm lined with shell-white beaches. Foxe guessed that the coral was supported on a volcanic cone which had never reached the surface, because the further island was just an upthrust, a ravine-creased pillar of black rock, formed in the complex upheaval that had shaped this part of the whole archipelago. Fall Bay had been made of the same stuff.

'What are they called?' said Foxe.

'The tall one is Trotter, the reef Afenziah. I persuaded Doctor O to rename them. I told him it shamed us in the eyes of the world that the map of our country should contain obscene words.'

The tone warned Foxe not to smile.

'Are they inhabited?' he asked.

'It is forbidden to land on them.'

'Why on earth?'

The steward came trembling back to put Foxe's cup in front of him and with a darting movement to shove a saucer of salted nuts towards Quentin. Foxe caught Captain Angiah's eye and saw a new look there, a sort of fury and repugnance. He felt too tired to work out the cause of it – it was safer to change the subject – but his unconscious mind must have made the leap.

'Is there a lot of magic on Main Island too?' he said.

Captain Angiah snapped his beer-can down and started to rise, staring hotly at Foxe for several seconds, then settled back into his seat and drank.

'You are a scientist,' he said softly. 'How can you talk about such things? You do us damage, you people, coming here and gossiping about these things as if we were animals in a wild life film. How can we stop being animals and become a modern people while you keep bringing your cine cameras and your tape recorders and pay us to do these stupid dances and sing these stupid songs? They are all bad, bad rubbish. They poison minds. How can a man do his work and earn his pay when he thinks that if he makes the right charm and gives the right gifts he can go into the forest and find pirate treasure? How can a woman be persuaded to use modern contraceptives if she thinks that she will not become pregnant when she binds four pieces of sharkskin between the toes of her left foot? You know that our enemies used this magic against us? We had Marxist guerrillas up in the Mountain, but they were not Marxist-Leninists, or Marxist-Trotskyites or anything like that. They were Magic Marxists. Only on our Islands, and perhaps on Haiti, would such a stupidity be possible. They did not take guns or grenades to terrorise a village, no. A man would walk up to the main hut in broad daylight with three sticks and a bunch of feathers dipped in blood, and lay them down on the path in a certain pattern. Then the villagers would take all the food in their huts and put it outside the door and hide, while the terrorists took what they wanted and left.'

'It sounds a bit more humane than guns,' said Foxe.

'You are wrong, Doctor. It is by these means that the people are degraded and kept at the level of animals. One of my own men, a soldier, was sentry at a camp. A woman came and stood in front of him. She blew on her palm at him and said "Man, you do not see me." He let her pass. In his own mind he never saw her. I questioned him closely, and even in front of the firing squad he would not believe that he had seen her.'

'You had him shot!'

'That man was no more use as a soldier – he had become an animal. Listen, Doctor. These people are like your rats. I think you would say they are conditioned. Your rats go along your mazes because that is all they know. Our people believe in this rubbish because that is all they know, and because they believe in it the rubbish works. You can only fight that sort of superstition with beliefs of the same power. Now my sentries are at least conditioned not to allow women to come close enough to blow on their palms.'

Foxe sat silent, full of that sort of numb lethargy which always overcame him when laymen used technical terms in an argument; it was hopeless to begin to explain where and how they got things wrong. He watched Quentin, interested in one corner of his mind to see whether he would even recognise salted nuts as food.

'You know how we broke the hold of the terrorists on the villagers?' said Captain Angiah.

'No.'

'We used conditioning. We sent Mrs Trotter up into the Mountain. They call her "The Old Woman" and they are more afraid of her than they are of any Magic Marxist.'

'And at the same time you reinforced the superstition,' said Foxe.

'Yes, that is the dilemma,' said Captain Angiah drily. 'How do you abolish the tools which you need to govern?'

He began to suck meditatively at his beer-can. Foxe watched Quentin, who seemed to be perfectly familiar with nuts, taking them one by one out of the saucer, nuzzling them about on the table till they lay to his satisfaction and then splitting them efficiently into two halves with his incisors. Mysteriously he ate only half of each nut, leaving the other half as if for someone else – his doppelganger, perhaps. Vaguely Foxe wondered whether this was a typical piece of aberrant Quentinry, or whether it was some left-over fragment of wild-rat behaviour, surviving through generations of laboratory breeding. The stupor of exhaustion washed across him. The white fur blurred in his vision, and the violet Q swam and changed. He was seeing it upside down and for a moment he was seeing something else – a white wall in Back Town, on which was painted a large circle with a vertical bar at the top, an upside-down Q. He blinked the blur away and it was still there. That explained Ladyblossom. That explained the steward. If the letters of the alphabet were not an important part of your mental make-up, then what you saw when you looked at Quentin was the illegal symbol on the dance-hall.

Tiredness made it a strangely tedious discovery. Anybody more interested in his surroundings would have spotted it weeks ago. Or perhaps Foxe's own turn of mind had made him blind to this trivial link between the two worlds Mr Trotter the herbalist had talked about.

'Now there,' said Captain Angiah. 'That is Main Island. Ten minutes before we land.'

Foxe looked out of the window and saw that night had become plain day. The sun, flush with the horizon, was streaming its light across the wave-tops, and already all the colours were too bright to seem natural to Foxe's northern eyes, though still far short of their noon-day garishness. Foxe had sometimes wondered on Hog's Cay whether any work had been done on the colour perception of tropical peoples, compared with that of races bred to a mistier light. The plane tilted through a change of course, and when the horizon steadied it was now blocked by a hulking cliff, a mile or so away. The usual flush of tropical brilliance crowned the rocks and streaked the ravines, and the blue sea sparkled into white foam at the shoreline, but the view was sombre; so much of the black volcanic rock stood apparently unweathered since the new-born mountain had come steaming from the sea. On these rocks the tropic sun, which made all other colours blaze as if with their own light, had no effect; their blackness drank it in and sent out nothing in return. Even the mountains of the main massif, twenty miles beyond the cliffs, had the same look, though distance and the dawn air produced a certain blueness and softness; Foxe could see that these tones existed between him and the mountains, and that the rocks themselves must be of the same unmitigable black.

'Mount Trotter, three thousand two hundred and twenty-six metres,' said Captain Angiah. The number came off his tongue with the lilt of something learnt by rote. He had evidently ceased being the military philosopher, and was now the polite courier. Foxe found this persona more frightening than the other.

The pilot changed course again, swinging round the south-western headland and losing height as he did so. For a few seconds Foxe was gazing along the southern coast until eyesight dwindled where headland after headland plunged in ragged parallels to the sea, each with its chain of rocky islets reaching beyond the shore-line, as though the Island were an enormous old instrument designed to comb the waves for wrecks.

Then they were flying along this coast and looking into the individual bays, which turned out to be barely more inviting than the reefs which divided them, at most a narrow curve of steep, dark pebbly beach separating the water from sheer rock blotched with shrubs. A fishing boat in the second bay had the imperilled look of one of those small fish that scavenge for parasites along the jaws of sharks.

The fifth bay was different, though Foxe could see no reason why men had chosen to make it so; it looked no wider than some of the others, and the cliffs behind were just as steep; perhaps there had once been a beach here where pirates could careen, or perhaps the reefs happened to give better shelter. But here a town of a sort had been built, tin shacks clinging to the cliff, a little sugar-icing church on a ledge, and at the bottom warehouses, quays, cranes, an old castle at the far end of the bay and at the near end what looked like a modern hospital or hotel. The town seemed far too small to support the level of commercial activity which the harbour implied; scattered along the cliff face its shacks looked as though a monstrous wave had hurled a mass of driftwood against the rock and left it clinging wherever a niche or ledge caught it. Often Foxe could see no means of access to these dwellings; and though there were signs that the town continued beyond the cliff-top – the plane was now flying too low to see for sure – there did not seem to be any road up the cliff.

But there the harbour was, with a couple of fair-sized merchantmen moored at the quays, as well as a few fishing-boats and three new-looking MTBs; no lissom yachts or gaudy cruisers to add their note of rich frivolity. There was an airstrip too, a concrete deck laid along the further reef and reaching the land at the foot of the old fort. At first Foxe hadn't noticed this last building, so closely did its black walls and crenellations match the cliff behind it, and before he could look at it properly the plane was swinging out to align with the runway; but in his mind's eye there was something wrong with it, a sense that it couldn't somehow fit into the narrow site between the cliff and the sea.

The plane whined in, flaps down. The glittering sea raced past so close on either side that Foxe felt they were about to pancake on the waves, but then the wheels banged into concrete and juddered with fierce braking. There was none of the normal sense of easing up which comes when a plane has slowed to its taxi-ing speed and can rumble safely to its berth; this one stopped like a car pulled up suddenly at traffic lights. Captain Angiah rose, stretching and yawning.

'Every time I think he's going to hit the castle,' he said. 'This runway is too short for jets.'

'I'm glad you didn't tell me,' muttered Foxe, collecting

Quentin from the table, and sliding him into the pocket of his jacket.

The pilot came laughing out of the flight-deck and opened the door. Short steps unfolded themselves downwards. Foxe put on his sunglasses and climbed down into the heavy glare of another Caribbean morning. Two other aeroplanes – naval fighters to judge by the way their wings were folded back above their cockpits – were parked opposite him, and a little further off a large helicopter. Only twenty yards away to the right the castle wall rose impressively into the hot blue sky, too close for Foxe to judge why it had seemed from the aeroplane to be a mere façade; but it was certainly theatrical in another sense, with the muzzles of ancient cannon jutting from its battlements, black as the black stone. Although it was obviously old it had none of the weather-gentled look of European castles, which had ceased to be guardians or oppressors and become playthings. This one was functional.

The sleepless night and the long tension made Foxe feel as though he'd just finished a fifteen-hour flight, so it was odd to find that there were no airport formalities at all, beyond a slouching salute to Captain Angiah from a sentry at the base of the runway. The Captain nodded and strolled on; Foxe had to trot to catch him up.

No car was waiting for them, neither jeep nor Rolls; in fact there was a curious lack of transport of any kind along the quay, where one might have expected to see queues of juggernaut lorries waiting to load or unload, or at least the battered and panting trucks that swarmed like horseflies round all minor Caribbean harbours. The only wheel Foxe saw in two hundred yards belonged to a barrow, laden with one bulging sack, which a gaunt-cheeked labourer was trundling towards the castle. But this was clearly a working harbour; the merchantmen were there, the derricks gesturing beside them like insect antennae wavering above dead prey.

Captain Angiah led the way over cobbles which looked

ancient but were in far better repair than any Foxe had seen on Hog's Cay; their path lay mostly across open stretches of quay, but sometimes twisted among sheds and warehouses, and they were just reaching the largest of these, into which the merchantmen seemed to be unloading, when the growl and clatter from the derricks was drowned by an appalling whistle, so shrill and loud that Foxe's ears continued to wince from the sound of it for some time after it had stopped. Captain Angiah halted and gestured to Foxe to do the same.

For a moment the warehouse seemed to be on fire, with an eruption of black and yellow smoke streaming through its open end and up into the virgin sky; then, out of the black and reeking pother crawled an extraordinary machine. It ran on rails, but was otherwise quite unlike anything Foxe had seen before; it looked like part of the innards of an early industrial pumping-house, staggering over the cobbles, flailing brass crankshafts, gouting steam and smoke. From the front it seemed absurdly broad, but when it rounded a curve and came thumping across Foxe's path, it looked stunted fore-and-aft. It was a steam traction-engine, eighty years old perhaps, but looking as though it had been built from a drawing in a medieval manuscript, with all its perspectives wrong. The harsh clarity of the tropic morning was smudged and then lost in the smoke which rose in gulping puffs from its tubby funnel, but before this smut-raining cloud engulfed Foxe he saw that the four wheels at the corners ran free on ordinary rails, while in the middle, just behind the furiously shovelling fireman, the rods of two colossal cylinders rose and fell, driving a monstrous cog. The device, trailing a short line of quite ordinary-looking trucks, moved towards the cliff at the speed of a fast walk. A lot of its energy was dissipated in noise. As the cloud thinned the awful whistle drowned the racket once more.

Foxe stopped choking and saw the last of the three, or possibly only two, trucks vanishing beyond a shed at the back of the quay; it seemed a foolishly little burden for that huge display of effort, and to add to the absurdity there seemed to be nowhere for the monster to go; Foxe was unconsciously readying his nerves for the crash of its collision with the cliff when a couple of men in blue overalls emerged at the point where the engine had disappeared; they had the same starved, exhausted look as the man with the wheelbarrow and were covered with sweat and grime. When they saw Captain Angiah they halted and backed to the corner of the shed, where they stood in feeble parody of the attention position. Meanwhile the rhythmic racket of the engine continued, slower now and more muffled, and the smoke of it streamed up the cliff face.

Captain Angiah, who had been picking smuts from his uniform, paid no attention to the men but gestured to Foxe and strolled on across the rails. There were three of these, the outer two like any railway tracks anywhere in the world, but the middle one a continuous rack of cog-teeth, four inches wide, very solid, mostly black with grease and soot but gleaming like a sword wherever the great driving cog of the engine engaged. From the track Foxe could see the mouth of the tunnel into which the thing had crawled; smoke still poured from it, and it boomed monotonously with the distant piston-strokes. Foxe stared like a tourist, then trotted to catch Captain Angiah.

'That's an unusual sort of gadget,' he said.

'I guess so. Only one in the world. One time the Americans were going to build us a road up the cliff, but . . .'

He shrugged. Foxe guessed that that was one of the projects which had lapsed when Doctor Trotter took over. 'How long has the tunnel been there?' he asked.

'Million years. I don't know. Volcano made it. There's no good harbours except on this coast, and no way up the cliffs except this tunnel. British put the railway in – before that it was mules, carrying every parcel of goods up and down from Saint Foudre at the top . . . That engine, that's our colonialist past – you could say it made us what we are. Listen, it will take trade in and out, everything the imperialists wanted off us, everything they pushed on us. But while it's working a man can't use the tunnel. Goods, yes. Men, no. They would suffocate to death.'

The Captain had changed. His enormous nostrils, tunnels themselves, seemed to stare at Foxe in accusation. His voice had lost its accentless neutrality – almost scholarly in its detachment – and become more lively, more like the sing-song of peasant Islanders. It was as though he felt the freedom of his native soil. Suddenly he lengthened his stride, as if determined to outdistance Foxe, the representative of imperial-mercantilist oppression.

Foxe didn't try to catch up, but followed in a daze of weariness, his mind still full of the strange machine. There was something about its age and dirt and peculiarity that marked very clearly the difference between Hog's Cay and Main Island. There such a machine would have been prettied for the tourists, driven by electricity, emitting white, hygienic, smut-free puffs of artificial smoke, but most of the time it would be out of action, waiting for spare parts. Here it was what it had always been, an ancient, clumsy, labouring slave, still working. Somehow the noise and stench of it told Foxe that certain illusions and pretensions, customary or necessary in most parts of the modern world, did not exist in this place.

2

The constraints of politeness can be extraordinarily powerful, especially when allied with fear. A man is arrested, absurdly and inconveniently, and as it were shanghaied to an island where he has no wish to be. He has been kept awake most of the night, but has not been allowed to ring his friends or his consul. There has been no warrant, no judicial safeguard of any kind. So he has every cause to complain. But when he finds himself, showered and shaved and dressed in clean clothes, breakfasting with the only man to whom there would be any point in complaining, a strange inward protocol prevents him from mentioning the subject until his host chooses to do so.

'More coffee, Doctor?'

'Er, yes, thank you, sir.'

Foxe had been watching half-hypnotised while a white-coated servant standing beside his chair stirred scrambled eggs in a little porcelain saucepan over a silver spirit-lamp. Beyond that another servant was turning bacon in a frying-pan, and beyond both of them the sea glittered through inch-thick glass that ran from floor to ceiling across one end of the room. Foxe and the Prime Minister were breakfasting in the President's palace, the modern white building which Foxe, seeing it from the aeroplane, had thought might be a hospital. They were looking sideways across the harbour towards the old fort at the other end of the quay.

'My mother was very impressed with you, doctor,' said the Prime Minister affably. 'She will be sorry to learn

103

that you have arrived in her absence. She's attending a convention.'

'I'm sorry to miss her too, sir,' lied Foxe. 'What sort of a convention?'

'People with similar interests, you know.'

'Oh . . . er . . . you mean . . . I thought . . .'

'That sort of thing was illegal? Quite right. But we are intelligent men, Doctor, and we know that the law has its limitations. You have to realise that these people I am trying to govern are the scum of the earth – I mean that in a quite scientific sense. They are the product of negative evolution, the survival of the unfittest. My islands, you see, are physically the worst in the Caribbean, with the poorest land, the rockiest coasts, the worst harbours. Until tourism came to Hog's Cay we had no natural resources at all, no tar lakes, no tungsten, nothing. In five centuries we have been ruled by four imperialist powers – Spain, Holland, France, Britain – and not one of them was not glad to haul their flag down. In the days of slavery the planters came, and they all went bankrupt and their slaves were sold, the strong men and women to richer planters on other islands, while the weak and the diseased stayed here. Other people arrived because there was nowhere else to go – usually because they were running away from the consequences of some crime. And meanwhile those who chose to leave the Islands were the men and women with initiative and intelligence. Through fifteen generations we have attracted the worst and then lost the best of that worst – that is the stock from which we are bred, you see. Now, how do you govern a people like this? On the one hand you must labour to help them see the world as it is, and to fit them to cope with that world, and so you must wean them or bully them away from superstitions which distort their vision of the world. That is the task of the right hand of the law. But on the other hand you have to control them with rewards and threats which they can understand, and this is the task of the left hand of the law. The central brain co-ordinates the left hand and the right. I use the left hand to help the right. I set a witch to catch a witch. Especially I set the older witches to catch the younger witches, and that means that in a few years, when the older ones die off, the problem will suddenly have almost cured itself. It is a sort of social homeopathy. There are not many witches of your generation, Doctor.'

He closed with a curious vague tone of threat, to which Foxe had no idea how to respond, but at this moment the egg-scrambler decided that the eggs had reached their peak of succulence and made a signal to the bacon frier, who sidled forward and deftly tweaked the rashers on to Foxe's plate. One might have thought that the events of the past twenty-four hours would have jaded Foxe's appetite beyond stimulus, but at the prickly odour of crisped fat his mouth glands jetted with saliva and his fingers twitched for knife and fork.

Quentin responded even more violently to the signal. There had been nowhere sensible for Foxe to leave the rat in his room, and he had seemed after the erratic lights and darks of the night to be ready to go into a doze, so Foxe had kept him in his pocket. Now he woke into startling life, scrabbled the flap open, dashed up Foxe's lapel and leaped on to the table, only to find that Foxe's plate was too hot for him to get anywhere near the bacon. He halted, a quivering blob of sleek mottled fur with the violet Q glowing on his back.

He had arrived at the plate the same time as the egg-scrambler, who started, dropped the little saucepan and rushed from the room. With a lucky snatch Foxe managed to catch the pan as it was going over the table-edge without spilling more than a spoonful on the glossy rosewood. Quentin stopped sniffing at the unreachable bacon and started to groom himself, apparently unperturbed by the Prime Minister's volleying laughter.

'I'm sorry, sir,' mumbled Foxe. 'I thought he was asleep.'

Doctor Trotter laughed all the more. Foxe spooned

egg on to his plate and a servant came to take the saucepan from him and to wipe up the spill with a trembling hand. Foxe reached out to put Quentin away, but Doctor Trotter said, 'No, leave it there. That is your subversive rat, I think. He is running true to form.' So Foxe cut a corner of bacon for Quentin and put it on the table for him, thinking it was remarkable that the Prime Minister should remember something about an individual rat. No, perhaps not, if the upside-down Q had a special magical meaning.

Foxe was about to ask what this might be when the Prime Minister said, 'Now we must get down to business. I mustn't waste your time. It is very good of your company to release you for a few weeks to help me.'

Now was Foxe's chance.

'I haven't really been consulted about this, sir . . .' he began.

'That is why I am consulting you now, Doctor.'

The reproof, though quiet, was loaded with extraordinary energy, like a suddenly switched-on magnetic field which grips movement into stillness. The effect lasted even while Doctor Trotter took a gross cigar from a silver box on the table and began to go through the ritual of getting it alight. Foxe waited.

'You told me a story about a substance called SG 19,' said the Prime Minister suddenly. 'It appeared to make a group of rats under stress more virtuous than rats which were not injected with it.'

'Yes, sir, but . . .'

'You are going to tell me that it was only a sedative.'

'No, sir. We stopped evaluation at an early stage – I don't know why. That quite often happens. My guess is that it was a mild sedative. Experiments have been done with rats to study the effect of sedatives on over-crowding, and it is well known that they reduce the stress-symptoms. The minor difference in this case was that only some of the symptoms, the fighting and cannibalism, seemed to be reduced. And I can't even be sure of that.

That's the whole point. This wasn't an experiment – it was just an incident. Nothing was measured or recorded. If I'd been an academic researcher with nothing more important to do, I might have checked it out a bit, perhaps, but . . .'

'That is what we are going to do now. Check it out. You may not think the manipulation of social behaviour important, doctor, but I do. I do.'

The Prime Minister took a long suck at his cigar, then laid it aside and leaned forward in a pose which made his head seem too large even for his enormous body. He stared, unblinking, at Foxe. His eyes were very bloodshot, and seemed to waver slightly as the smoke from the corners of his mouth floated up past them. Foxe found it very difficult to look elsewhere until, in the periphery of his vision, he glimpsed a movement of white and brown and violet. Almost without noticing what he was doing he reached out a hand and picked up Quentin before he could reach the Prime Minister's cigar, smouldering its blue wisp on an ash-tray. The touch of fur broke the half-trance.

'Honestly, sir, I wouldn't know where to begin,' he said. 'This is the sort of project which, supposing there's anything in it, takes years to map out. It's so vague. You have to find areas where you can get animals to behave in specific ways in which a particular, measurable alteration in their behaviour can only be interpreted as the result of your experiment. And there's practically nothing on it in the literature – that's what I mean about not knowing where to begin. The only thing I can think of off-hand is some work by Franck on flight behaviour and submission behaviour which in human terms might have something to do with cowardice. And that's another point. I don't think any reputable scientist would consider making the leap into human terms which is what you seem to want. So I . . .'

Doctor Trotter cut him short with a gesture of his cigar and a dragon-spout of smoke from his nostrils.

'You are making difficulties,' he said. 'It is excellent that there is nothing in the literature, because there is no literature available. I am not asking you to map out the whole area, I am asking you to do a preliminary study to see whether there is anything in this drug worth further investigation. As for the leap into human terms . . .'

He shrugged, inhaling a long draught of smoke, which oozed from his lips as he spoke again.

'You can spare us the time for that, Doctor?'

Now or never! Foxe, half way to trying to make the point about the difference between animal and human behaviour in a way which this suave maniac could grasp, changed tack.

'Apparently I've got to spare you the time, sir. Captain Angiah says I'm under arrest in connection with a murder. But I haven't seen a warrant. I haven't even been allowed to see the British Consul.'

'A murder? Whose murder?'

'I went to my laboratory last night – I always do that – and I found the body of one of the cleaners on the floor. I thought it was a heart-attack, but Captain Angiah, who'd been following me for some reason, turned up and said it was a magical murder. He arrested me as what he called a potential witness.'

'How unfortunate,' said Doctor Trotter soothingly. 'We must see what we can do.'

He strolled to a side table, picked up a telephone and spoke quietly into it. For a while he stood listening and nodding, then put the receiver down and turned, shaking his head.

'Most unfortunate,' he said, as solemnly as a solicitor breaking the news of a death. 'I cannot even say that Angiah has exceeded his duties, though he could certainly have been more tactful. He's a good man, but he has strong views on magical practices, and a death like this – snake-apple poison by the sound of it – might throw him off his balance. No doubt that was it. I imagine you have a work-permit, Doctor.'

108

'Yes, of course. But what's that got to do with it?'

'It means you are not a tourist. I've explained to you, doctor, the nature of this people I try to govern. You can imagine that when a crime occurs the witnesses vanish, like water into sand. So we have to arrest them. Of course we make an exception for tourists, or they would not come, but as you have a work-permit you are subject to this law. You will see that it is politically impossible to make an exception for you simply because you have a white skin. But do not be alarmed. I, personally, will see that the case is investigated with the utmost vigour, so that it is cleared up by the time you have finished our little experiment. And meanwhile you can reside here . . . in a way the death of this poor woman is fortunate, because as you say it means I can ask you to spare the time for this experiment without either of us feeling that I am robbing you . . . Oh, yes, the consul. Mr Palamine. A helicopter has already been sent to bring him here. A very good man. He will explain the legal position to you with great clarity, I am sure. He will be here in half an hour, and that will give you just time to present yourself to my brother, the President. It is he, after all, and not I, who is your host. And after you have seen Mr Palamine Captain Angiah will take you and show you the resources we have arranged for your experiment. Now, if you will excuse me . . .'

Foxe waited for Mr Palamine in a large, plush, characterless room like a hotel lounge. It too was lit by a single huge window facing the harbour. Foxe was glad to be alone for a moment, after his battering from the Prime Minister and his eerie interview with the President – Doctor Timothy Trotter.

Foxe had been led from the breakfast-room by another of the white-jacketed servants, elderly and plump, with the solid walk of the traditional butler but with a haggard, greyish face and ceaselessly flickering side-glances. This man had shown him into a much smaller room, windowless, with a curious sweet reek in the air. After a few minutes another door had opened and two men had come in, the first moon-faced, yellow-grey, enormously fat, a little shorter than Foxe, wearing a crumpled linen suit; the second another palace servant, but with the rubber-muscled face of a professional boxer. All in one sentence the second man had said, 'His Excellency Doctor Timothy Trotter President of the Southward Islands tell him your name, mister.'

'I'm Doctor David Foxe, your excellency.'

At a nudge from the servant Doctor Timothy had moved forward, extending his right hand for Foxe to shake. His fingers seemed to have no bones in them. He began to mumble in a gasping bass that made the loose folds of flesh round his chin, like the pouches of a male orang, quiver in sympathy with the incomprehensible syllables.

'I'm very honoured to be staying here,' said Foxe when he paused.

The servant had nodded, touched Doctor Timothy on the elbow and led him away. The first servant, who had been waiting by the door, had then shown Foxe to this other room and left him here.

Although he was standing at the window, watching the work of the harbour, Foxe didn't notice the Consul's arrival because he was distracted by a belch of black-and-yellow smoke up the cliff face. It was so large and sudden that it looked like a signal – of the election of an anti-pope, perhaps – but then the ancient steam-engine emerged into daylight and with its extraordinary waddle chuntered into the sheds. Only when the smoke cleared did Foxe notice that the helicopter had returned to the landing-strip and its rotors were still moving.

A fat little man wearing a pale blue suit and carrying a black brief-case climbed down. A soldier, not Captain Angiah, followed and pointed directions. The man in the blue suit began to walk along the quay, unescorted. Soon he was visibly European. There was something about his walk – a rapid but short-striding bustle, a sense of hurry without actually moving at all fast, a likelihood that he was about to trip over something and fall flat on his face – that extinguished the last flicker of Foxe's hopes; and when at length Mr Palamine was shown into the room this impression became still stronger. He picked his way between the chairs, smiling with the affable smug incomprehension of a cuckold in a French farce.

'Well, well,' he said. 'Doctor Foxe, I believe. We're in a bit of a mess, aren't we?'

'You make it sound as though I was in hospital and I'd been sick in my bed,' said Foxe.

'Do I? Palamine's the name. Oh, you're not in any serious trouble. Time will come when you look back on all this and laugh, I daresay. Now, let's sit down while I take a few details, name, next of kin, passport . . . I imagine they've nobbled your passport, though.'

'That's right. But I made them give me a receipt, with the number.'

'Good man. Shall we sit here?'

They settled side by side on to, or rather into, a too-luxurious sofa and Mr Palamine took notes of Foxe's history and predicament, pausing almost between every question to gaze round the room or out of the window. His hand trembled as he wrote and he kept licking his lips.

'That's all,' said Foxe at last. 'Now the point is this. It's very simple. The Prime Minister asked the company I work for to lend me to him to do a job. I was going to refuse, but then this happened. His line is that now I've got to stay here anyway, so I might as well do the job. Is that right? Can he insist on my staying?'

'Oh, I should think so, Doctor Foxe. Indeed I should think so. First time I've been to the President's Palace, but in my opinion you're very well off as you are. Last case I had like this was a sommelier from one of the hotels on Hog's Cay – a Gibraltarian, as a matter of fact. Silly fellow.'

He paused, smiling softly, as if in pleasurable contemplation at the idiocy of British subjects who get into trouble in foreign parts.

'What happened to him?' prompted Foxe.

'Gone to one of the dance-houses the night it was raided.'

'That sounds fairly harmless.'

'A dance-house is different from a dance-hall, my dear chap. Curious practices, not to say, er, disgusting. My bloke was only there out of curiosity, he said, but they flung him in the hoosegow with the rest. Took me three weeks to get him out.'

'Three weeks?'

'Oh, don't pin any hopes on that. Special case. That's to say I worked a wangle. I got a line on the Minister of Tourism. In fact I took his sister and brother-in-law out to dinner at my chappie's hotel, and fixed to have them served with warm champagne and shook-up claret, and told them what a pity it was that the fellow who knew how to do the job right was in jail, and what damage that was doing to the tourist trade. He was out next day.'

Mr Palamine nodded, smugger than ever at his own astuteness.

'But . . .' began Foxe.

'Wait a moment, my dear chap. I haven't got to the point yet. What I wanted to tell you was that this chap had a pretty rough time of it till I got him out. Eight in his cell, one with DTs and one with dysentry, and that was on Hog's Cay. Prisons on Main Island are – well, one doesn't care to criticise, but I'd be surprised if they were better than the ones on Hog's Cay. So I'd say you were pretty well off here.'

'Look, so far I've been told that I've *got* to be under arrest because that's the law. But they let your wine-waiter out, law or no law. So why . . .'

Mr Palamine stopped smiling and sucked his lips in, shaking his head slowly from side to side.

'That is not the kind of point I would advise you to

take, Doctor Foxe,' he said. 'In your position, the more valid an argument is, the less tactful it becomes.'

'What you're telling me is that I've bloody well got to go along with them or they'll put me in a real jail and keep me there as long as they like. Aren't you going to do *anything*?'

'Of course I am. I shall cable London immediately. I shall point out that you are accepting this job under protest ... you are accepting it, aren't you? I strongly advise that.'

'I suppose so. Listen. What about Ladyblossom?'

'Who?'

'The woman whose body I found, for God's sake! Now listen, can you check that they're doing something about clearing that up? They sound quite capable of dragging their feet over it just to keep me here as long as they want. In fact, can you check that the old biddy's dead at all? I'm beginning to think that the whole thing might be a charade, just to get me here and keep me here, because they'd decided that I wasn't going to come unless I had to.'

Afterwards Foxe tried to work out how long this notion might have been floating around, a vague unformulated unease below the surface of rational thought, before his tongue so suddenly brought it to his mind's attention. Now, having said it, he paused to think it out. Was there anything to support it? Captain Angiah had arrived remarkably pat. The skin diver in Fall Bay might after all have heard Foxe say he wasn't going to Main Island at any price. He could have radioed ... Ladyblossom's arm had still been warm ... on the other hand Charley's glimpsed face had shown real fear and horror ... Perhaps she *was* dead, killed just to fix Foxe. Were they capable of that? Were there any moral limits to caprice? None, Dreiser would say ... and why the hell was Quentin loose?

'Oh, come,' said Mr Palamine patiently. 'They could hardly hold you if the lady wasn't dead, could they?'

'There might be a so-called failure of communication, mightn't there?'

'All right, all right. I'll do my best to check. But . . .'

'And check what she died of, if she did. I mean, suppose it was only a heart-attack, after all . . . Have you heard of snake-apple poison?'

'Can't say I have,' said Mr Palamine, rising and gazing at the view. 'Look, Doctor Foxe, I'm going to do what I can for you, though honestly I think your company's got a lot more leverage than I have. I'll be in touch with them, of course. I'll cable London, and I'll make it clear that you're taking the job under protest, so we've got that position reserved. I'll find out what I can about the murder. But when all's said and done I don't think you've got a lot to worry about. I mean, it isn't as though you were one of those beggars there.'

He gestured towards the harbour and Foxe stood up to see what he was talking about. At the far end of the quay the gates of the castle had been thrown open and for a moment – rather as one sometimes sees a face or an animal in just one place among the repeated pattern of roses on a wallpaper – the castle became a face, a stone mask of tragedy propped against the black cliff. The crenellations were its crown; two wide slits, cut later than the other fortifications to take more modern weapons, were its eyes; it had no nose, but the black arch of the gateway was its wailing mouth, out of which a drab tongue began to protrude. Foxe shut his eyes and shook his head, letting the blood which his sudden rising had drained from his tired brain come back. The mask was gone. A gang of men, guarded by soldiers, was being marched out of the castle gate. Foxe realised all at once how the dock got its labour force.

'They'll be on indefinite sentences,' muttered Mr Palamine.

'Jesus! What do you get that for?'

' 'Political.'

*

Foxe, Captain Angiah and Mr Palamine walked back along the quay together. Once again they had to halt and wait for the engine to pass, and this time Foxe watched it with a sense not of strangeness but of familiarity; the feeling puzzled him for a moment, because he knew it traced back to long before yesterday, and then he found that his mind had meshed unlikely images together, human and mechanical. The machine was a Dreiserism, in fact it was very like Dreiser himself, in its jerky and flailing motions, its intricacy and inefficiency, its huge effort to moderate ends . . . This time too, because he had approached from the opposite direction Foxe saw the driver and fireman leap from the footplate just as the cliff began to swallow its meal of smoke and iron. Mr Palamine chattered questions which Captain Angiah answered in mutters and monosyllables, strangely more contemptuous than his earlier replies to Foxe. Together they saw the Consul into the Presidential helicopter and then stood clear while it battered its way aloft.

'Now I must show you your animals,' said Captain Angiah, pitching his voice above the thudding of retreating rotors and at once turning on his heel.

I won't do it.

Afterwards it was impossible to remember at what point Foxe realised what he was being asked, or ordered, to do. Was it at once, clued by the dryness of the Captain's tone and the manner of his turning? Was it as they were ducking through the little wicket in the vast, iron-studded gate? Foxe would have liked to think so, but in that case why had he said nothing, merely gazing with a growing sense of uneasy dread at the scene inside the castle wall? In a way it was like Back Town all over again. The courtyard was about fifty feet deep from the gate to the cliff, but four or five times as wide between the two points where the masonry met the living rock, and the whole of this area was crammed with ramshackle hutments, far larger than the Back Town houses but with

115

the same improvised and tumbledown air. The place stank.

As Captain Angiah led the way through this muttering barracks towards the cliff, Foxe's sense of dread increased. It was this that later made hindsight so difficult. At one point he was looking, weary and frightened but still with daytime eyes, at the prison camp and the castle, and next everything became wavering and monstrous through the lens of fear. Not even the normal processes of self-respect, which after a crisis tuck away the loose ends of nightmare and repattern one's cowardice and stupidity into a memory one can live with, could change that. Fear was, and remained, the major colour of the next few minutes – like one of those obscure Rembrandt etchings so hatched with burin-strokes that seeing it one is more conscious of the experience of ink than of anything the picture portrays – a blackness, in the middle of which something is happening.

In a clearing of consciousness Foxe waited swaying at the door of a hut by the cliff while Captain Angiah, just inside the door, snapped orders at a lounging soldier, who picked up a telephone and spoke. Outlined against the brilliant sky and seeming black as masonry and cliff two soldiers manned a machine-gun on the castle rampart. Laughing they traversed it across the courtyard and sighted on Foxe. A motor purred. Captain Angiah shouted angrily at the men with the gun, then took Foxe by the elbow and led him between still-sliding doors into the cliff.

'Volcano made this one too,' he said.

'Uh.'

Even in his stupor Foxe was aware that the tunnel was not man-made, only man-improved. It was lit by electricity and its floor was smooth, but the walls and roof were unchanged since the raging gases of the volcano had burst out through the rock, leaving a tunnel that widened and narrowed erratically, like the intestine of a stone giant. It seemed to suck Foxe along; his legs, against all

116

his mind's desires, followed the Captain's loping stride as if they'd been taken over by this autonomous nervous system. These effects he later guessed had a cause outside the rationale of nightmare, because the tunnel sloped steadily down, swinging to the right as it did so. The sharp lights passed like the hammer-pulse of fever. The air was dry and cool and almost odourless after the reek of the castle courtyard. The Captain's crêpe-soled boots set up soft whimpering echoes, the footsteps of invisible companions. The lights were too close together to cast any real shadows. Foxe longed to fall, to crumple, to faint and be unconscious, but his legs refused even to stumble.

And then there was an end. A big man seemed to emerge from the tunnel wall and saluted Captain Angiah, beyond whom the monotonous glare of the tunnel changed. There was a brighter, whiter light below and real darkness above, and between them a sharp line of black which Foxe only focused into a handrail when Captain Angiah stopped, leaned on it and looked down. Foxe's legs drifted him forward to stand beside him.

'There are your animals,' said Captain Angiah.

'I won't do it,' said Foxe, speaking all at once with the clarity and firmness of plain day.

They had come out from the tunnel on to a narrow timber gallery which ran out of sight along the rock face to left and right. The handrail was its balcony, and beyond that was a huge pit, fiercely lit. The effect was as if Foxe was standing on one of the lower tiers of a Roman circus arena. Up here was safety and relaxation – a couple of soldiers, a few feet along the gallery to Foxe's right, were lounging against the rail, smoking, bored; down there on the pocked and scuttered sand were the victims of the show. The lights were fixed below the gallery, leaving it in deep shadow and thus adding to the sense of privacy and security. The difference between the two levels was only about twenty feet, but it seemed as sharp as the difference between night and day.

Foxe didn't at once grasp the size of this cavern. Later,

when he was used to it, he guessed that a great plug of lava must have risen inside the rock like a piston rising up a cylinder, compressing above it the superheated gases which had first melted this bubble in the solid rock and then escaped along the fumarole which was now the entrance tunnel. Then, miles below the surface, the pressure had eased and the lava plug had sunk, again like a piston, leaving this pit. No doubt there were other tunnels, many undiscovered, riddling the now-cold rock, a meaningless maze. There was the one along which the mad engine crawled, too.

But for the moment all Foxe saw was an over-arching darkness beneath which on the flood-lit arena was a kind of crude encampment through which men moved. Foxe's words came back as echo, hovering in the dark.

'I won't do it.'

3

Negotiations. No doubt, Foxe slowly realised, this had all
been foreseen – not in exact detail of how he would
behave, but as far as the need to weaken him with loss of
sleep and to disorientate him with sudden changes from
horror to luxury and back, from sympathy to insolence.
They sat, Foxe and Captain Angiah, in a small room above
the castle gateway, part office, part bedroom with filing
cabinets along one wall, a table with an ancient typewriter
in the middle, and beneath the window a mattress and
tousled blankets. The place smelt of sour old sweat, and
tobacco, and stale food, all mixed with the more excre-
mental odours of the courtyard. Captain Angiah never lost
his monotonous calm, but Foxe's own voice slithered
uncontrollably along the gamut between scream and whee-
dle. Occasionally this antiphone was varied by the Prime
Minister's bass coming through the radio set. Foxe didn't
know how much he listened, but Angiah sometimes
seemed unable to contact him to settle a point – or
pretended to be.

Foxe had always refused to read stories, whether fact or
fiction, about torture and interrogation, or to listen to
victims, however brave and worthy, talking about their
experiences on radio or TV. Why should he be got at with
other people's sufferings? Even so, despite this willed
ignorance, he was aware that a bond tends to build up
between oppressor and oppressed, and was only surprised
by the speed with which this happened. He could detect
no sign of response to his feeling in Captain Angiah, who
maintained throughout a formality which became yet more
punctilious the more obscene were the threats and pres-

sures he had to apply. At first Foxe longed for some flicker of feeling to show in the fine, ascetic countenance – rage or impatience would have done – anything to prove that the man was more than a totally neutral tool in the hands of the monster at the other end of the radio link. Then, slowly, he began to persuade himself that the relationship wasn't like that – not monster / tool / victim but monster / victim / victim – that Doctor Trotter had set them down in this arena as gladiators, so that he could watch the contest with Olympian amusement. If so, Captain Angiah was fighting with a far more admirable style than Foxe, stoic and professional in his degradation. Discovering this, Foxe managed to pull himself together a little. Perhaps it wasn't true. Perhaps the Captain was enjoying his work. But even imagining that he might not be was a help.

The descent into the pit lay along the traditional helix, spiralling down. While Foxe believed that his choice lay between doing what Doctor Trotter wanted and enduring for a few weeks the kind of jail Mr Palamine had described, it had been fairly easy to continue to refuse. But slowly Captain Angiah, without directly telling him, let him become aware that there were a number of ways in which Ladyblossom's murder might be solved, and that the choice of whom to accuse and the verdict of the court lay completely within the Prime Minister's whim. He even referred to Foxe's talk with Mr Trotter the herbalist as evidence of Foxe's interest in magical practices. Other witnesses could be found. A snake-apple could be discovered in Foxe's flat. Charley would say that his wife knew Foxe for a powerful witch ... so the weeks could be months, years ... ah, no, there was no death penalty on the Islands, but nobody was immortal. Men died, slowly or suddenly ... and wasn't the court likely to consider Foxe's refusal to take part in a scientific experiment as evidence of his conversion to magical practices?

The first step down the spiral had seemed hypothetical. Suppose Foxe were to agree to conduct the experiment, then what would his conditions be? It must have taken almost an hour for Captain Angiah to coax and bully Foxe past that point, and then he was walking down the slope. He had agreed. All he could do now was safeguard his position as far as possible. The subjects must be genuine volunteers. If less than twenty forthcoming, Foxe to return to Hog's Cay under house arrest. Foxe to have complete charge of the experiment – no guard, police officer or other person to address, contact or discipline in any way any of the subjects of the experiment, except as specifically ordered to by Doctor Foxe. The drugs administered to be only those already supplied by the Company, etc, etc, etc.

While Captain Angiah typed the agreement out on the ancient machine, Foxe ate a pappy roll and greasy hamburger, and thought. He tried to pin his mind down to further safeguards. Secrecy first; if that was broken, proof that he'd been blackmailed into this fix; proof that he thought the experiment harmless; proof that the subjects were volunteers. The headline ran threading through all his thoughts: *Prison Camp Doctor Conducts Human Experiments.* Now, Doctor Foxe, you claim that you were forced into this situation. But surely . . .

His digestive juices seemed to make no contact with his meal, which lay in his stomach like a stone. He had stopped asking himself, Why me? because now half-knew the answer. The Prime Minister was not merely interested in Foxe's experiment on the prisoners, he was also conducting his own experiment on Foxe. He had chosen his victim that morning at the laboratory, because of something that Foxe represented, something perhaps that Foxe had said to Mrs Trotter – not a logical choice, of course, but a sudden, passionate interest, like love at first sight.

The Captain pulled the paper out of the machine, read it slowly and passed it across the table. The sentences were meaningless, read by Foxe's prickling eyes like words in a dream, but not reaching his brain. He put his hand in his pocket to look for his pen but found Quentin instead. Quentin had slept since breakfast, but now seemed to be stirring, so Foxe lifted him onto the table to clear up the crumbs, but he seemed more concerned to witness Foxe's signature. Foxe wrote his name in an angry scrawl. Captain Angiah added his, slow and clear but surprisingly florid. As if adding a seal Quentin excreted neatly onto the paper. Quite right. That was about what it was worth.

The arena where the prisoners were kept was called the Pit. Once you were down in it, standing on its sand-strewn floor, the glare seemed less – certainly less than the afternoon sun in the castle courtyard. The overarching dark lay close above, making the gallery invisible behind the lights; it was impossible to tell whether one was being watched by twenty guards, or two, or none.

'Do they all speak English?' said Foxe.

'Yeh. Some of them may pretend not to understand you.'

'OK. Thanks. Now I'm going to need an assistant, somebody who can read and write and add up. Not a guard or a soldier. Shall I pick one out of this lot?'

'No,' said Captain Angiah firmly. 'The Prime Minister says they've got to be all in the experiment.'

'Provided they volunteer.'

'Sure. I'll get you a prisoner from outside.'

'Fine. Now will you go back to the gallery, please?'

'I better stay here, Doctor.'

Foxe's hand seemed too tired to quiver as he snatched the agreement from his pocket and thrust it under Captain Angiah's monstrous nostrils, pointing at clause (iv). For the first time that day Captain Angiah smiled; he nodded to the two armed guards who had accompanied them to the floor of the pit and led the way up the flight of wooden steps to the gallery. Foxe waited till they had reached the top and with a squeak of pulleys and creak of hemp the steps were hauled up into the dark. Then he turned to the silent prisoners, paraded in three ranks in front of him.

'Perhaps you would all sit down,' he said.

The large eyes stared at him from drawn and sunken

122

faces. Nobody stirred. A voice bellowed out of the darkness.

'Siddown, yah black bastards, when the white man telling you.'

As the ranks collapsed to the sand Foxe turned.

'Captain Angiah?'

'I am still here,' said the darkness.

'Will you see that the guards understand their new orders? Interference of that kind will make the experiment valueless.'

Slowly Foxe turned to face the prisoners, aware that for almost the first time that day he had spoken with real confidence. This glaring arena was now his laboratory, the world where he was himself, solid, in control. He was aware too of a strange surge of excitement, far below the rational level, at the prospect before him. Reason might surface in the end – it might, for instance be possible to set something up which paralleled a known animal experiment closely enough for actual comparisons to be made – probably nothing quantifiable, and of course never publishable, but still an experience, an insight, a colour that might tinge future experiments, back in the sane world where rats were rats and you could do what you chose with them.

He looked along the ranks. Four-fifths males – that was good. A few impossible to sex at a glance. Condition poor – in fact appalling by normal laboratory standards. But the starved eyes seemed bright, watchful, interested. His own eyes locked to a particular glance, a hard, strong face surrounded by a frizz of tight-curled hair, the eyes sunken and very dark, a look both withdrawn and speculative. He stopped inspecting a group of laboratory animals and realised that he still had to make contact with each individual mind. Rats don't volunteer.

'My name's David Foxe,' he said. 'I've been asked, or rather I've been forced, to conduct an experiment. I can promise you it will do no one any harm. I can also promise that no one need take part unless they want to. Everybody in the experiment must be a volunteer.'

Arms rose at the word, like the tentacles of some sea-bed creature wavering for prey above the sandy floor.

'That's no good,' said Foxe, wearily. He was cross with himself for not having guessed that one of the guards would already have been down here, telling them what would be done to those who failed to volunteer. The Prime Minister had probably given the orders even before he'd allowed Captain Angiah to concede the point. Foxe was tired of the sheer crudeness of the machinery of despotism – surely they must know that he'd be aware that if he failed to get the volunteers he wanted there'd be no question of the clause about his going back to house arrest on Hog's Cay becoming operative – he'd simply vanish, or fall into the harbour and drown, or eat something poisonous from Mrs Trotter's recipe book, or . . . Part of Foxe's anger rose from feeling that he was being treated as almost totally naïve, but more from this being a further interference in the domain of his laboratory.

He waited till the arms had returned to rest. A few of the faces looked puzzled, but one or two were smiling, in a remote sort of way, as if his refusal to accept their offer had been a small victory for them.

'Now listen,' he said. 'First I will tell you what I can offer to those who do volunteer. I cannot work with you if you are ill or starved, so I will see that you get proper food. You will not do any work except what is needed for the experiment. You will have no contact with any of the guards. I think the experiment will last about five weeks.

'Now, as for the experiment itself. I can't tell you the details of it, partly because I haven't worked them out yet and partly because if you know what the purpose of the experiment is that will affect your performance. But in general terms it is to study the effect of a particular drug on human behaviour. I myself believe that this drug probably has no effect at all, or is if anything a mild sedative. To prove that this is so, I will inject myself with the same drug. I'm not doing this only for that reason, but because I've been forced to conduct these experiments, and I need to be able to show that I'm not asking you to undergo anything that I'm not prepared to undergo myself. For the same reason I need to be able to show that everyone taking part in the experiment is a genuine volunteer.

'The only other thing I can tell you at the moment is that the experiment will consist of your doing certain tests, which will probably be more like children's games than anything else, and I will measure your performance. Are there any questions?'

There was a brief silence. They stared at him with a strange look which he found hard to read. If they had indeed been children he would have said it was that sense of desolation which comes when an expected treat is cancelled by the mysterious whims of the adult world. A deep voice spoke.

'This what you come to tell us? We play games?'

The words seemed to come from nowhere in particular, like a medium's ventriloquial trickery – a useful knack among prisoners.

'It's not exactly games,' he said. 'I haven't worked out the details, because I've never done anything quite like this before. My proper work is with animals. Rats, for instance. I make them do rather simple tricks, such as finding their way through mazes, and I measure how fast they learn to do it. I've got one here, as a matter of fact.'

He put his hand in his pocket and held Quentin up by the scruff, legs and tail dangling. Some rats don't mind this treatment, but Quentin started to wriggle so Foxe, unwilling to lose the slight hold he now had on the prisoners' attention, put him on his left sleeve and let him run up to his shoulder. All along the ranked faces before him eyes opened wider, a movement both involuntary and unanimous, like a bed of mussels opening in response to a change of current.

'The rat has a name?' asked the sourceless deep voice.

'Quentin,' said Foxe. 'That's what the Q stands for.'

They laughed, loud and all together, with a note of surprise and delight, as if what he'd said had been a brilliant, unpredictable pun. The noise startled Quentin, making him nuzzle into Foxe's ear. Abruptly the noise cut out.

'What he saying?' whispered two or three voices together. Foxe shrugged, wishing he could think how to erase the violet dye and return Quentin to ordinary rathood. He didn't want a lot of magical nonsense messing up his task. Probably it was best to treat it all as a joke, he decided.

'I don't pay much attention to what he says. He's a bit mad, if you want to know.'

They stared, so silent that it was hard to believe they were even breathing – stared not at Foxe but at Quentin on his shoulder, making him feel that they were actually looking past him at some monster of the volcanic pit creeping up behind. Carelessly he plucked the rat from its perch and slid it into his pocket. They breathed. They fidgeted.

'OK,' he said. 'I suggest you take a few minutes to think about it. I'd better remind you that I'll need to be satisfied that anyone who volunteers is doing so because he wants to, not because he's been ordered to.'

Foxe strolled away, trying to undo by his walk the mischief he'd done by producing Quentin. He ought to have been frightened; it looked as if he'd now be faced with a batch of prisoners too scared of Quentin to volunteer, and it would be the harbour for Foxe, or the poison, or perhaps a fall from a helicopter ... He didn't care much. It wasn't because he was too tired to care – in fact, despite his exhaustion, he was full of a strange eagerness to begin. His mind was like a student's on a first project, running ahead in an undisciplined way to future details, with none of the groundwork cleared. But a lot of the groundwork was irrelevant in this loony set-up – most of the logical safeguards for a start – you couldn't even arrange for a double-blind system, with only Foxe to do all the work ... Games ... he'd used the word almost unthinkingly, but now it flashed on him that it solved huge problems. In the world of games there is only one vice, which is cheating ... Cheating should be measurable, if the rules were clear enough ... they'd have to think they were being tested for something else, of course – it wasn't Foxe's field, but he'd once shared a flat with a psychologist who was interested in competitiveness and was telling his subjects that he was testing their hearing acuteness ... so you'd need games which seemed to measure something else, but you wouldn't even tell them that ... let it slip, perhaps, and see who passed the word to whom ... no dice, that'd be measuring group-loyalty against rule-acceptance ... no, keep all aspects, both apparent and real aims, *inside* the games ... Umm, umm ... Doctor Trotter wasn't going to fancy any of this ... what he'd liked about Foxe's original story was the stress, the breakdown of social behaviour, the mindless blood and dirt; and that was what he wanted here, more stress, more starvation, the legitimised torture of his enemies in the name of science. Well, he wasn't bloody going to get it. He was going to get games – not for reasons of morality, or of cowardice, but because they'd work. Games.

Vaguely as he strolled around Foxe took in details of the Pit, rather as if he'd arrived too early for an interview in a strange town and was wandering about, his main attention fixed on the coming encounter, but still subconsciously registering elements which combined into an impression of a life-pattern. The walls were rough rock, their monotony relieved here and there by sharp-shadowed crevices into which even the two dozen arc-lights did not shine. It was only rock, and the light only light, and the darkness overhead an unmysterious space beyond the light; but in the arena itself a life-mode had evolved, parts of it – for instance where he passed a block of improvised patched screens from which came the sharp odour of latrines – obvious, and parts alien. Foxe, without much

127

thinking about it, realised that the sand which floored the Pit was not its natural surface, but was brought in to provide some sort of cleanliness. He halted, still considering the problem of games and cheating, and stared at a patch of this sand, one of the alien bits of Pit life, where the surface had been carefully smoothed and covered with a pattern of symbols through which footsteps threaded a spiral path.

'We ready, then,' said a voice.

Foxe looked up and saw a gaunt young man with a pocked face had come up.

'Fine,' said Foxe. 'Any volunteers?'

'All the lot of them, man.'

Foxe didn't sigh or shrug, though the news should have been no less irritating than it had been ten minutes before. But now, OK, he'd lost a point, but he'd got his volunteers.

'You think it will work?' said the young man in a low voice.

'I don't know. It's pretty difficult. This isn't really the right place – and as far as I know nothing like it's been tried before.'

'Seems it begun working this same morning,' said the young man.

'Umm,' said Foxe. He was half way back to the group of volunteers before he was far enough out of his abstraction to realise that the man had been talking not about the experiment but about the pattern on the floor.

4

Foxe lay on a huge soft bed dreaming that he was looking for Lisa-Anna in a strange city. It should have been an anxiety dream, but had none of that feel about it because he was certain of reaching her in the end, and was bitterly disappointed when a voice woke him, speaking close beside his ear.

'Doctor Foxe, you there?'

'I suppose so,' he muttered.

'The President dining in forty minutes. Request your company, uh?'

Foxe groaned, opened his eyes and half sat up. There was no one in the room.

'You hear me, suh?'

The voice came from among the luminous press-buttons on the console beside the bed.

'OK, I'll be there,' said Foxe. 'I haven't got much to wear.'

'Tuxedos, suh. Plenty clothes in closet. Guests assemble at twenty-forty hours in ante-room to left of elevator lobby, first floor.'

The speaker ceased its subliminal hum. Foxe peered at the luminous buttons and pressed the one with the lamp-symbol on it. Light began to glow through the room, increasing in intensity while he kept the button pressed and stopping when he released it. Another button slid the window-shutters away, revealing equatorial stars over the oily harbour and the black hulk of cliff that hid his new laboratory. Yet another, with a temperature-setting knob beside it, started to run a bath next door.

Foxe rose and walked to the clothes-cupboard, which

disappointingly opened with a manually-operated catch, but turned out to be as large as a fair-sized room. Rack on rack of clothes, male and female, seemed to inspect him as he entered. It was like a roomful of ghosts, no, not ghosts, for these presences were nothing if not material, hanging there, waiting to be reanimated. For a moment Foxe, perhaps because his mind was still full of Lisa-Anna who had enjoyed playing with such notions, considered the possible combinations of spirit, flesh and clothing. There are seven in all, one with the set complete, the living man, three with one element missing and three with two. They had names, moreover, even the two-combinations: spirit and clothes were the ghost; spirit and flesh were the savage; clothes and flesh the corpse — no, you'd got the corpse already, as a one-combination. Clothes and flesh were the walking dead.

Foxe made his face grin at the idea, as if to appease Lisa-Anna's ghost. He deliberately didn't look to see whether any of the dresses would have suited her, but went and found a white suit of roughly the right size, a new shirt, tie, socks, shoes even, and carried the loot back to his bed, shutting the ghosts away. As he dumped them something scuttered close by. His heart gave a nervy flicker, then he remembered what it must be and opened the drawer of the bedside table. Quentin peered up at him, jet-eyed.

'Sorry, mate,' said Foxe. 'I forgot. I should have taken you with me — you wouldn't have let me muck around with that sort of stupid fancy, uh? Come and have a bath.'

As he spoke it occurred to him to wonder whether the room was bugged. Probably. In which case he had added yet another involuntary pebble to the cairn of Quentin's supposed magic powers.

The bath-taps might or might not have been gold. The gadget by the bed had got the temperature wrong, so Foxe adjusted it by hand, then climbed in for a long soak. Quentin skated round the bath's wide rim but never quite slithered in. He ate some pink soap which sadly didn't make him froth at the mouth. Foxe watched him, and continued his line of thought. Was he in fact, subconsciously but deliberately, engineering incidents which built up Quentin's reputation? The way he had used him in the pit had, at a rational level, been fairly childish, and at the same time the subconscious motive had been close enough to the surface for him to be vaguely aware of it. In fact his subconscious might long ago have registered the magical symbol on the walls of Back Town, and made the connection with the letter Q. It was even possible that that had influenced him in deciding that Quentin was a nutter . . . And thus made Quentin a nutter?

Quentin, for reasons beyond research, was now trying to drag a large sponge to the corner which he seemed to have decided was his own territory. Foxe watched him with considerable affection, a sentiment strong enough to draw attention to itself. He, Foxe, also seemed to believe in the power of the rat, not as a bearer of mighty magics, but as a charm, a totem. He remembered how the touch of fur had broken the Prime Minister's hypnotic hold. It was only natural: his subconscious, much-repressed, would reach out for symbols of help from the region in which Foxe really did have power. On perilous journeys it would seek to take with it a piece of Foxe's home territory, where the kindly and predictable gods of science ruled. A lab-bred rat, for instance.

Again, Foxe's attention was caught by his own mental processes, by the fact that he had for once let his subconscious out of the dungeons for exercise and air, had even allowed it a momentary vote. The process gave him an odd feeling of being two people, one of whom lived and moved so precisely in the same space as the other that it was normally invisible, but now for the moment had shifted a little, so that its shadowy outline was there, like an image on an ill-tuned television, like Foxe's own reflection in the doubled glass of the laboratory window, that day when he had waited for the Prime

Minister to come and had watched the gardener killing the snake.

'Do you think I'm becoming a bit schizo, mate?' he said. 'They say it's a common response to stress.'

Startled by his voice Quentin let go of the sponge. Because his paws got no grip on the glassy surface he had been using the curve of the rim for leverage and now, without the sponge's weight to hold him back, he fell with a plop into the bath.

'Twenty-thirty-five, now, suh,' urged the voice from the speaker.

'Coming,' said Foxe.

He picked Quentin from the huge warm towel on which he'd been grooming himself dry and put him in the pocket of his dinner-jacket. It was a tightish squeeze, but Foxe didn't want him nicked by some magical power-maniac. And besides that, he thought, I'm scared, so I take my totem along.

The lift worked. The white-jacketed prisoner-slave in the lobby where Foxe had been told to wait made an excellent Martini. The air-conditioning was well-tuned, producing an atmosphere that smelt and felt like fresh air and yet was cooler than a tropic evening. In a way this was a contrast with the outside world even more striking than the one between the luxury of the palace and the emaciating poverty beyond. That it should actually be possible to buy efficiency here! But why not? It was ridiculous to suppose that nothing on the Islands ever worked properly. Captain Angiah, for instance, gave an impression of dedicated efficiency, and according to Dreiser the secret police did their work with skill ... It was even possible, Foxe thought, that Doctor Trotter regarded efficiency as a luxury, to be enjoyed by the few, that for the masses he *preferred* the bus services to be erratic, the electric supply to keep failing. His bent, certainly, was towards chaos.

For at least twenty minutes Foxe waited, gazing out of

the window at the dockyard scene. Gangs of men were still unloading the ships, sharp-shadowed under bluish floodlights. Above the castle's silhouetted crenellations the same acid light glowed, a Satanic aureole, showing that the courtyard, like the docks and Pit, knew no proper dark. While he watched the gesticulating derricks a fresh shift arrived from the castle, so he guessed the work went on all night. Soon after that the steam-engine started another run, its fountain of smoke glowing orange and pricked with upshot sparks. The previous shift staggered away into the dark, one or two of them leaning so heavily on comrades' shoulders that they were really being carried. At last came the sigh and suck of a moving lift and the whisper of doors. A familiar voice filled the air.

'. . . when I say bad time coming, then bad time do be coming. That's sure. Here you are, my clever honey boy, condriving yourself to be Prime Minister and this and that, and still you never know to be serious. Who's an empty man?'

Her voice was blanketed by the Prime Minister's laugh. Nape prickling, Foxe turned and watched her waddle towards him.

'Hi, Foxy!' she cried. 'Coming home special for to see you!'

She was wearing an extremely décolleté long dress of coffee-coloured satin, covered with seed-pearls and sequins. A display of opals lay on the broad shelf of her bosom, as if being proffered for Foxe to choose from. Strings of pearls and other jewels threaded the amber stook of her hair. She was still wearing her reflecting sunglasses in which Foxe could watch himself, double and miniaturised, bowing like a stage count. At the same time he registered that her greeting, if taken at face value, meant that she at least hadn't been expecting him to arrive that day, so that if Ladyblossom's death was part of a long-planned plot to trap him onto Main Island, she was not in the plot. Small comfort.

'It's an honour to meet you again, ma'am,' he said.

'Just the family tonight, Doctor,' said the Prime Minister. 'Come along, mother, we mustn't keep His Excellency waiting.'

'You take my arm, Foxy,' ordered Mrs Trotter.

She hauled him close against her side, like a liner warping a tender to her. Foxe was thankful that Quentin was in his opposite pocket or he would have been pulped against her corsetry.

They ate in what Foxe guessed was the state banqueting room, just the four of them sitting along one side of the table on the end dais and looking down the length of two more tables, all set with cutlery and plates and glasses for something like a hundred diners, and decorated with gushers of exotic flowers and ziggurats of fruit and tall candles, every one of them burning. Some twenty of the prisoner-servants stood around the walls, as if ready for an inrush of guests; in fact Foxe wondered whether a hundred servings of the nine or so courses which he was offered had been prepared. He drank champagne, then hock, then better claret than he'd ever tasted, then port of the same snob-value. The Prime Minister and Mrs Trotter drank milk and the President Coca-Cola. At first Foxe thought that this had been laid on as part of the Prime Minister's deliberate caprice, a super-luxurious prelude to some new degradation of him; but slowly he came to perceive that it was normal, that even when the others were away the President would dine thus alone, humming and fidgeting.

The President said nothing throughout the meal and appeared not even to notice Foxe sitting on his right. He showed himself quite capable of handling a knife and fork, if with rather messy results, but mostly his mother, sitting on his left, would lean across and cut up his food for him and then feed him mouthful by mouthful. A couple of times she opened her reticule and withdrew a little sachet of paper from which she sprinkled a powder on his food. While she did so she muttered rapidly. One of these ingredients sent the President into a convulsion of coughing, and Foxe saw out of the corner of his eye the President's attendant – the same whom he'd seen that morning – moving forward with an enamel basin but it wasn't needed.

Mrs Trotter treated all these distractions as negligible, talking almost continuously either across the President to Foxe or across both of them to her other son. Foxe was naïvely surprised how much of the world she'd seen, and what a collection of notables she had met. For instance, she was critical of the decor of both Buckingham Palace and the White House, but considered the Shah of Iran 'discriminading'. She spoke at length of a meal she'd had in Taiwan as 'best in the world, better than the President of France giving me.' This was all small-talk, but had to be listened to, as she snapped for attention the moment Foxe's mind began to wander.

Somewhere around the middle of the meal – after a course of plump little birds which had been delicately boned and then stuffed, so that they could be eaten whole – the President gave a long, gargling sigh and fell asleep. Mrs Trotter patted his cheek fondly, then nodded to the attendant, who brought up a gadget like a small fork-lift truck, ran it under the President's chair and wheeled him away.

'The Lord give,' said Mrs Trotter, her voice thicker than ever with solemnity and emotion, 'and then He rob you blind with His free hand. He give me one clever son and then He say "That's enough for this old witch," and he give me one stupid son. You think I treating the boy right, Foxy?'

'Well, how are you treating him, ma'am?'

With an eager sweep of her arm she shoved the President's remaining cutlery to one side, like an old general clearing a space to demonstrate how he fought his last campaign, and emptied her reticule onto the table – leaves, sachets, ampoules, pill-boxes and withered shreds of what looked like skin and sinew.

'Lord, Lord,' she croaked, 'the things a woman carries

135

round. That marra root stale, for sure. What this bit? What you think this bit, Foxy?'

She had been peering at the collection with her nose a scant couple of inches from the table, but still didn't remove her glasses, which must have been almost opaque in the candle-light. Foxe looked at the leaf-like scrap she poked towards him. How on earth could he be expected . . . but there was something familiar about it.

'Some kind of ear,' he said, decisively. 'Not a rat's – it's too large and thin. A bat's, perhaps.'

'Right. Bat-ear,' she mumbled, snatching it back. She had known, of course, and wanted to see if he knew. 'Still good, but don' give him that, for sure. Snake-apple – that last for ever . . .'

'Mother, you're not carrying snake-apple round with you?' said Doctor Trotter in a teasing voice. 'There's a law against that, you know. Interesting plant, Doctor – at one time I hoped your Company might find a pharmaceutical use for it, but it seems that the Creator planted it for no other purpose than to kill people.'

'So I gather . . .' began Foxe, but missed his moment.

'Foxy know all that,' snapped Mrs Trotter, as if calling an unruly meeting to order. 'Now *this* I give my boy Mondays, 'cept when the moon full.'

'What is it?' asked Foxe, eyeing the greyish granules in her palm.

'Owl-crap.'

'Aha.'

She seemed to take the grunt for qualified approval, and throughout the next course rattled on about her campaign for the President's health. It was like street warfare: in every artery, lurking along the bowel, holed up in pancreas and kidney, were hostile troops that had to be winkled out with high-explosive laxatives and herbal flame-throwers and the hideous hand-to-hand of charm and philtre. Meanwhile the city was under siege, assassins ringed its walls with knives and spells, and other-worldly enemies hovered above it, hoping to snatch its chief treasure, her son's mighty soul. To Foxe the spells she used, the dangers she named, were mostly silly mumbo-jumbo, but slowly a historical logic became clear. Like a child playing hospitals with a doll, she had dosed her son since he was born with any ingredient that amused her. It sounded as if he might have been a comparatively normal baby, and now he was this . . . this thing.

'What you think, Foxy?' she snapped, catching him by surprise because she didn't seem to have finished her recital.

'Oh . . . Well, I think perhaps you're overdoing it,' he said. Very little of him wanted to laugh. Her methods were ridiculous, but the horror of the effect kept his tone grave.

'What you mean?' she said sulkily.

'You see, drugs aren't simple things. They have more than one effect on the body, and if you use them together they affect each other's effects. Sometimes you have to use more than one drug, perhaps to suppress a side-effect or something like that, but you don't if you can help it. And on top of that two drugs may have a side-effect which neither of them has alone. A lot of my job is looking for things like that, but even so we sometimes make mistakes. I remember a couple of years ago we had to withdraw a stuff we'd just brought out, a decoagulant for thrombosis cases, when we found that if the patient had been taking a very common tranquilliser – even if he'd stopped taking it several weeks before – he got severe bleeding of the intestine.'

The pout of her mouth lessened, she began to nod, assimilating Foxe's mumbo jumbo to hers. The Prime Minister laughed.

'You'll have a job persuading my mother to leave anything out of her recipes. You're a vicarious hypochondriac, Mother.'

'Nothing to do with you, O,' she said. 'The Lord cheat me there, Foxy – give me this clever son with no soul, and that stupid son with a 'normous soul – soul big 'nough for two men.'

'The Lord arranged things very well,' said the Prime Minister, somehow adjusting his tone to share amusement and disbelief with Foxe and acceptance and credulity with his mother.

'That for sure,' she croaked, appeased. 'That why this my son get so strong, Foxy. Enemies, they can go for to shoot him, go for to poison him, but they can't lay for his soul, cause of for him an empty man. Right, and you tell me I giving that my other son too many these things?'

'I'd have said so, though it isn't my field, really. Perhaps rather more exercise, to let them work out of his body . . . I don't think you need cut down on the incantations, because I doubt if they have side-effects in the same kind of way . . .'

'Right. Right. You're a good boy, Foxy. You help this my son, I look after that my other son.'

She swept her ingredients into her reticule, rose and waddled away down the hall. The servants shut their eyes and bowed as she passed.

'You managed that very well,' said Doctor Trotter. 'It is important not to treat my mother as a fool. She is a woman of very great . . . abilities.'

The last sentence was clearly a euphemism. As a man of education and experience Doctor Trotter could not of course say that his mother had the power, but that was what he meant.

'Yes, sir, I know, but . . .' Foxe began.

'Now you must tell me how you are getting on with my experiment,' said the Prime Minister.

'I've hardly begun yet, sir,' said Foxe. A dark hand, white-sleeved, emaciated, slid in front of him a plate of ice-cream sculptured to the shape of a turtle. It snagged his attention.

'I'd rather not talk about it till we're alone, sir,' he said.

'We *are* alone. Ah, I see. These people are hardly likely to bear witness against you, doctor.'

138

'It isn't that,' said Foxe, with some of the energy and confidence which came from stepping into his own field. 'You want this experiment to work – to produce a result which has some meaning. I don't think it will, but I'm going to do my best, so it's not my fault if it doesn't. Now, one thing which will make any results completely useless will be if the subjects know what's expected of them – or even guess. If the slightest rumour got back . . .'

'They are totally isolated, Doctor.'

'Yes. That's what makes the whole thing even faintly possible. But I'm not taking any risks. I've not read a lot of prison literature, but I do know how people seem to smuggle news in and out of what look like totally closed situations.'

Doctor Trotter's face darkened, perhaps at Foxe's obstinacy, perhaps at the notion of his victims eluding his power in even so slight a fashion. He ate several spoonfuls of ice-cream.

'I have a country to run, Doctor,' he said. 'There are many things I can afford to leave to no one else, so I have not much time to spare. One advantage of bringing you here is that it means we can discuss the experiment over dinner, like this. My mother and brother usually leave well before the meal is over. I wish to follow your work very closely.'

(Meal after meal, night after night, in this place, under this pressure – the sirring, the baaing ma'ams, the soapy assents and cringeing disagreements – watching the President being fed, adjudicating on the dried entrails of frogs . . . Foxe could see only one way out, and started to work towards it.)

'It isn't like that, sir. I mean there's often nothing to discuss. I once spent three and a half months working out the details of a job which took eleven days to run.'

'I am not a patient man, Doctor.'

'You're an intelligent one, though. You can see that it's going to be much harder to get valid results from an experiment like this than it would be with rats. Everything

139

about my rats is known and controlled – their heredity and their rearing. Any which show the slightest sign of abnormality are weeded out. You know that rat which you called subversive – the first thing I shall do when I get back to Europe is to see that all his first-step and second-step siblings are removed from the breeding pools. That's the measure of control I expect.'

Doctor Trotter nodded vehemently, several times, as if to show he understood, approved and hoped to emulate.

'Well, sir. This new group of, er . . .'

'Subjects.'

'OK. Subjects. I know almost nothing about them . . .'

'I will see that you have their police records.'

'I suppose that will be a bit of help. But for instance I've obviously got no control over their genetic inheritance. They've all been reared differently, fed differently. They'll have widely different metabolisms. I shall have to start with a whole series of tests – psychology, intelligence, physique – to establish even a vague norm. But more important than that, I shall have to get to know them. I shall have to rely on my experience as an experimenter – my nose, you might almost say – to tell me where that norm lies. This is all going to take time.'

'I am not a patient man.'

'I know. The only way I can think of to speed the process up is to go and live with them.'

'Don't try to cheat me, Doctor. The only way you can think of to prove to the world at large that you are not guilty of experiments on unwilling prisoners is to become a prisoner yourself.'

'I hadn't even thought of that,' said Foxe. 'I don't think it would help much. But the last experiment I did in Europe involved keeping a batch of monkeys under continual stress, and to all intents and purposes I lived in my lab while it was going on. It's the way I work, in tricky experiments. I'm very grateful for the President's hospitality, sir, and obviously I would be much more comfortable here. But, for instance, how can I know what the guards are up to when I'm not there?'

Foxe found that he was, and had been for some time, facing the Prime Minister's direct stare. It was like a tiger's mask, the deep-folded brow, the hard hypnotic gaze. He was conscious of the warmth and softness of Quentin, asleep in his jacket pocket. Doctor Trotter spoke at last in a tiger's rumbling, jungly purr.

'Very well. I will give the orders. You shall live in the Pit.'

5

Next morning Foxe walked alone to the Castle, carrying his own bag. He had a slight hangover – enough to make him realise that he must have been about one-third drunk when he'd made his suicidal suggestion the night before. He stared about him at the glittering sea and the gawky shapes of the harbour, trying to absorb and somehow store away the feel and smell of liberty against the weeks of imprisonment ahead. Not, of course, that he was free here; the cliffs looked mostly unclimbable, and all along the top ran a complex of chain-link fences which marked the edge of the prison area. No doubt escapes from the working gangs were rare.

Quentin's biorhythms were still in a tangle. He had slept most of the night, woken before dawn and was now at his most active, refusing to stay in Foxe's pocket and insisting on riding on his shoulder. As they reached the railway line a group of guards came out of the tunnel, returning to duty no doubt after a night in the town at the top of the cliffs. They were teasing and mocking a large corporal, who returned their jeers with cheerful swagger, but when they saw Foxe they all fell silent and came to a shuffling halt to let him pass. It seemed an appalling omen, this sudden solemnity at the sight of the man walking towards his doom, and Foxe's nape began to prickle with their sensed stares. He could hear them start to move again, following him towards the castle. Their voices murmured at the fringe of earshot in tones of serious discussion. Foxe was almost at the gate before he guessed that it was not the sight of him that had changed their mood, but of

Quentin, though the mark on his back was surely invisible from the angle at which they'd seen him.

'Hey, you're famous,' he muttered. 'Classic bit of rumour-spreading, uh? Still, you're going to have to go in my pocket now, or they won't let us through the gate.'

He reached up, plucked the rat off his shoulder and held him for a moment in front of his face.

'You might have been a bit more on the spot last night, mate,' he said. 'Kept me out of this.'

Quentin paid no attention. He just crouched in Foxe's grip, beady eyes unblinking, nude tail dangling, refusing to be anthropomorphised. This time when Foxe stuffed him down into his side pocket he stayed there. At once the sound of the soldiers' voices changed its tone. One pair of footsteps quickened, and by the time Foxe reached the ominous black gate the large corporal was striding beside him.

'Hi, Doc,' he said, as though they'd known each other for years. 'I'll see you through. I'm Louis. I look after those dumb bastards in the Pit.'

Close too he didn't look quite so big, about Foxe's size and build. It was the uniform and the swagger and the attention of his comrades which had given him added appearance of mass. He was a black-brown Negro, big-lipped like the old cartoons of darkies, with blood-shot eyes under almost hairless brows. He had the confidence of animals which exist fully inside their own brute nature.

'Oh, thanks,' said Foxe. 'I think I'm expected.'

'Sure,' said Louis, not seeming to notice the silliness of the cliché in this context. He grunted at the sentry, kicked at the wicket till it boomed and stepped at once into the gap when it opened. Foxe and two of the other soldiers followed him across the reeking courtyard to the gate into the cliff and then waited as he had for Captain Angiah while Louis went into the little guard hut. This time, being merely frightened and not wholly dazed by terror, he was able to sort out a little of the routine; the guard in the hut telephoned through to the guards in the Pit to check that all was secure both sides before the doors were opened. Very likely there was some kind of switch inside which also had to be pressed before the motor would turn. In a way it was curiously like some of the gadgets which Foxe had devised in his time to test the ingenuity of rats – only, of course, he had always given the rats an answer . . .

At the far end of the tunnel, black against the white glare from the Pit, three guards were waiting to go off duty.

'Where you been, man?' said one.

'Up the town,' said Louis. 'Got to wait twenty minutes top of the line. That damn engine running slower and slower.'

'And that girl Louis got in the Avenida wanting it more and more,' added one of the relief guards.

'You owing me half an hour each morning, Louis, soon you owing me whole night. I be taking it off your girl, uh?'

They all guffawed, and the men going off duty began to shamble into the tunnel.

'Hey!' called Louis. 'Who that fellow down there, that new man? He ain't meant to be in the Pit.'

'They send him in jus' before you coming,' called a voice, already blurred with echoes. 'Man to read and write for Doctor Foxe, they saying.'

'That's right,' said Foxe. 'I know about him.'

He glanced down into the arena and saw why Louis had picked the newcomer out so quickly. It wasn't just that he was separated from the other prisoners, a thin shape sitting on the sand with his head buried between his up-drawn knees. The man's shirt, though tattered, was still of such harsh unmitigable violet that Foxe recognised him at once for Mr Trotter, the herbalist.

However long he stayed in the Pit Foxe never became quite used to the sense of being watched. It wasn't the guards that bothered him, it was the feeling that he inhabited a globule of relentless light, like a drop of

144

infected water illuminated for inspection through a microscope. Somewhere above, beyond the furry dark, a stupendous eye peered down. The feeling was already strong in him as he walked across the sand that first morning.

'Mr Trotter?'

The thin, scholarly face looked up, haggard with apprehension.

'Holy Bridget! You! You get me in here, uh?'

'I'm afraid so. I'm sorry. I didn't know it would be you. I just need somebody who can read and write to keep records for me while I do an experiment. You won't be hurt – and nor will anyone else. I hope.'

A change came over Mr Trotter's face.

'Science?' he said, breathing the word as if it were somehow holy.

'As far as possible,' said Foxe. 'It's not going to be easy, but we've got to do the best we can. I dare say I could exchange you if you don't want to take it on.'

'No. Sure,' said Mr Trotter, scrambling almost eagerly to his feet. 'Better than shovelling coal into that bloody engine. Every time she come to the cliff I been all scared she going to take me with her. Right. What we do?'

'We start by taking records of all these people – age, name, and so on. And I've worked out a rough IQ test. There's supposed to be a trestle table and chairs for us, and paper and things. Ah yes, over there . . .'

Ten minutes later Foxe and Mr Trotter were sitting behind the table and the first of the 'subjects' was ready to begin. He was a pale-skinned man, his haggard cheeks fringed by a tight-curling black beard, and with eyes so large and fiery that he looked as if he were in the grip of some drug.

'Please sit down,' said Foxe. 'Now, what's your name?'

'Plantain.'

'Uh?'

'Musa Paradisiaca,' said Mr Trotter. 'No relation of your European plantain.'

'It is my naming name,' said the man. 'On the mountain we are reborn. We take a true name which we tell only to the Secret Ones, and a naming name for men to use. My naming name is Plantain.'

He had a deep, priest-like voice which made Foxe guess that this had been the ventriloquist. A nutter, too. A pal for Quentin. But OK, if you can name experimental rats after people you can name experimental people after plants.

'Age? From your, er, pre-mountain birth, I mean.'

'Twenty-eight years.'

'Trade?'

'Magician.'

'I will put down "Social worker",' whispered Mr Trotter.

'OK,' said the man, indifferent. 'Provided Doctor Foxe know the truth.'

Foxe tried to grunt as if he had the slightest idea what was going on. The selection of experimental rats was never like this. As if to counterbalance the man's nonsense he fished Quentin out of his pocket and put him, drowsy now, on the table. The man glanced at him with interest but without fear.

'All right,' said Foxe. 'Now, the next thing is an intelligence test; it's very rough, but it's the best I can do in the circumstances. I'm going to ask you six questions, and I want you to answer as quickly as you can, or to tell me if you don't know the answer or can't understand the question. Ready?'

Foxe had no professional experience of IQ tests, and regarded them, even at their best, as outside the boundaries of genuine science. But six years ago he'd lived for one winter with a dark, giggling, motherly girl called Margaret, who'd had a job with an Educational Research unit as a test-tester. There'd been a fuel strike that winter and she and Foxe had spent their spare time in bed, taking turns to extrude a chilling arm above the eiderdown to hold the paper on which she was working at the time and then pick holes in her colleagues' logic. This remembered smattering was enough for the moment; it didn't matter that it was going to be statistically valueless, because its main function was to mislead the prisoners about the actual nature of the experiment. Still, the man who called himself Plantain scored pretty high.

'Thank you,' said Foxe when he'd finished. 'Now will you go and sit over there, away from the others? I don't want any communication between those who have done the tests and those who haven't.'

Plantain rose and glanced down at Quentin, who was sleepily gnawing a pencil.

'We will not cheat you,' he said.

Hm. We'll see about that, thought Foxe. That's the whole point.

'Next, please,' he called.

A woman rose and came striding across the sand. She was pale fawn and quite pretty, apart from her emaciation and sadly protruding teeth. Her ragged shirt was open to her navel and she stared blazingly at Foxe as though daring him to glance below her neck-line.

'Please sit down,' he said. 'What's your name?'

'Cocoa Bean,' she snapped.

They were in their twenty-third interview – a man who called himself Lobelia – when the darkness above found a voice.

'Dinner time, Doc. You wanting it now?'

'Three minutes,' said Foxe.

He finished his questions and called again. A basket came dangling down on a rope, and then a plastic dustbin. Mr Trotter sniffed with flared nostrils.

'Hey! That smell like *food*!' said Mr Trotter. 'They been feeding us on shit outside!'

He sprang to his feet and rushed towards the bin, a one-man stampede. No one else moved.

'And there's plates too!' he cried.

Foxe reached him before he could actually plunge into what looked like a goat-meat stew.

147

'Hold on,' he said. 'You and I come last, I'm afraid. But I'll see you get your share.'

'Holy Bridget! That's *oranges*!'

'Right,' said Foxe, feeling absurdly smug and competent at having thus far managed to keep his side of his bargain with the prisoners. 'Now, I want to see that they all get equal rations. What we'll do is this . . .'

It took less time than he expected, because the prisoners accepted the discipline of exact rations with complete understanding. The stew was already tepid, and accompanied by greasy rice, but nobody began to eat until they were back in their separate groups. They chanted what sounded like a grace – solo and response, and ate in silence. Foxe and Mr Trotter returned to their table with their own share.

'Pardon me, sir,' said Mr Trotter. 'I ain't exactly superstitious, but you mind putting that rat away while I eating?'

'No, of course,' said Foxe. 'Come here, mate. Now, you go to sleep for a bit. Look here's a bit of orange peel to take to bed with you.'

He slid Quentin away and settled to his meal, a soapy mess of meat-shreds and gluey blobs of starch, almost saltless. By all rights the contrast with last night's dinner should have made it inedible, but Foxe felt strangely hungry and ate with appetite. He must have burned a lot of fuel in the last mad days, but now he was settling to something like his proper work. He reached for the morning's records and began to browse down the columns of figures, all in Mr Trotter's looping, slanted Victorian copperplate.

'It reads like a cast-list for *Watership Down*,' he said.

'Uh?'

'Kid's book about rabbits, all named after plants. It's been a sort of cult success, not only with kids. My last girl thought it was the greatest thing since Shakespeare.'

It was odd to be suddenly freed to talk about Lisa-Anna in this place.

'I could put you in the Latin names,' said Mr Trotter. 'That way we can talk about them, you and me, and they ain't knowing who we're naming.'

'I don't know. They're a very bright bunch – that or I got my IQ test wrong. Who are they, do you know?'

'You didn't know?' whispered Mr Trotter. 'Holy Bridget! They's all that's left of the Khandhars. You 'member we been talking 'bout that, back in my hotel. Doctor O sent the Old Woman up the Mountain, so all the people been too scared to help the Khandhars, an' the soldiers ain't scared no more. There's two sorts of Khandhar – all one movement, but some of them taking more interest in the political side. Doctor O shot all those sort when he caught them, and now there's only a few left in New York and places. These fellows in here are the religious sort. I don't know why he don't shoot them too – maybe he likes to see he's got them trapped and wriggling.'

'I see,' said Foxe. 'I wonder how Plantain knew my name – I'd been meaning to keep that quiet. Perhaps the guards told them when they were ordering them to volunteer.'

'Khandhars know a lot of things.'

'I suppose so. Never mind. The real thing is that a bunch of highly motivated revolutionaries aren't much of a cross-section. They're probably all outside the curve of normality. Though I suppose you could say that's true of most people who find themselves in jail.'

'Not on the Islands, so, sir. Look, in my hut outside there was two fellows I know from Hog's Cay. One of them was arrested for loving up the Mayor's daughter. Mayor's wife, she finds them at it so Mayor tells the police this fellow's subversive and pow, he's in the Castle. The other fellow, Mayor's daughter makes a play for him, but he heard about this first fellow, so he tries to excuse himself. And the Mayor's daughter she gets angry and tells her Papa this fellow's subversive, so pow, he's in the Castle

149

for not loving up the Mayor's daughter. Mayor's cousin of Doctor O, course.'

'Yes, it certainly sounds like a random process. But I'd have thought Trotters got left out. What happened to you? I came to look for you a few days after we met and they pretended they'd never heard of you.'

Mr Trotter smiled wearily as he peeled his orange.

'You remember that bird Daisy-Daisy?'

'The barmaid in the Igloo Bar?'

'That's the one. This morning I am a little drunk – hell, I am a little drunk all the damn time I am running that hotel – so I loose off at you about these Khandhars. Now, this Daisy-Daisy wants to buy a Chevvy for her man, and she come to hear about this other cousin of mine wanting my job, so she goes to him and he gives her the money and she tells the police. So me too, I'm in the Castle for a clapped out Chevvy for a bum fisherman. But I guess my Mamma will start working on Doctor O, soon, get me out of here.'

'I hope so. I'll do my best, too, though I'm not at all sure how much leverage I've got. Do you want me to stop calling you by your name? I mean, would you be in any danger from these Khandhars if they found out who you were?'

'Hell, no. That fellow calling himself Plantain, he's my cousin Denver. Played with him most of the time when we was kids, and he liked to boss us other fellows around even then. A real Trotter, Denver.'

Foxe suddenly found he could eat no more of the clammy rice, so he lifted Quentin out and showed him the remnants of his meal. Yes, Quentin understood about rice and nosed over the rim of the metal plate, whiskers quivering. Foxe felt Mr Trotter stiffen away from him.

'I'm sorry,' said Foxe. 'I forgot. Do you want me to put him away again? He's got to eat sometime.'

'I ain't superstitious,' said Mr Trotter. 'And it's *your* plate.'

'What's this all about, anyway? The servants at the

Palace and the guards here seem dead scared of him, but you aren't and the Khandhars aren't. I've guessed it's something to do with that mark, because I've seen it on walls and places, but on him it's only a Q upside-down.'

'Bridget! You don' know what you is carrying round,' gasped Mr Trotter, lapsing deeper into Island patois. 'Yeh, course the mark am there for accident. Much stronger this way than if you is putting it there of purpose. This am meaning *he* want it put there.'

'Who?'

Mr Trotter made a curious wavering sign with his left hand.

'The Sunday Dwarf,' he breathed.

The calendar in the Pit was going to be marked only by meals. For the time being these arrived regularly, according to Foxe's contract, but when that evening he tried to have the arc-lights dimmed for sleep he found that there were clear limits to his command. In the end he lay down like the others on a roll of sacking on the shadowless sand and hoped that his residual exhaustion from the last three days would drag him into oblivion.

It didn't work. He could sleep for a while, a dull, unrestful doze, but then he would wake with his mind already active. It was as though a flywheel had been unable to stop and now, lacking the control of having to raise a work-load, was spinning faster and faster each time he slept until it was almost at the point where its own centrifugal stresses would tear it apart; then an alarm signal fizzed inside his mind and woke him to slow the flywheel down by thinking. At one moment, he would be asleep and the next awake, with his brain already in the middle of a train of thought . . . *clumps . . . eight groups, four control . . . say five games to establish norm . . . allow for increasing expertise . . . later begin to exchange players between groups, but of course keep controls separate throughout . . . let them think it's a test of magical powers . . . that gives them greater incentive to cheat and*

151

*it's the kind of thing Doctor O might be after ... time
games ... if all four control groups score score higher –
improve their score faster ... well, it might have signifi-
cance ... If they were rats ... rats under unvarying light ...*
All of a sudden Foxe dropped into darkness, to wake again
after an unguessable interval and find he was thinking
about drug-doses ... *Four groups experimental ... could
have four dose-levels ... much less flexible when it comes
to interchanging group-members ... one level then –
fairly high for quick results, but leave room to increase
dose if tolerance builds up ...* Only once in the whole
night did it cross Foxe's mind that it was absurd that he
should be applying this intensity of mental energy to a
problem which he knew quite well was a nonsense.
Carefully, trying not to rouse his body to the level of his
mind's activity, he turned on his other side, keeping his
eyes screwed tight against the glare. It's only natural, he
thought. Trapped in a maze it doesn't know, the mind tries
to recreate familiar mazes. To-morrow I'll wear a blindfold.

They were playing a trial run of clumps next morning
when the pulleys of the gangway started their tortured
creaking. Foxe pushed his stop-watch across to Mr Trotter.

'Can you manage by yourself for a bit?' he said.

'Sure.'

'The important thing is not to let a messenger from one
group overhear the word you've given to another one. If
two of them come together, see that one stops at the line.'

'OK.'

Mr Trotter was too languid and self-confident to make
a good lab-worker – he'd need a lot of watching ... Foxe
waited for the gangway to touch the sand and at once
began to scamper up. Half way he was met by legs,
uniformed, supporting large buttocks, black against a
dazzling lamp while the upper torso shaded into darkness.

'I can't have anyone in the Pit just now,' said Foxe.

The man's right arm moved up and out of sight, so that

152

Foxe thought he was about to be struck. In fact he was being saluted.

'Prime Minister here, Doc,' said Louis. 'He say you to come up.'

'Oh. Hell. OK. Thanks.'

Foxe followed Louis up into the delicious semi-dark above the lamps and found Doctor Trotter leaning on the rail of the gallery and gazing down into the arena. The upshot shadows gave his large face a look of whimsical malevolence, and there seemed to be no eyes in the sockets.

'What is happening, Doctor Foxe?'

Foxe looked down at the brilliant, shadowless circle, thinking how strangely the few feet difference distanced him from the scene below. A minute before he had been a participant, a creature in the maze; now he was leaning above it, explaining the activities below in much the same manner as he'd once explained the performance of his rats to Doctor Trotter.

'This is a trial run, sir,' he said. 'It's based on a game called clumps. Each group is trying to guess a word which only one of them knows; they ask him questions, which he can only answer by nodding or shaking his head.'

'A game?'

'I can control a game, you see. I can devise it with set limits. And then I can make it to the players' advantage to cheat, and I can measure how much the drug affects the tendency to cheat. You could say it's a small-scale model of your people's tendency to break the laws you make.'

'But if they know you are expecting them to cheat . . .?'

'I hope they won't get that far. I'm setting it up so that it looks like some sort of experiment with intelligence, but I'm going to let them guess that it's really to do with psychic abilities, telepathy and telekinesis and so on. When we start taking the drugs . . .'

'You are going to take this drug yourself, Doctor?'

'Yes. I thought . . .'

'What if it makes *you* virtuous?'

153

Doctor Trotter exploded into one of his monstrous laughs; it seemed not so much to pierce the darkness as to impregnate it, a booming mass of sound hovering above the arena. The scene changed at the signal. Foxe had noticed a girl half-running from the tables back to her group, and had been thinking he'd have to see they all moved at a regulation speed, when she stopped dead at the sound. Heads, hitherto intent over the game, looked up.

'Now that,' said Foxe coldly, 'is a good example of how to spoil an experiment. The whole timing of this section of the game isn't any longer comparable with other sections . . .'

'Games,' said Doctor Trotter. 'I am not very interested in games. When will they start taking the drug?'

'As soon as I've got enough data on their performance without it. About five days, with luck.'

'I am not a patient man, Doctor.'

'You don't imagine I want to hang around here longer than I have to?'

'Do you normally talk to Prime Ministers in that tone of voice? Or is it because I am a black man?'

The tiger-purr was deliberate now, inciting Foxe towards punishable rudeness. He drew a breath and spoke as neutrally as he was able.

'We are looking for a significant change in behaviour. To do that we have to establish what normal behaviour consists of.'

'We know that already – not how they behave in children's games, but how they behave in real life. Our interrogation records are very thorough. We know that these people are, and what they have done, in great detail. Their normal behaviour is shown in contexts of stress and violence, not in the relaxation of childish pastimes. What you must do is set up a similar context here and study their reactions. Suppose, for instance, they were allowed to think that violence might achieve something – their freedom, for instance – you could then study how far the drug

154

affects their readiness to attempt to escape. What are your objections to that?'

Foxe managed not to sigh. It was, *mutatis mutandis*, a typical layman's suggestion.

'Well,' he said. 'A sedative would have the same effect. Then it's something you could only do once, and that's statistically useless – in this field you prove things by showing that they happen with measurable frequency. And however detailed these records of yours are, I don't imagine they were compiled with this idea in mind. It might take me months – years even – to extract statistics from them which could be compared with anything I can lay on in here.'

'How can you know that? You have not listened to them. I insist that you will at least do that before you dismiss their usefulness – in fact I shall give orders for them to be brought in here – the guard-cell at the mouth of the tunnel would be suitable. Your assistant down there is clearly capable of supervising these games, once you have told him what to do, and that will give you time to listen to the records. Is there anything else?'

'I don't think so,' said Foxe dully. 'Oh, yes – my assistant – I believe he's a relation of yours – he oughtn't to be here. He was drunk and he talked a little indiscreetly to me, and a girl who overheard him was bribed to tell the police so that someone else could have his job.'

Doctor Trotter turned from the rail, benign and patronising.

'I read the files, Doctor. Cousin Paul is being punished for running an important hotel badly. My justice is more even-handed than you think.'

He nodded and strolled away. Foxe moved to the top of the gangway but didn't at once go down it; instead he stood there, trying to master his shudders and swallow away the taste of vomit in his mouth. The usual taut anger that built inside him when anyone interfered with his work was now mixed with fear. Why me? he thought; and then, Why anyone? There was something more here than what

Dreiser had called caprice, something more than mere boredom of superfluous power playing a kind of patience, with human cards, shuffling and reshuffling the pack to see how long it took for the card that was Foxe to emerge at the very bottom. Certainly there was that – Foxe guessed that long ago Doctor Trotter had started to play the same game with Captain Angiah, and had now nearly got it out – but there was something more, which the one word 'Game?', breathed with questioning contempt, had expressed. This was not a game. The mad and evil tyrant genuinely wanted to make his subjects good, and thereby make himself a kind of god. This was a serious political aim, such as another government might have proposed about agricultural reform or educational expansion. Foxe was unable to explain to himself why it should seem more monstrous than any catalogue of tortures and degradations, but he found his shudders gone and was able to walk down the steps. As he came into the glare Mr Trotter made a performance of demonstrating how neatly all the papers were stacked on the tables.

An anomaly began to emerge. Group D won that game, and the next, and the next – each time by a whole round or more. After the third win, while the other groups were still playing, Foxe went to check on them. Each group seemed to have elected itself a leader without argument or discussion, and Group D had chosen Vine, a wiry little man, older than most of the others and very black; he had once been trained in physical education and something about his bearing, a characteristic combination of stiffness and alertness, helped Foxe to distinguish him among the so far half-sorted faces. The five players in Group D squatted in an arc on the sand, heads bowed, silent and relaxed. They all looked up as Foxe settled in front of them.

'You're doing well,' he said. 'I just want to check you've got the rules right. The person who knew the word was

156

only nodding or shaking his head? He wasn't making any other sign?'

'Sure, sure,' said Vine.

'Um,' said Foxe. 'Take the word "Shoes" in the last game – can you remember how that went?'

Three of the group looked at Vine. He glanced across the arena to Group B, which included Plantain. The fifth member of the group, a girl, bowed her head.

'This is Cedar's word,' said Vine in a low voice. 'We begin to ask him two, three questions – can't remember those – then Cactus say "Shoes".'

'What about "Helicopter"?'

'My word,' whispered Vine. 'They ask a whole lot of questions – is it food, is it houses, is it people – not getting anywhere. Then Cactus say "Bird" and I shake my head. Then she say "But it fly" and I nod. Next somebody say "Aeroplane" and next Cedar say "Helicopter".'

'I see,' said Foxe. The girl still wouldn't look at him – he remembered her now, mainly for her quite inappropriate name. Mushroom would have been better. She was grey-skinned, sleepy-eyed, shy-spoken; her skin looked loose on her, as though it was used to being filled with blubbery flesh; her other distinguishing feature was that she had scored bottom marks on Foxe's improvised IQ test.

'Was it like that with most of the other words?' he asked. 'A sudden intuitive guess?'

'Yeh, but Plantain don' like we talk about her,' whispered Vine.

The other men's glances flickered towards Cactus and away.

'OK,' said Foxe, rising. 'Look, Group C's finished – you weren't that far ahead. Thanks.'

Funny, he thought as he went back to the tables. If they thought Cactus had telepathic powers which they wanted to conceal they could have told her to ask the wrong questions. They were quite bright enough for that. He wondered how she did it – hypersensitive hearing, perhaps.

157

Anyway, he told himself, we've got our nutter. You always get at least one.

For variety they switched to psychokinetics – a blindfold player trying to toss the metal plates they ate off into a target area, while the rest of the group, silent, willed him to throw in the right direction. The Khandhars took this game too with unnerving seriousness, so that Foxe began to feel that even rats, and certainly monkeys, would have shown more reaction to their fellows' antics; but these people played as though the game were part of their life's purpose – in fact Foxe began to worry whether they were too high-minded to cheat at all, and was brooding on possible incentives when a voice hissed out of the darkness above.

'Got a load of stuff for you here, Doc. You coming up?'

The usual anger burned, useless.

'OK, lower the steps,' he called.

He found Louis waiting at the top of the gangway, smiling uneasily, a child not sure whether he is going to get away with some blatant misdeed.

'Now listen,' said Foxe, 'the Prime Minister doesn't want my experiment interrupted. Not at all. If I tell him you keep calling down to me, he will have you punished. Do you understand that?'

'Yeh, yeh,' said Louis, cringeing a little but still smiling. 'It's just he send all these tapes and we don't know where to put them.'

'In the guard cell, he said. I'll listen to some of them later. Now . . .'

'Doc, while you up here, you tell us the rules you playing? We can't bet on the game less you tell us the rules, uh?'

'You're betting on my game?'

'Sure,' said Louis, gesturing along the gallery to where the other guards, five or so, leaned on the rail discussing the scene below with jerky intent mutters. 'I'm a fellow

158

will bet on anything. I got a pair of cocks up the town will beat all the birds in the Islands.'

Foxe hesitated, trapped by a sudden notion. There is no sharper observer than a man with money on a game, and the people below wouldn't know they were being watched in this way. He couldn't think of an immediate use for this odd lab facility, but it was too potentially valuable to refuse.

'OK,' he said, beginning to walk along the gallery towards the other men. 'It's very straightforward.'

'Yeh, bit too simple,' said Louis, following him, jovial with success.

'I could complicate it a bit, I suppose,' said Foxe.

'Fine, fine. Hey, man, why you not fix these bastards to fight, like the cockfighting?'

For emphasis he slapped Foxe's ribs with the back of his hand.

'Watch it,' said Foxe. 'A bit lower and you'd have got my rat?'

The warning was a blast of frost, shrivelling the tendrils of comradeship. Foxe heard the indrawn sigh of shock.

'It's all right,' he said. 'He's been asleep all morning. Now about this game . . .'

They had reached the lounging guards, who listened, discussed the rules and suggested a few variations which would make their gambling more amusing, until Louis re-introduced his suggestion about the cockfight. At once all interest in the game below vanished. Foxe found himself saying over and over, 'I'll think about it,' when he knew quite well that his mind had closed like an anemone at the first touch of the idea. In the end he dropped his hand into his jacket pocket and said, sharply, 'Louis.'

The enthusiastic mutter stilled. A tick appeared at the corner of Louis's mouth, and the nearest of the guards made the same sign with his left hand that Foxe had seen Mr Trotter use.

'Where are these tapes?' he said. 'I've got a lot to do. I'll think about this other game, but I can't promise anything.'

'I show you,' said Louis soberly. 'Going off duty now – only hung around for the betting. Coming, fellows?'

Two of the other men grunted and Louis led the way into the tunnel. A few yards up on the left he pushed open a steel door, nodding to Foxe to follow him through. The room was another cave, but made, or at least adapted, by man; Foxe could see on the walls the slant parallels left by the hacking tools that had shaped this cramped cuboid. It was lit by one bleak bulb, and the furniture was a plain table and two crates. There was a cardboard carton on the table, with a tape-recorder beside it; on a side-wall hung a small control panel with switches and lights and sockets. This cell had a strange, musky smell, like an animal's lair – a reasonably cleanly animal, but one which over the years had impregnated the place with its own faintly foetid odours; it reminded Foxe of the room of misogynist dons at old universities.

Louis went to the panel and spoke into the air.

'Coming out now, Robbie.'

'Why you been so long?' said a tinny voice. 'Andy's lot been in twenty minutes.'

'Setting up a game. Tell you. Now I just got to show the Doc these tapes, right?'

Louis turned to the table, unravelled the flex of the recorder and plugged it in on the control panel. The machine must have been already loaded and switched on, but it didn't seem to Foxe to be working because an extraordinary whining wail filled the room.

'Hi! Turn that stuff off!' called the tinny voice. 'I studying, I tell you!'

Louis prodded a big finger onto the recorder and stilled the racket.

'He got to listen to this,' he said. 'Doctor O says.'

'OK,' replied the voice. 'Show him how he take this circuit out.'

'Right,' said Louis. 'Watch here, Doc. When you listening to these tapes, you cut out the mikes. This the switch here. Ready, Robbie? Three, two, one, now.'

160

At the last syllable he pressed a switch to the left of the one he'd shown Foxe. A green light glowed above the panel. Louis grunted and strode away, and Foxe stood listening to the pad of soles up the tunnel. In the silence a faint voice muttered.

'Group A. Twelve throws. One hit, one on the line.'

'One and one, OK,' answered Mr Trotter's voice, just as faint.

A red light began to wink on and off and a loud bleeper drowned all other sounds until one of the fresh guards scampered in and threw another switch, which stopped the bleeping and let the light glow steadily.

'OK. Shut them now,' said Robbie's voice. 'Three, two, one, now.'

The guard clicked switches and turned.

'Coming out, Doc?' he said.

'When I've checked this recorder. It was making a rum noise.'

'OK,' said the guard and left.

By training and instinct Foxe always checked machinery the moment it was delivered. Now he closed the microphone circuit to the outer guard-hut and started the recorder again. The same racket filled the cell, but before he could switch off the noise stopped and was replaced by a heavy, quick panting, unmistakably non-mechanical.

Captain Angiah's voice said, 'Your name is Lucilla Banker.'

Another voice, still panting, said, 'My name be Cactus.'

Immediately the wailing began again.

6

The girl who called herself Cocoa Bean had been educated by a nursing order of nuns. She scowled at the large needle.

'This will hurt,' she said.

Foxe shut his eyes, thinking of the thousands of superfine needles he had in his life slid painlessly into the animals he'd handled. He felt Cocoa Bean's fingers exploring for the best spot in the fiab of his upper arm, and then the sudden stab of pain.

Did the decision date from that moment? Sometimes Foxe could distinctly remember the change of attitude flooding through him as the pain dwindled to soreness: a second before he'd been thinking of fine disposable needles and cursing himself for not realising that if he didn't insist he'd be offered these iron-age prodders; the next he was thinking, We've got to get out of here. Not I but We. At other times, and equally distinctly, he could remember not thinking about that at all at that moment, but experiencing a gradual change over several days from a state when his mind in spare moments automatically turned to the details of the experiment to a state when it turned to the experiment only as part of the machinery of escape.

There were only three hypodermics, all blunt, so injecting the Khandhars took almost an hour. Mr Trotter sterilised the needles over a butane flame and Cocoa Bean did the actual injections, leaving Foxe free to check who the next sufferer was and fill his needle with SG 19 or saline solution, working behind a screen so that no one else could see who was getting what. He'd made it clear that they could select any single dose prepared for one of them and ask Foxe to take it instead (the only way Foxe

162

could think of to prove that he hadn't been giving himself the saline every time) but this first morning Plantain had given one of his rare, bleak smiles and asked Foxe to go first. Plantain was in one of the SG 19 groups, so Foxe got his dose.

Last of all Foxe injected Cocoa Bean. As he was looking for a spot on her shrunk arm where there might be muscle enough to take the dose she began to mutter.

'Screwy jabs! Why you not get us good hypos? Cactus say Old Woman. Screwy jabs. Up above. Hell that hurt. Watching. Finished? Sorry. Even jabs with a good hypo I hate.'

Foxe nodded to show he'd understood the message, buried almost inaudibly among the gasped complaints. For the moment what impressed him was not what Cocoa Bean had said, but that it had been she who'd said it. Though she played her part in the games with the same surrender to the group will that all the other Khandhars displayed, in her individual contacts with Foxe she had been chilly and brusque; so it was a measure of how far the Khandhars assumed that Foxe was wholly on their side that she'd, so to speak, given Cactus as a hostage into his hands. From his one brief talk with Plantain about Cactus Foxe had discovered that the Khandhars were touchily protective of her, and also that they guessed the whole arena was bugged.

His mind had switched to this last point, and the problem of how to organise any kind of escape if you might be being listened to at any moment, when a voice yelled from above.

'What they signs? Foxy, what they signs?'

Foxe had almost forgotten the ritual pattern in the sand through which the Khandhars threaded their gawky dance each evening. He was unwilling either to exploit or to deny his supposed magical powers, so it had seemed simplest to take the pattern for granted and ignore it – though he'd noticed that Mr Trotter, who'd become sufficiently accepted among the Khandhars to sit with them and talk herbalism, kept well away from the area. But yes, it was old Mrs Trotter's sort of thing, of course.

'Can't come now,' he called.

'Foxy, you come right up an' tell me.'

'I'll be free in about ten minutes.'

The gangway ropes creaked. Foxe ignored them, prickly with anger and frustration at his inability to control these irruptions into his kingdom. He stowed and locked drugs, needles and dose records in the file cabinet that now stood on the sand like a fragment of Dali landscape. As he turned he saw a guard coming towards him. He knew most of the soldiers by name now – this one was Andy, a black, wiry, slow-witted man with a strong resentment at anything that lessened his own authority over the creatures of the Pit.

'Mister Doc, when *she* say, you come,' said Andy. His gun was slung over his shoulder, but in his right hand he held a thing like a flattened truncheon, bound in leather, and he slapped this against his thigh as he spoke. Foxe stared at him, aware of the man's hatred and contempt, but at the same time of an odd undercurrent of nervousness, as though he half-expected Foxe to produce some threat more powerful than his own truncheon or Mrs Trotter's anger.

Foxe smiled, unlocked the cabinet again and took out a couple of sheets of paper which he thrust at Andy, who stared and backed away.

'You take those up to her,' said Foxe. 'Tell her to try and work out what ought to be in the missing picture. I'll be up by the time she's done that.'

Andy hesitated, frowning. In the silence Foxe heard Quentin begin on one of his rampaging scuttles round the second drawer of the cabinet, which was now his home. At the first scrape of sound Andy's face changed; he snatched the papers, backed a couple of steps away, turned and then only just managed to keep his walking pace from teetering into a run. Still smiling Foxe locked the top drawer, opened the second and took Quentin out. Wher he turned to the Khandhars his fingers automatically fondled the smooth fur, soothing the fret away. They watched him with none of the fear that the guards showed, but with a sort of deepened seriousness, as though he were about to demonstrate some difficult and important technique.

'Right,' he said. 'Now we've got to take a bit of exercise to distribute that stuff round our blood-streams. Vine, you use to teach this sort of thing, didn't you?'

'Sure.'

'OK, will you organise something while I go and talk to our visitor? Nothing too violent, and if you can manage it everybody using about the same amount of energy. OK?'

'I get you.'

As he started to climb the steps Foxe was thinking that not having proper lab facilities was a great time-saver. A guess is much quicker than measurement. Next came tests for sedative effects . . .

'What you try to do to me, Foxy? What these pictures? You can't tie me with no pictures.'

She was waiting for him at the top of the stairs, a squat idol. Further along the gallery the President leaned on the rail, scratching his buttock, while his white-jacketed keeper stood impassive against the rock. Foxe discovered that he was still fondling Quentin, so he slipped him into his pocket but kept his hand caressing the soothed pelt.

'It isn't a spell, ma'am,' he said. 'It's what's called a matrix test – it's a way of measuring intelligence. Look, this one is a single bar, and in the second picture it's turned through forty-five degrees. This one's a double bar, and in the second picture it's turned through ninety. This one's a triple bar, so in the missing picture it's got to be turned through a hundred and thirty-five. Good morning, sir. How are you?'

'He's OK,' said Mrs Trotter. 'I doing what you say, Foxy – I cut out the owl-crap and the marra-rood, and I sing for Bakubaku to ease his bowels, and like you say he getting

165

better, a little. But those signs on the sand – you telling me they're the same like these pictures?'

'The same sort of thing, only much more complicated. They've got to find the right way through – do you remember the mazes in my laboratory? I wanted these people to do a difficult intelligence test . . .'

'They ain't indelligent! They stupid!'

'Everybody's intelligent about some things and stupid about other things.'

'That's right, Foxy! My clever son, he's stupid about his soul, and my stupid son, that's the only thing he clever with.'

She cocked ahead and frowned again across the arena, not looking at the ranks of Khandhars swinging from the hips in time to Vine's monotonous chant, but at the magical pattern in the sand.

'Some of those look to be snake-signs,' she said.

'You're looking at them upside down,' said Foxe blandly. 'It's the same with the Q on my rat's back – people look at that upside down and think it means something else. Look, you can see the marks of the footprints going through the maze.'

'You let my son see your rat, Foxy? Hi, Dimmy, got something to show you.'

The President grunted and came shambling along the gallery, followed by his keeper. Very reluctantly Foxe drew Quentin from his pocket and held him up, stroking his nape with his free hand. The President gave an extraordinary little chortle and reached forward with his own hands cupped like a beggar's.

'I've got to have him back, ma'am,' said Foxe in an urgent whisper. 'He's essential for the experiments.'

'Sure, sure,' said Mrs Trotter. 'Just let the boy hold him a little.'

Quentin didn't seem to object to being dropped into the pudgy palms, but sniffed at the new, strange reeks with an eager nose. For a moment the President peered crooningly at his prize, then swung ponderously round to face his keeper, raising his hands as he did so until they were directly between the two faces. The man stared, the mask of numb detachment suddenly vanishing, replaced by the shock of ambush. The President blew at him, a long sigh of a breath that fluttered Quentin's fur on its way, and the man seemed to go into trance, his lips parted and his eyes wide and staring. The President chuckled and stepped forward, letting Quentin drop as he did so. Foxe saw him nudge his keeper on the shoulder, and the keeper beginning to collapse with the slow-all-of-a-piece sway of a demolished chimney-stack, but by that time Foxe himself was on hands and knees, grabbing at Quentin before he could recover from the shock of his fall and scuttle into some cranny. It seemed overwhelmingly important to regain control of his totem before anything else happened. He felt the jar of the man's weight hitting the boards just as his fingers closed round the fur, and by the time he rose to his feet the President had taken another step forward and with happy little cries was kicking at the inert form.

'You see, my son got the power, 'cept he don' know how do use it,' said Mrs Trotter with sad pride.

'Yes, so I see, ma'am. Er, I ought to go back now or the experiment will get out of hand.'

'Sure, Foxy, sure. I get these stupid soldiers help carry Marcus out. Be lucky.'

'And the same to you, ma'am.'

Only on his way down to the arena was Foxe struck by the fact that it had seemed completely natural to lie to Mrs Trotter about the meaning of the pattern on the floor.

Time, not measured in days, ground past. Foxe felt no impatience, because his mind was filled with the work; everything became subsumed to it, even the most meaningless elements of the routine of the Pit. It was like the sand which, despite the still air, found its way into food, under clothes, between sheets of paper, into Quentin's drawer, into ears and nostrils. Not even the bout of reeking diarrhoea which afflicted the party for four days was free of the question, Does it help? Just as, earlier, Foxe had woken with his mind already buzzing with the experiment, now he woke with the mechanisms of escape half-built behind the façade of dream. In one sense the escape was an experiment too; even guessing at the reactions of guards had affinities with guessing at those of rats and monkeys. Only an occasional freshet of panic served to remind Foxe that there was no question of tinkering and then running the work again if it failed first time; but mostly the details of planning, which included organising games in a way that allowed small moments of whispered or coded conversation, numbed such fears, though he was never infected with the Khandhars' almost loony certainty that all would in the end be well.

It took a dream to remind Foxe why he was in the Pit at all. He woke vaguely aware that Ladyblossom had brought him a present in a brown paper bag, and the picture vivid in his mind as he eased his eye-bandage up, screwing his eyes tight against the glare of the floodlights, was of a red-cheeked apple crawling with caterpillars. Peeling his orange in the mid-morning break he remembered about it.

'What's snake-apple, Mr Trotter?'

'*Pseudodatura Wilsonii.*'

'Is it common? What does it do. How does it work?'

'No, not common at all. I never see it. Grow only two places, and the Government put a big fence round them. Say it for to protect the plants, but course it for to stop people getting to the snake-apple.'

'It's against the law to carry it, isn't it?'

'Yeh, but you can't carry the apple round – it rot too quick, and it only get poisonous just before it begin to rot. You take an apple and stick it full of thorns while it still on the bush. When it fall down to the ground and begin to rot, you come and pick your thorns out, and if you lucky all the poison gone into them. Some old witches still got a few thorns left, I guess, but there ain't many about.'

'Presumably the Government could still manufacture them if it wanted to.'

'Yes, I guess so. I guess the Old Woman got a few. But it ain't that good for a poison – there's plenty better. Snake-apple were a witch-poison, cause of when it work the man go walking around for a while, like one of the Secret Ones come into him . . .'

Foxe stopped listening. It was all irrelevant, merely confirming guesses. If the Government controlled the supply of snake-apple, then it was fairly clear that they had had Ladyblossom killed, merely in order to trap him into this work. That didn't matter now. What mattered was the escape.

The Prime Minister came twice more – at least Foxe had to go up and talk to him twice more, but according to the girl Cactus he was once there, watching in the darkness, not making his presence known. Foxe had no idea whether this was true – he had been too busy to test her subliminal hearing.

On Doctor Trotter's first acknowledged visit he merely grumbled about the childishness of the games and the lack of progress or of results, not being much appeased by Foxe saying that he had found no measurable sedative effects in SG 19. This was a gross overstatement, of the sort that Foxe had despised all his working life. It was only not a lie because the measurement techniques had been so coarse – Foxe was fairly sure in his own mind that the stuff was a mild general sedative. No doubt that was why the Company had been interested in the first place.

On the second visit Doctor Trotter seemed much more intently concerned. He watched with real absorption while the subtle pattern of cheating emerged among the games below, and purred with pleasure when he spotted Mace fudging the mark where a plate had landed in the throwing game. Plantain had been reluctant, almost obstinate, about introducing any kind of cheating into the games, which seemed to have become to the Khandhars part of the ritual of their strange beliefs, but once they had agreed to do it they did it well – Foxe had not managed to spot quite how Group F were getting such good results in one of the games. Now, as he craned over the rail, he felt an odd pang of loss – not loss of scientific innocence, because the set-up in the Pit was barely concerned with science – but for the brief period then his relationship with the Khandhars had seemed to provide him with ... had he ever really thought of them as animals, like his rats and monkeys? It was a measure of the power of Doctor Trotter's personality that for this moment that longing came back.

'This is progress,' murmured the deep voice in the dusk, giving the last word a strange, almost magical weight. 'Now I think it is time to move your subjects to conditions of greater stress. Have you any ideas yet?'

'Yes, sir. One of the guards made a suggestion I think I can use. I want to keep to a basic game-structure, but there's no reason why we shouldn't introduce an element of physical contest. This will be modelled on cockfighting – the subjects will be led to understand that we are measuring their endurance and tolerance of pain, when in fact we will be studying what they are prepared to inflict on each other.'

'Ah.'

It was a strange sound, barely audible but full of satisfaction – not merely at the prospect of his enemies suffering pain, but at something much more complex. At the first of these meetings above the Pit Foxe had thought Doctor Trotter was driven by a muddle of motives, but now he saw that the experiment in goodness and experiment in the degradation on Foxe were parts of one structure. Why had Foxe been chosen? It had seemed a malignant whim, like love at first sight; but they say that even the victims of that passion recognise in each other submerged potentials, and so perhaps on Hog's Cay Doctor Trotter had recognised Foxe's moral neutrality – what Lisa-Anna called his emptiness. He had decided – he

170

was his mother's son – that such a victim was necessary to his grand experiment, a spiritual sink, or sump, into which the wickedness of the people could be drained . . . The Khandhars were another part of the structure, because those who recognised a different 'good' from Doctor Trotter's must be led to deny it by cheatings and betrayals . . .

'You have been listening to the tapes, Doctor Foxe?'

'Yes.'

'You find them interesting?'

'Only very occasionally. Mostly I find them disgusting.'

'Ah.'

'Disgusting' was the wrong word. In a strange way the tapes were refreshing. Foxe listened to them quite often, because he needed to learn the exact drill for the guard-change. Some of the tapes consisted of nothing but screams. Some of grunting silences interspersed with questions, some of magical mouthings. Suddenly the tension would ease and a couple of clicks would mark the space during which the machine had been turned off while the victim hid in the cave of his own darkness. Then the sounds would begin again. They were horrible, but each time Foxe left the airless, animal-smelling chamber he felt an impulse of moral energy, of fresh will to carry through what he and the Khandhars had begun.

He had one of the spell-weavers – they were the easiest to endure – on the machine when Louis came into the cell. He listened for a moment, head cocked, as his own voice said, 'How long you been up the Mountain, bastard?'

'Hey, that me!' he said, delighted.

'Is it?' said Foxe, clicking the machine off. 'I can never recognise my own voice on tape.'

'Yeh, sound kinda stupid, don't it? Play us some more.'

'No, I wanted to talk to you. I've been thinking about this cockfighting thing – in fact I was talking about it to the Prime Minister just now – and I think I can lay that on.'

'You can? Man, that's fine! Lots of fellas wanting to see that!'

'Well, they can't. About a dozen at the most. If we get a crowd up here it'll spoil the experiment.'

'That bad. They all wanting to see it.'

'Perhaps we might be able to lay it on later, when I see how things go. But I thought there might be a day when there weren't a lot of you on duty, for instance. I mean, if most of you had the day off, then we could put on a show for all the people who had to stay behind, d'you see? That wouldn't make too big a crowd.'

(Would he get it? Foxe had no idea how the Khandhars knew all they seemed to know about the outside world – how, for instance, they'd known Foxe's name – and the chances for private talk in the Pit were too precious to waste on that sort of inquisitiveness. They just knew, but now it would be much better if Louis thought Foxe didn't.)

'Carnival you meaning?'

'What's Carnival?'

'Next Sunday. Everybody go up San Andrea, dance in the roads, make music. Lotta masks, lotta costumes. Even the port close down for Carnival.'

'What happens here?'

'Everybody go off, 'cept the guard on duty.'

'What about you?'

'I got to be on duty.'

'OK. Well, suppose we fix some cockfighting for that night. How many people will want to see it?'

Louis began to check off numbers on his fingers. Four men on the walls, sentry at the gate, five in the guardroom, guard commander, Robbie – the one who was studying to become a lawyer – in the shed by the Pit entrance – apparently that left nine soldiers free to join the guard in the Pit. Twelve in all.

'All right,' said Foxe. 'You bring them along and we'll try it out then.'

On the control panel a red light glowed and the bleeper began to sound a continuous note. Louis, who had come in to be ready for the guard-change – which was why Foxe had chosen to be there at that moment – pressed the switch to open the microphone circuit which Foxe had shut off while he listened to the tapes, did the count-down and pressed the gate-switch. The red light changed to green.

'Got to go now,' he said, 'you'll make it so they fighting for real? Like cocks, uh? Plenty blood?'

'I'll try to. I'll need about four broom-handles and some cord.'

'OK.'

The red light flickered and the bleeper chirped. Eleven seconds, Foxe knew, though he couldn't time it openly with Louis in the room. Then another fifty-three seconds of silence and the green light while the relief guard came down the tunnel. The automatic brief bonhomie of changeover, and fifty-five seconds for Louis and his two companions to get back up the tunnel. Eleven seconds to get out.

7

Waiting for the gangway to reach the sand, Foxe was
suddenly pierced by a conviction that he was being
inspected from above. It was not the gaze of the guards
that he felt, but of the huge eye in the higher darkness,
a surrogate sense, linked directly to Doctor Trotter's
brain. All this had been foreseen. In half an hour it would
be over, they would all be back in the Pit, except a few
Khandhars chosen for detailed punishment. Foxe himself
would not be punished, only now he would be a whole
winding further down into the vortex. He put his hand
into his pocket to still Quentin's sudden fit of energy. The
creaking contraption reached the sand. Foxe scampered
up.

'Better leave it down,' he said. 'I'll probably have to
keep running to and fro.'

Louis grunted. Without waiting for him to object Foxe
walked to where the guards were gathered in their usual
watching-place, a little beyond the tunnel mouth. Their
faces turned eagerly to him. The rhythm of his heart
hiccupped. Now I might do it, he thought – if it's going
to work on one, why not on twelve? His arm seemed to
lack the muscles to draw his hand from his pocket. Too
late.

'Right,' he said. 'I hope this is what you want. It's an
experiment in joint will-power. Those are your birds,
down there, with the broom-sticks strapped behind their
knees. You see they can only hop – it's a very exhausting
position, and I've sharpened the ends of the sticks so that
they can hurt each other a bit. They score a point for

174

their side when they knock the other man over, and three points if they drive him out of the circle. OK?'

'Sure, sure.'

'One team's green – you can see that bit of green rag tied to the back of his belt – and the other's yellow. The whole team's willing their man to win – that's the point of the experiment – and I want you to do the same. Six of you for greens, six for yellows, OK? You can bet how you like – who wins, how long the fight lasts, how many points scored – it doesn't matter – but my side of the deal won't work if you aren't rooting hard as you can for one side or the other. Right? I'll give you a couple of minutes to settle the betting while I get my notebook out of the guard cell.'

'Yeh. Saw it there,' said Louis absently, turning away at once to join in the babble of argument about the bets.

In the guard cell Foxe picked up the notebook he'd left there and crossed to the control panel.

'Robbie, that you?' he said.

'Sure. How the cockfight going?'

'Not started yet. Listen, I want to turn one of these tapes on.'

'Why the hell?'

'Part of the experiment. Increase the tension. It'll be pretty loud. Do you want me to turn your circuit off.'

'Yeh. Sure, I still studying.'

'Good luck,' said Foxe and closed the switches. He turned and saw Louis in the doorway.

'Hey, Doc, I come to ask . . . Hey, what you doing with the circuit?'

This time, though it would have been perfectly possible to produce the same mumbo jumbo about needing the tape-noise, Foxe's arm moved unwilled. Louis stared and their gazes seemed to lock together until Foxe's hand had risen far enough and he was looking along Quentin's spine as if along the barrel of a gun. The breath came out of his lungs in a sigh of tension, getting under the sleek fur which rose all round the crouched body in a staring

175

halo. Louis's eyes widened and bulged. At the corner of his mouth a tic started, like a monstrous pulse, then stilled.

'You saw nothing, Louis,' whispered Foxe. 'Go outside and turn round. Ask your question when I come out.'

He put Quentin back in his pocket and waited, counting a slow five, then went to the door. Louis was standing in the tunnel, expressionless.

'Hello, Louis. You want something?'

Life came flooding back as if Foxe had thrown a switch.

'Yeh, Doc. I come to ask is there going to be more 'n just the one fight?'

'Yes. We'll have a couple of the women next. I've arranged for six fights in all.'

'OK. When we starting?'

'Soon as you're ready.'

'Ready now.'

'OK. Let's go.'

Foxe walked to the gallery and called down.

'Give them the starting signal please, Mr Trotter.'

Shadowless, insect-like in their movements, Ginger and Vine hopped into the circle. Their bare chests glistened already with the sweat of the crouch to which the broomsticks constrained them. Each man had his ankles tied together, and his wrists lashed in front of his ankles, with the broomstick, sharpened at each end, thrust through the gap behind his knees and in front of his elbows. A hop was the only possible gait; fall, and you had to be helped back to your feet.

The cheering began, whoops and shouts from the guards, and from the two groups of Khandhars a strange noise, an indrawn gasp – almost a gulp – of air with a vibration in the throat. The individual pulses of breath sounded like something percussive, a loose-skinned drum perhaps. Each group made its noise in unison, slowing and speeding the beats in response to the rhythm of the fight but out of time with the other group. The effect was hypnotic but far from somnolent, and much more expressive of sustained fierce effort than the more orthodox crowd-noises from the gallery.

Without feint or warning the circling ended as Vine and Ginger leaped at each other and clashed. For a second they were still, necks strained at each other's shoulders, and then they were toppling apart. As they fell Vine twisted violently so that the pointed end of his stick raked across Ginger's torso. The beads of blood welled on the blue-black skin, glittery under the arc-lights, then joined in runnels like a ragged comb as Ginger's handlers pulled him to his feet and set him opposite Vine. The Khandhars' chant slowed to a mutter, and the yells of the guards, which had doubled at the fall, dwindled as if in sympathy. A bet was settled without argument.

'Fight on,' said Mr Trotter, strutting at the edge of the ring, stopwatch in hand.

Since the fight had begun Foxe had been conscious that his body was trembling all over, his elbows pressing at his ribs and his knees clenched to each other, as if his whole being was trying to cringe away into an inner self. He was in a sort of trance, hypnotised half by the fight and half by the consciousness of Louis standing beside him, inside whose mind, flimsily buried, lurked the fatal bit of memory of what had just happened in the guard-cell. How long would it stay buried? Foxe remembered what the President had done to Andy. He remembered Captain Angiah's story about the sentry whose mind stayed blank even in front of the firing squad, but they were like dreams, things that couldn't have any mass in the waking world.

A crash of yells burst from the gallery, a mixture of rage and laughter. Down in the Pit Ginger had managed to upset Vine and instead of backing off was trying to nudge him out of the ring with his knees. Mr Trotter said something inaudible, and Ginger's handlers stepped out and pulled him off. His chest was more red than black, and there was a smaller but fast-flowing wound below Vine's left ear. Once more the fight began, the gulping

177

chant fluttered round the Pit and the guards' yells rang out from above. Both combatants were tiring now, oily with sweat and blood, smeared with sand and gasping like stranded fish, but they came at each other as though that were all that mattered in the world. Ginger wheeled round as Vine came in, but Vine avoided the slash of the broomstick and bowled him over with his charge. Mr Trotter held up his hand. Plantain rattled two of the tin plates against each other, and Vine too collapsed, chest heaving. Their handlers untied them and stood them up. Cocoa Bean took their pulses and spoke to Mr Trotter, who made a couple of notes. The fighters blew into plastic bags, with Mr Trotter counting the breaths they needed to blow them tight. Cocoa Bean inspected their wounds and led them, leaning in apparent total exhaustion on their handlers' shoulders, away to where the surgical dressings were laid out on the table, in its usual place along to the left near the foot of the gangway. The guards sorted out their finances.

'Great fight, Doc,' said Louis, grinning.

'Glad it was what you wanted,' said Foxe politely.

'They do sure go at the other fellow. You think the girls fight as tough?'

'We'll have to see,' said Foxe. 'They're using that smaller circle over there.'

Down below the Khandhars shifted position, now taking station round the ring which Foxe had drawn over to the right. The watching guards slouched along the gallery for a better view, but naturally didn't go the whole way, halting to watch at an angle which focused their attention away from the gangway. The two women, Hibiscus and Lettuce, crouched at the edge of the ring. Foxe didn't dare look anywhere else, but out of the corner of his eye he saw the handlers of the previous fight come quietly back to join their groups. Mr Trotter gave the signal and the women hopped into the ring. The same chant from below, the same yells from above, filled the cavern.

It hadn't been possible to choose the women for their

178

physical attractions; starvation slims nobody to cover-girl shapes. Their thin and wrinkled breasts flopped with each hop, their lank hair clothed their shoulders, and their ribs stuck out all down their straining sides. They clashed, toppled, were righted and leaped at each other again.

'Hey, Doc! She's biting! That right?'

'Oh yes, I think so,' said Foxe in a detached voice. He let his glance flicker across the arena to the table. There was no one there, but a movement on the gangway. He counted five and tapped Louis on the shoulder. Impatiently the big guard turned. Foxe already had Quentin poised between their two faces, and as soon as the eyes, glimmering in the upshot light, met his he sighed out a slow breath, this time barely ruffling the rat's fur. Louis froze, glaring with blind eyes at Foxe, who reached out with his free hand and gently eased the gun from where it was slung on Louis' shoulder.

'Stay still,' whispered Foxe. 'See nothing.'

He passed the gun behind him without looking round. A hand took it. One.

The next man, apparently sensing the stillness on his left, turned almost before Foxe was ready, but Foxe caught his eye, blew and froze him with the look of surprise and query stiffened on to his face. Two. The third man was leaning right over the rail, gesticulating at the fight below and wouldn't take any notice of Foxe's polite tap for attention. Impatient and panicky Foxe snatched at his arm and spun him round into the gust of breath. Wrong technique. The man almost shouted, looked over Foxe's shoulder, back at Foxe and was caught. Three.

As the fourth man froze unresisting the women below toppled from their clinch and all along the gallery the strained attention on the scene below lost focus. Someone yelled inarticulately. A shot swamped the yell. Foxe flung himself flat on the boards and covered the back of his neck with his hands thinking Not enough – Not enough – Angle too fine – Men this end screen rest. The noise

179

was like pain. He couldn't tell how many guns were firing. A large, soft weight slid slowly across his spine and stayed there, and then another, more sudden and stunning, collapsed on his head, muffling the last stammer of firing. A bare foot kicked his wrist. That's one of us, he thought. One of us still alive. His ears rang with the whining remains of deafness and his heart slammed and pounded. At last he took a half-stifled breath and tried to rise, but at the movement the man who was pinning down his head quivered and groaned. Appalled with the shock of it, Foxe's body went rigid, and before he could force his muscles into another effort he felt the body on his back being hauled slithering away, and then the man on his head was lifted clear.

'That one's still alive,' he gasped.

A single shot banged, very close.

'Not now,' said someone.

Foxe forced himself to hands and knees, crawled to the edge of the gallery and vomited over it.

'You hurt, Doc?' said someone.

'Don't think so,' he gasped, and retched again.

As his head cleared he saw that the Pit was almost empty. Hibiscus was lying panting in the fighting-circle, still lashed into her crouch, and Cactus was bending over Lettuce to untie her ankles. A little further off lay Mr Trotter, face down, spreadeagled. Directly below Foxe scarlet blotches appeared and spread on the sand, where thin streams of blood trickled between the boards of the gallery, breaking into drops before they reached the bottom.

'Vine, he's dead,' said a calm voice.

'How be Cocoa?' said another – Plantain.

'Bleeding bad. Cut across the scalp. Bone feel OK and she breathing steady.'

'Fetch her some bandage from that table. Anybody found Sonny?'

'He here,' said a voice further down the gallery. 'I think he dead too. Yeh.'

180

Foxe got to his feet and stood, gripping the gallery rail and shaking his head in a stupid way. Sonny was one of the guards, surely, a quiet, smiling man with a flat face like an orang's.

Down below, moving very slowly limb by limb, like a dreamer easing out of the rigidity of nightmare, Mr Trotter rose to his knees and looked around.

'How long we got?' said Plantain. It was strange to be able to discuss plans thus openly.

'About twenty minutes, I think,' said Foxe. 'I said six fights, say five minutes each. We've had two of them. I know which switches to press and what to say, but I don't think I can do Louis' voice well enough to fool Robbie.'

'Uh. Yeah. Maize do that. You tell him what to say.'

'OK. I don't know much about what happens beyond the gates. There'll be Andy in the shed there, and four men manning the machine-guns on the castle walls, and about half a dozen in the guard room and a guard commander, Louis said. Oh, yes, and a sentry at the castle gate – outside, I think.'

'Hey, Doc,' called a voice. Foxe looked round. The dead guards sprawled along the gallery, two or three still dangling half across the rail. Several of the Khandhars crouched among them, stripping off weapons and uniforms. One man was already easing his legs into a pair of trousers, and others were standing examining their guns, their poses confident and calm.

'No, this side,' said the voice.

Foxe turned, still gulping at saliva that wasn't there. The taste of his own vomit stayed sharp in his mouth. He picked his way between sprawled limbs and slithery pools of blood to where two of the Khandhars had drawn back from a body and were gazing at it in the attitude of kneeling angels on a Victorian tomb. The dead man was the last in the line, or rather the first, and that meant it was Louis; his face still wore the look of numbness which Foxe had breathed on to it, and his body seemed unmarked. One of the kneeling men pointed at the cave between arm and torso. For a moment Foxe could see nothing, then two pale flecks gleamed. Foxe slid his hand into the cranny and felt Quentin trying to cringe still further away, but making no attempt to bite or struggle as Foxe took him gently by the scruff and hauled him out. The whole of one flank was scarlet, and his coat was all on end with fright, but he seemed unhurt. The blood must have come from Louis.

Without a word the men bent back to stripping Louis, and as they turned him over Foxe saw that all the left side of his shirt was soaked with blood, with three round holes, neat as a dice-mark, pocked across the scarlet. He shook his head and swung away, still cradling Quentin in his hands, fondling the staring fur, using the familiar touch to soften his own shock as well as the rat's.

Down below, in the arena, Mr Trotter was now sitting on one of the chairs by the table, hunched and gazing down at the space between his own feet, quite motionless. Foxe stared at him, thinking not of the deluded assistant in the experiment but of the drunk young man in the hotel. He felt a pang not exactly of guilt or responsibility, but of sympathy for someone else – a fellow scientist – unwillingly caught up in the bloody mechanisms of tyranny and revolt. Time to spare. Time better filled than left blank to the scrawls of horror at what had happened and fright at what would happen next. He walked along the gallery and down the gangway. Mr Trotter didn't look up.

'You coming with us?' said Foxe.

The dark head shook from side to side.

'Sure?' asked Foxe. 'It'll be hairy either way, but if they find you alone here . . . We could tie you up, I suppose. But once the gates are shut I don't know how you open them if there's nobody on the inside to press the switches.'

'My Mamma coulda got me outa here, couple of weeks. Now you done this.'

'Listen,' said Foxe. 'The best I can think of is to get them to take you with us, as a hostage. Then if we get

182

out you can escape. It's quite plausible. You are a Trotter, after all.'

'I just got to come along,' said Mr Trotter despairingly. 'That hostage stuff, that no good. No good staying here, either. When they find me they torture me, just making sure I never knew what you was doing.'

'OK, I'm sorry about this, you know. I had to do it.'

'I guess so.'

'Come up now and wait with the others, so you aren't left behind when they go.'

As Mr Trotter groaned, Plantain's voice called from above.

'You better get dressed now, doc.'

'Coming.'

While Foxe was climbing the gangway a series of dull thuds broke the stillness as one by one the bodies of the dead guards were tipped naked to the sand below. The Khandhars had Louis' uniform hung out for him along the railing, as if to dry. There was no escape from wearing it because Louis' large figure was a necessary part of the guard detail, and none of the Khandhars was nearly big enough to play the part. Foxe found the process of dressing difficult and repugnant in itself, and not simply because it committed him to the next stage of the escape. The clothes smelt of Louis, oily and animal, and even where they were free from blood were greasy to the touch.

When he was dressed he joined the group, also armed and uniformed, who were already waiting by the mouth of the tunnel.

'That's fine,' said Plantain. 'OK, we ten go out, because that's the number would be coming out after the cockfighting. Maize, you come and do Louis's voice, and watch how the switches work so you can open the gates again when we've done finish the soldiers in the castle. And listen, brothers. Remember you the guards now. You been in here watching the cockfighting, an' some of

183

you won an' some of you lost, but you all been having a good shout and a happy time. How long now, Doc?'

'Foxe looked at his watch. Time was moving with weird slowness.

'Ten minutes at least,' he said.

'OK. Sit down and rest, everybody. How Cocoa getting along?'

'Still the same,' said a voice.

'Bad thing about Sonny,' said someone else.

'Was he one of us?' asked Foxe.

'Yeh. He tell us things. Tell us about you, and the fellow who making the life pill, and the other fellow keeping all the secrets. He say he want to join with us, but we don't know if he be a spy, perhaps.'

'He knew a lot about the labs,' said Foxe. 'That's odd . . . oh no it isn't – he must have been Ladyblossom's son who went to join the army. Do you know if . . .'

'Rest now, brothers,' said Plantain's velvet voice. 'Put your minds to the Secret Ones. Put your hearts to the Secret Ones. Put your souls to the Secret Ones. Peace.'

As he walked beside Plantain along the tunnel the drying blood on Foxe's left boot sucked at the bare rock floor.

'You walking all wrong, Doc,' said Plantain. 'You walking like you got no arse. Wave your bum around. Yeh, that better. And feel like putting your boot down on somebody's fingers. That's a good feeling, uh? Make the feller squeal, right?'

Conscientiously Foxe brandished his hams and slapped his blood-squelching boots down. The tunnel seemed impossibly shorter than it had been when he'd first followed Captain Angiah down it, but there was an echo of that time in the way Plantain walked, with something of the Captain's loose-jointed swagger. He at least looked entirely at home in his disguise, but the rest of them were less convincing. Though they moved with the right half-disciplined slouch, they looked flimsy, lacking the bulk of

184

professional thugs; their uniforms were loose on the starved bodies and their hands on their rifle-straps were skeletal, almost transparent. Still, they held themselves with total confidence, as though fulfilling some God-ordained purpose; only Foxe seemed to be conscious of their feebleness and fewness, as he marched in his Louis-smelling clothes with Louis' blood drying stickily against his ribs; his mind's eye saw the stony mass of the castle, and the warren of guard-rooms and cells, and the machine-gun nests on the battlements. For a few uncanny paces Foxe became two consciousnesses, one still inside his body and one marching in an invisible body a few inches to his left, so that its immaterial limbs actually overlapped with his limbs of flesh. The double being filled him with a new terror. I'm going mad, he thought. But now, here, refocussing the soul-squint, were the steel doors closing the tunnel. A white light blinked above them.

'Look big, brothers,' whispered Plantain. 'Feel big and happy.'

His strange eyes stared at them, as if hypnotising them into greater bulk, until the winking light steadied and at the same moment the doors whined into movement. The light through the crack was violet-blue, streaked as it widened with strips of impenetrable shadow where the arc-lamps failed to reach. Now, surely, would come the ambush.

'Walk from your arse, Doc,' muttered Plantain and ambled through the gap.

The lights glared down from above, casting night-black shadows under the peaks of their caps, hiding all their faces. Swinging his rump like a Scot in a kilt Foxe walked the few paces to the guard-shed, pushed at its door and went straight through. The familiar buzzer was sounding. The small room reeked of sweet tobacco, whose streaky haze dimmed the already feeble light. A stronger lamp made a white cone onto an open book on the table, and almost invisible beyond that a man standing by a control panel on the wall.

185

'OK?' he said, pressing the switches down. The buzzer stopped.

'Robbie, look at me,' croaked Foxe.

The man turned slowly, as though he foreknew the horror. Foxe had Quentin raised on his palm and waiting, pointing like a weapon. The man stared, silent, numb Foxe blew, gently, almost unwillingly. The blood-clotted fur on Quentin's flank refused to ruffle, but the man froze just as the others had done.

'Don't move,' whispered Foxe. His eyes were locked to Robbie's, but in his peripheral vision he saw Plantain coming past him and the blur of his striking arm. The rustle and thud of it too seemed faint, dimmer than the movement of his own blood. The life died from behind Robbie's staring eyes like a picture fading on a TV screen. Plantain caught him and lowered him against the wall, pulling a knife from his side as the other filed into the room.

'OK,' he said. 'Guard off duty goes to get a meal – six of us – Doc, me, Ginger, Date-palm, Coffee, Mace. I guess it be over at the tower by the gate. Clean up there, then go up the tower to the battlement, clean up the machine-gun men. Rest of you stay in here, but soon as you hear any shooting, you pull down those switches – show him the ones, Doc – let the others all out of the tunnel. You hearing me in there, Maize?'

'Sure,' said the voice from the microphone.

'OK. Let's go. I guess you better march us across the courtyard, Doc. Remember to walk like you be stamping on kid's fingers.'

As Foxe reached the door he heard, far off, the crackle and snap of distant explosions. He hesitated.

'Fireworks up at Carnival,' whispered Plantain. 'C'mon.'

They lined up, Foxe muttered an order, and they swung out across the shelterless and violently lit courtyard. Plantain led the file. Beneath his left armpit Foxe could see a patch of wrong-shaped shadow which was really the smear of blood round a bullet-hole. It seemed to empha-

186

sise the sheer implausibility of all their disguise. He cringed inside his skin, telling himself that the perspective from the battlements would make heights and shadows unreadable, but always expecting the shout of query, and then the hose-flow of bullets. The crêpe soles of their boots whimpered stickily on the cobbles; otherwise the castle was silent as a ruin. He forgot to give the order to halt and dismiss, but Plantain filled the gap with military murmurs, and then once more Foxe found himself leading the way through a narrow door into a new unknown.

Three worn steps led up to a stone landing and another door; the close air smelt of spice and grease; a mug rapped on wood; men's voices rumbled.

'Above five, I guess,' whispered Plantain. 'OK, Doc?'

He swung the door open.

It was a large room, running away from the base of the tower and filling the width between the inner and outer wall of the castle. There were tables for about sixty men, but now only a small group hunched over a card-game near the kitchen hatchway; their weapons hung from pegs on the far wall. The men didn't look up as Foxe came in, but a cook slouching against the far side of the serving-counter glanced across the room, then away, then back, staring now, at the newcomers. Foxe showed him Quentin and puffed a breath at him, not even bothering to raise his palm. The man stayed still.

The sense of his own power appalled Foxe. It isn't me, he thought. It isn't me. There seemed to be some other being crouched inside him, seeing through his eyes, moving his limbs, exercising these explosive bouts of will that could lock men helpless while they waited for their deaths, like animals in an abattoir. This creature walked his legs to the table where the men sat.

'Look at me,' it croaked.

They looked. It blew across Quentin's ruffling fur.

This time the spell didn't work completely. A soldier sitting close to the end of the table stared for a moment like the others, but his mind remained free. His chair

187

scraped, and now he was jumping to his feet and twisting away towards the dangling guns. He hadn't reached full acceleration before Plantain met him and hit him behind the neck with his knife. Blood gushed, the man staggered, but even while he was collapsing his legs continued to run, stumbling him on till Plantain hit him again. This time he fell and lay still in a yard-wide pool of his own blood.

'Disbeliever,' said Plantain.

'Do we have to kill them all?' whispered Foxe.

'I guess so.'

'No.'

'You been listening to those tapes. These were the fellows did the work.'

'No.'

'That mark on your rat – know who it means?'

'Yes,' whispered Foxe.

The creature with the power spoke.

'It is not their time to die,' it said in a voice that wasn't Foxe's at all.

'OK,' said Plantain immediately. 'Date-palm, Coffee, strap these fellows up, good and tight. Gags. Mace, you be covering them, case they come round. Doc, will you wake up this cook-boy?'

Foxe slipped Quentin back in his pocket and crossed to the counter. The cook's head had nodded forward since Foxe had blown at him, making it seem as though he'd dropped off to sleep in a standing position, but when Foxe put his hand under the man's chin and tilted it up he found that the eyes were still open, unblinking, glazed as if with drink.

'Wake up now,' whispered Foxe.

The eyelids stirred. The eyes crossed for a moment in an awful squint, then looked weepingly at Foxe. The man began to shiver all over, so that a pile of plates on the counter rattled gently.

'How much men in the castle now?' said Plantain.

'Sergeant upstairs – got a woman to-night,' muttered

the cook. 'Fellows in the Pit, gone to see the cockfighting – round about twelve of them. Four fellows with the guns on the wall. Sentry outside the gate.'

'The men up top, an' the sentry – when they be relieve?'

'Five minute? Ten minute? Soon as these fellows finish the game.'

'OK?' Now, brother, hear this word. You know who been in here?'

The man's face went grey. He nodded feebly.

'OK,' said Plantain, 'he leave you 'lone now, but he put this on you. You stay here. If any of these fellows try get loose, you strap him tight again. One hour gone, you find all the keys, you go roun' all the huts, you tell the people how the Khandhars been here, set them all free. You do all that, an *he* leave you 'lone. Right?'

The man looked as though he would have fallen to the floor but for the support of the counter, but he nodded, trembling.

'C'mon, Doc,' said Plantain.

In the upstairs room where Foxe and Captain Angiah had threshed out the contract for the experiment they caught the guard-sergeant, naked, leaning his gross buttocks on the edge of the table and smoking a small cigar. A scrawny girl, also naked, lay panting on a mattress by the wall. They were both believers. Though the girl was clearly a prisoner, Plantain insisted on having her tied up like the men, saying that you couldn't tell what she might do if she were left loose.

They climbed the tower stairs to the starlit battlements, where they split into two parties to tackle the men who manned the machine guns. Below them the castle courtyard lay empty under the unchanging flood-light. The windows of the prison huts were dark. The place was like a stage, waiting for the first actors to saunter on and tell each other necessary bits of plot. On the other side of the wall the quays were floodlit too, and just as silent, the cranes still, the ships unworked. Presumably even twenty-four-hour shifts stopped to let the guards attend Carnival.

189

Maroons banged in the distance. A speckle of coloured stars showed in the sky above the cliff-top, and died. The sea, black as the pupil of an eye and flecked with a few quick glimmers, shuffled against rocks and wharves. A man came striding along the battlement walkway.

'You bloody slow,' he said angrily, and then with a sudden change of tone, 'Who that?'

'The Sunday Dwarf,' croaked Foxe's other voice.

The man started violently, but made no attempt to avoid Foxe raising Quentin close between their faces. The breath must have gone right up his nostrils. He gave a moaning gasp, and half collapsed against the crenellation behind him.

'Stand up. Wait there,' whispered Foxe, and strode quickly on. The other guard was still in the little wooden gun-post, bending down and collecting equipment. The tin roof made it too dark for him to see properly till he came grumbling out into the open.

'Look at me,' whispered Foxe.

The man dropped his load with a tinkle and a clatter, and the reek of rum swam into the air, but the man himself was unentranced and almost had his pistol out of its holster when Ginger hit him across the back of the neck with a clubbed rifle. The night silence closed quickly in.

'It sometimes doesn't work,' muttered Foxe to himself, in a vague daze.

'Maybe he wearing a good amulet,' said Ginger, bending. 'Dead. Broke my gun, too. Finish here, OK?'

They walked back along the wall and found the first man still in the precise pose in which they'd left him.

'You go on, Doc,' said Ginger. 'Plantain wanting you for that sentry.'

Before Foxe reached the tower he heard behind him a scraping rustle, followed by a second's silence before the thud rose from the cobbles below. He didn't look round. Plantain was waiting for him at the top of the tower stairs.

'OK?' he asked.

'Both dead,' muttered Foxe. 'One of them had an amulet or something.'

A minute later he was stepping through the little wicket in the main gate, head bowed to leave his face completely in shadow. The creature with the will-power seemed to have withdrawn, and Foxe went through the motions of enchantment with a sort of fumbling incredulity, much as he had when he'd first tried it on Louis in the guard-cell. But it didn't seem to make any difference. The sentry was trance-held even before Foxe blew at him. He was a believer all right.

8

They moved along the quay in three parties, each with its apparent guards and apparent gang of work-slaves. They trundled four barrows, two holding weapons, one the body of Vine and one Cocoa-bean, conscious now but very feeble. They moved from dark to glare to dark, because the floodlighting on the quays was not uniform, and they made no special attempt at stealth except for Mace and Manioc, scouting ahead among the warehouses. There were no other movements on the quays, and few lights showing among the huddled shanties on the cliff – all the life of the harbour had been sucked up into the glitter and rush of Carnival in the town above. Only the long windows of the palace laid great golden bars of light along the rock and were reflected almost as steadily from the water.

'We might get Doctor O just now,' murmured someone.

'Gone,' said someone else. 'Up in town.'

'Old Woman too – she never missing a Carnival.'

'I didn't see any helicopters on the airstrip,' said Foxe.

'Hear what Doc say?'

The last phrase was more than acceptance of rational corroborative evidence – it was a statement of creed. What Foxe said, while the power was in him, was true. Anything else was heresy. He saw several eyes glance at the breast pocket of his uniform jacket, which had been stitched to take bulky packets like maps, and where Quentin now perched with his front paws and head poking over the rim, peering ahead with his deceptively bright eyes. Even Foxe, who was used to the near-sightedness of rats, found it hard not to think of this pose as alertness for hidden dangers, as though Quentin were the true guide and leader of the escape.

Foxe was aware that this sort of feeling was a response to deep shock. His own ego was barely in control; his own mind seemed to go through phases of watching the whole episode from without, like a spectator – not an amused observer, but one forced to sit apart and endure and shudder while the ruthless farce enacted itself – a mind terrified not just for the safety of Foxe's body, the bullets slamming out of the dark before the sentry's challenge had ended, but for what it had seen. Had caused. At the same time this Foxe, this spectator, trembled with the exhilaration of the adventure, with the sense of approaching triumph that seemed to run like a current through the Khandhars. But then, as the spectator could see with ugly clarity but with no power to intervene, there was this other Foxe, this croaking magician, a puff of whose breath could lock men into obedience, into slaughter. The spectator Foxe said several times that this other being was a schizoid product, a thing from the inner deeps summoned by the smell of blood, invented after the first batch of deaths to take the guilt and let the ego stand aside, washing and washing its hands.

These doppelganger phases came and went like waves of fever, but even when he was whole for a while he found he still acknowledged a power, locating it now not inside himself but in Quentin. For all the ego might insist that the rat was just a lucky mascot, a comforter for a scared scientist, other parts of Foxe's consciousness continued to believe that he carried a power as real as a magnetic field or an X-ray beam. He teased himself with an image he had barely thought of all the time he was in the Pit, Ladyblossom dead and grinning on his laboratory floor. She had believed in the power, had accepted – had died by it? Foxe also knew that the mind that was thinking these thoughts, the helpless spectator, was no more real than the magician; it too was a construct, a mechanism for attempting to grapple together the centrifugal chunks of his whirling being. The only real thing was the body, walking on whimpering crêpe across oily or gritty stone, tense for the next instant when action would focus all the blurred elements of himself back into a solid-seeming man.

A jut of cliff narrowed the quay and created a wedge of deep shadow in which they could safely halt. Only fifty yards ahead stood the main unloading-shed, with a single ship moored alongside. There was a longish pause, broken by the crackle of maroons and very distant wafts of cheering and chanting, before Manioc came out of the shed. Plantain whistled. Manioc floated across the floodlit quay and into the shadow.

'One fellow on the ship,' he said. 'Sailor I guess. Let him be.'

'Where Mace go?'

'Trying the train-tunnel,' said Manioc.

'OK,' said Plantain, 'Pass round all the weapons – see everybody got a gun.'

The process took a little time, enough for Foxe to become aware of a change of mood among the Khandhars – not the expected surge of purpose as they transformed themselves into a fighting unit, but a slight diminution of that feeling, a hesitancy, as though on the edge of escape they had for the first time accepted the possibility of failure, or as though the touch of individual weapons made them aware of themselves each as a spirit apart, no longer a cell in the single, hive-like will they had seemed while they were in the Pit. One man close to Foxe didn't move.

'Aren't you going to get yourself a gun?' whispered Foxe.

'Not me. Don' know nothing about guns,' muttered Mr Trotter.

'I'm glad you decided to come,' said Foxe, as though welcoming a fastidious guest to a potentially tiresome party.

'Couldn't do nothing different.'

Now came a change, no more than a rustle and a panted whisper on the other side of the group, but somehow to tense senses the sounds had the accent of bad news. Foxe moved towards them, half-conscious of Mr Trotter still at his side.

'Where's Doc?' said Plantain. 'Uh, Mace been up the tunnel, Doc. Big steel doors across the top, shut solid. What do you think?'

Foxe shrugged. You're a rat in a maze and you meet a blank wall, so what do you do? Turn round, go back, look for some other way out.

'There must be somewhere we can climb the cliffs,' he said.

'There ain't,' said someone. Other voices agreed. It was a known fact.

'Could hijack the ship there,' suggested a voice.

'Who know how you drive a bastard like that?'

'Doc O get his planes out, bomb us to scraps.'

Now, even more strongly, Foxe felt that something which had kept the Khandhars together was loosing its hold, that like his own their personality was falling apart, leaving an undisciplined gang of rebels arguing in the dark about a hopeless chance. He closed his eyes and drew a deep breath.

'The engine,' said his other voice. 'Send it up the tunnel. It will be strong enough to get the doors open.'

The Khandhars stood in silence.

'Sure,' said Plantain at last. 'Anybody knowing how to make her go? We been in the Pit all along, Doc.'

Again there was a silence.

'I been running her,' whispered a new voice. Like Foxe's, though to a much lesser extent, it seemed shocked at the sound of itself.

'You?' said Plantain.

'Sure,' said Mr Trotter, more confident now. 'I been stoking her, but I guess I can drive her. She'll have fire up, too, for of being an old bastard when she cold. Somebody got to stoke for me. Yeh, I'll do that for you, Denver.'

This time the silence was of a different sort, almost a chill of social outrage at Mr Trotter using the name which

Plantain had discarded when he was reborn on the mountain. Foxe thought Mr Trotter had said it on purpose, and with a bit of swagger, as though to show his too-dominant cousin that he also was master of something. Plantain snorted a small laugh.

'Thanks,' he said. 'Coffee, you go stoke for him.'

'Wait,' said Foxe in his ordinary voice. 'Captain Angiah told me that you couldn't use the tunnel while the engine was working or you'd suffocate to death.'

'He get it wrong, then,' said Mr Trotter. 'Ain't much room there while the engine going through, but I heard story about a soldier was caught there, and he lay flat on his face against the wall, and all he suffer is a hole burnt in his pants where a spark lit.'

'OK,' said Plantain, in total command once more. 'We go up first, 'cept for a rearguard, lie against the wall, run out when the engine break the doors. Four five soldiers up there, maybe – everybody else at Carnival. Got to come out shooting, for of they'll hear the engine and perhaps be ready for us. Pine, your men stay down behind, case of somebody coming from the palace . . .'

'Engine throw sparks way up,' interrupted Mr Trotter.

'Yeh. How long you take to start her moving?'

'Ten minutes. Uh, bit more 'n that.'

'OK. Let's go. Mace, you got that lamp? You first, then me and Doc.'

Foxe had envisaged their groping their way up the tunnel in solid dark, stumbling on loose rocks with a constant clatter of dropped weapons. In fact three large torches had been looted from the castle, so they could move in light enough to pick out the individual ties that held the triple track in place, and to use them as the awkwardly-spaced steps of a shallow stair. The tunnel was less regular than the one that led to the Pit, with one or two stretches widening into caverns and others so narrow it was difficult to believe the engine had room to pass; its walls and roof were jet black and caked soot that gave off streaks of tarry glitter where the torchlight caught it; the side-rails had the dull shine of worn iron, and the cog-rack between them raised its endless rank of teeth like the spine of a vast lizard. Foxe's heart began to thud with the climb – it might be shallow by the standard of stairs, but it would have been steep on a hill – and his breath came in shorter and deeper gasps until he was genuinely panting. He knew that the Khandhars, still feeble from their long starvation, must be finding it even stiffer than he was, but he seemed to himself to be making more noise than any of them. Again he felt trapped. A picture kept forming in his mind of the burning gases of the volcano rushing through this place, with himself being whirled along, charred but still screaming, in the middle of them.

'Getting near,' whispered Mace.

'Shine your light at me,' said Plantain, and turning he halted his followers with an upstretched arm, like a prophet announcing the doom of cities.

'OK, Mace, I take the lamp. You get back down the line, tell 'em to find place to lay, tight along the wall, tell 'em to cut bits of shirt to tie across their face, against the smoke. Doc, you and me best look at this door.'

Foxe followed him on. The tunnel floor seemed to level out a bit, but otherwise there was no change. It took him several paces to see that the blackness before them, the wall of dark they'd followed all the way up the tunnel, was now no longer retreating but had grown solid, was in fact the surface of two soot-encrusted doors which filled the whole arch. Plantain was picking with his knife-tip at the crust.

'Yeh, that be iron,' he whispered. 'Like down at the Pit.'

'These ones are hinged,' said Foxe. 'That's something. Look, you can see there's a sort of rail to take the weight. Sliding doors would have been tougher. Still, I wonder if that engine's strong enough – it's pretty elderly.'

'You tell us she do OK,' said Plantain.

'Of course it won't be pulling any trucks,' said Foxe, determined not to take any responsibility for the magician inside him. 'It'll have power to spare.'

'Hark at that,' said Plantain suddenly. 'She started.'

Foxe had heard nothing, but at the next instant an enormously deep soft sound, like a giant throat being tactfully cleared, soughed up the tunnel, followed almost at once by a movement of sooty air that seemed to pad against the closed doors and fall back. The next throat-clearing reached them just as the air-puff died.

'She be in the tunnel,' said Plantain. 'Got to find us a place to lie.'

'Not right up here,' said Foxe. 'In case the boiler bursts or something.'

'Sure,' said Plantain, uninterested.

Twenty yards down, the tunnel was lined on each side as if with a neat row of corpses, head to toe, looking as though they had been stacked there for some purpose to do with the mechanics of the railway. There seemed to be no gaps on either side.

'I won't be much use up here,' said Foxe. 'I haven't got a gun. I'll go down to the back.'

'Might need you here,' said Plantain, not with any sternness at what seemed to Foxe to be his obvious cowardice, but more as stating a practical fact. Sulkily Foxe knelt and settled, straining away from the rails. In his memory the engine seemed to work with many flailing parts projecting beyond its carriage. The floor was a tacky mess of tar and oil, much the sort of mixture that is painted onto the shaved backs of rats in cancer tests. He tied his handkerchief across his face and eased his body up against the wall, trying to make sure that Quentin, who seemed to have gone to sleep, wasn't under any pressure.

The engine took an age to come. Each gasp of its progress was indistinguishable from the last, but the tone and duration of the pulses changed imperceptibly, building up the grudging rhythm of approach, menacing and mindless, so that suddenly he was back in the skin of childhood, enduring the old nightmare of hiding from the steamroller driven by the two brass dragons, crouched in an apparently safe cranny, and yet the passing monster stops, the dragons climb down and with echoing footsteps come straight towards the place . . . Under his left breast Foxe felt a stir and struggle like the palpitations of an external heart, hoicking him back into now. Evidently in the memory of nightmare he had been straining against the rock in a way which had trapped Quentin's paw or tail: he eased his shoulder up, put his hand into his pocket and gently lifted the rat out.

'Sorry, mate,' he mumbled through the handkerchief, teasing the fur behind the ear with his thumb. 'Where'll you be comfortable? You won't be able to breathe out here. Try right inside. Make yourself at home.'

He could feel that Quentin was jittery, feel too the slight easing of nerves as the rat slid under his collar, hesitated and began to rove around, sniffing the mixture of Foxe-smell and Louis-smell, as if looking for the extra nipple which witches carry in order to feed their familiars. Foxe had a large mole under his left armpit – Margaret used to say that she'd use it to identify him by when his dismembered body was found in packages in a Railway Left Luggage Office.

The engine was nearer now, the huff and puff of its cylinders filling the tunnel with more and yet more noise, none of it unbearably loud but covering an increasing width of the sound-band as secondary grunts and clanks added themselves to the implacable main pulse. Now he could smell, though the air was still just breathable, the sour, fat reek of cheap coal, partially combusted. As the engine came on Foxe's belief in its ability to break the doors dwindled away. It had never been *his* belief, for God's sake – just something he'd blurted out in shock which these peasants had taken for gospel because he'd said it in a funny voice. He tried to shake the fear out of his mind by imagining Margaret giggling at the idea of his having a familiar and a spare nipple, but then he was thinking about Lisa-Anna. If she learned what he'd done . . . all she was likely to learn, if anything, was that he'd died in a railway accident in a tunnel, honoured guest of the government, forty other casualties all local citizens (small sighs of relief round the rest of the world). No chance, ever, that she'd know about his leading an escape, nearly making it, and the engine blowing up when it hit the doors and becoming derailed and slithering back down the slope, all askew, smearing bodies against the rock as it went.

How long? How long? There was a new noise in the tunnel which he'd accepted as mechanical until the first hot, smut-bearing wave of smoke rolled over him and he knew that it was the convulsion of choking lungs. Stupidly he twisted his neck, hoping to see the orange glow of fire through the pother, but at once had to screw his eyes tight and hope to weep away the smuts under his eyelids. His own lungs heaved and gasped, building an explosion of coughing, quite unmasterable. He forced his lips shut between each bout of choking, sucking the needed air through his nostrils. His whole will focused on this effort, sometimes successful, sometimes not. The gases, air no longer, became hotter. The racket was the universe, frontierless, filling flesh and brain, tunnel and rock. In a little clearing of sense he saw that the guard Mr Trotter had talked about – the one who'd got his trousers burnt – had been caught when the tunnel was open at both ends, so that the heated air and gases from the engine would rush up the tunnel as if it were a factory chimney, dragging clean air behind it. But now the tunnel was closed and the gases had nowhere to go . . . the top end was the worst . . .

He twisted again, and felt rather than heard or saw that the engine was almost on him and there was no chance of creeping back down the line of Khandhars. He cringed into the rock, still convulsed with choking but now willing his flesh away from the slow-grinding wheels and the flail of shafts and rods and the jetted leaks of superheated steam. A spark landed on the back of his neck and stung like a hornet, but the terror of the blind monster pounding past blanketed out the involuntary twitch of pain. He could feel the rock jar each time a tooth of the engine's driving cog engaged its mate in the rack and transferred the contraption's whole weight another six inches. His mind dipped into blankness and out again, almost at once, because the wheels were still groaning past. He knew if he stayed where he was he'd be dead, but still he lay through two more spasms of choking, then flung out his left arm gropingly behind him. His knuckles rapped into greasy riveted metal, moving, moving away, gone. He rolled to his buttocks, feeling for the rail he was going to follow as he crawled down.

As he knelt the swirl of gases in the blocked tunnel changed their nature. They became a blast, a long gust moving all one way, up, out. Out. No kind of intelligence told him that the tunnel was no longer blocked – his body knew and was standing, stumbling up the track after the engine. He fell almost at once, bashing his right thigh against the cog-rack, but rose and staggered on. The engine couldn't have reached the doors . . . someone had opened them . . . the guards had heard the noise or seen smoke pouring from the cracks . . .

The movement of air changed, lost is onrush, swirled loosely up. A man was coughing and swearing on the left. Foxe flung himself that way, was only prevented from falling again by the open leaf of the doors, groped along it, choking all the way, and stumbled round the end, falling against the man who was standing there and beginning to push the door shut.

The man swore at him. Foxe fell to the ground with the pent and useless breath in his lungs bursting out of his mouth, and his chest heaving retchingly for more, and finding air. He opened his eyes and through the haze of weeping saw a man standing over him, black against the town-glow of the night sky.

'What in hell you doing?' shouted the man. 'You all drunk?'

The tone of voice was not that of a man talking to an enemy, or even a suspect, but the exasperated note of a responsible soldier to a feckless comrade. Of course – Louis' uniform. And a face blackened with smoke and

201

contorted with choking. Foxe might be anybody. He rose swayingly to his feet, his vision clearing, and saw the guard half-wreathed in a swirl of the smoke that was still pouring from the tunnel and streaming skyward. The nearest lamp was some way off along the tracks, but gave light enough for Foxe to be aware at once of the guard's posture beginning to change, of his arm reaching for the gun that had been slung from his shoulder while he heaved at the door.

Foxe was unarmed, and Quentin was out of reach in the slack of shirt at the small of his back. Helplessly he raised his left hand, cupped, fingers pointing at the guard, and as the safety catch clicked he blew. The puff ended in a cough. It was as though Foxe had had a bullet in his throat and had shot it out across his pointing fingers. The guard seemed to jerk back at the sound, then slowly crumpled to his knees. Foxe picked his gun from his hands, drew a breath and lurched into the smoke.

He met the other guard in the middle of it, chest to chest, but Foxe was heavier and moving faster so they both fell over the cog-rack with Foxe on top and the man shouting with surprise, losing all his breath, and gasping in a lungful of the smoke. Foxe managed to hold on to some of the air in his lungs and didn't need to draw a fresh breath until he had picked himself up, staggered clear of the smoke and turned, with the gun still in his hands. In front of him a swirl of smoke solidified and became the second guard, convulsed with choking but at the same time reaching for his gun. Without conscious decision Foxe pointed his own gun and pressed the trigger. The barrel jerked and threshed and the guard, as if connected to it by puppet strings, jerked and threshed too for an instant before collapsing back into the smoke. Foxe stopped pressing the trigger.

The bubble of clamour that had enclosed him while his gun was firing seemed to burst, letting in other noises again. The engine was still churning away between lit unloading platforms. Several men were yelling up there.

A gun began to fire – at Foxe, presumably – so he pointed his gun in that direction and pressed the trigger again. Five or six shots came out of it, and then no more. Empty? Jammed? Foxe shrugged, dropped the gun and sat down on the ground. He saw a man jump out of the engine and scuttle across a platform. Another gun started up, very close. Foxe looked round and saw someone lying on the ground and firing along the line of the tracks. Now people were running out of the tunnel through the thinning smoke, some of them shooting as they ran. It looked dangerous, and Foxe guessed that he ought to lie down too, but he stayed where he was, watching the scene ahead.

In the distance a rocket spangled the sky with green and pink spots, and beneath it the engine was still churning away, though it seemed to have halted. Its puffs had lost rhythm and were interrupted by erratic thuds and crashes, and some of its insect-like rods seemed to be flailing at random now. A tremendous jet of sparks shot up in its smoke, making the whole column glow like a roman candle in a fog. Now the machine seemed to be trying to free itself by jumping about. Its left wheels rose clear of the track, settled with a crash and rose again. There was a slow, wumping explosion. Large pieces of metal floated twirling up into the dark above the lamps. The whole contraption keeled over onto its side and stayed there, silent now, steaming and smoking.

Foxe watched it for a few seconds, and then as if in sympathy keeled over too, with a fresh burst of gunfire clattering beside him. As he dropped into the quiet dark he was thinking that they'd never be able to find spares for a contraption like that.

The Mountain

1

Four days later Foxe sat on the branch of a fallen tree in the rain-forest. The slope of the ancient volcanic crater was here so steep that the tree's fall had made a sort of window in the leaf-cover, and for once it was possible to let the eyes focus on something other than the shadowy maze of tree-trunks and rediscover real distance. What matter that all the eyes found in that distance was the tops of other trees, a shapeless spread of gigantic broccoli tops? It was better than the claustrophobic shadows.

Foxe had brought Quentin here to explore what might be an interesting source of edibilia under the rotting bark. Quentin showed no interest in it at all and was crouched on the stub of a broken branch grooming obsessively at the haunch which had been soaked in Louis' blood. To Foxe the place now looked speckless but the smell of it still seemed to worry Quentin.

Just as obsessively Foxe's mind kept tracking and re-tracking through images of the escape. Some deaths haunted, while others didn't. The man Robbie in the hut outside the Pit, for instance, whose gaze Foxe had held while Plantain came and stuck a knife between his ribs – the change in that man's eyes Foxe saw again and again. But the image of the man in the mess-room, sprawling to the floor while blood pumped from his neck – that didn't come unless Foxe summoned it. It was less strong, even, than the image of the naked sergeant, haunches on the table, puffing at his cigar while he gathered energy for a fresh bout of rape; and Foxe hadn't even seen that man die. He might have caused the death, but it hadn't happened until the cook had set the other prisoners free.

Then there was little doubt of what they would have done . . .

Foxe knew that this secondary escape had happened because some of these other prisoners had come up the tunnel while Foxe and the Khandhars were still at the top, recovering from their ordeal – those who had survived it. Foxe himself seemed to have been the only one of the leading party to have stayed conscious while the engine went past, no doubt because he was far fitter than the others, and but for him the doors would have been shut again before Pine and his rearguard, following up behind the retreating smoke, had reached them. But Pine had heard his gun fire and had come charging through, and the rearguard had driven off or killed the guards at the railhead. Then they had dragged the rest of their comrades out and tried to revive them.

Foxe had recovered from his faint during this process. As the Khandhars came to, however faint or feeble they were, they pressed out the perimeter of their bridge-head, moved off on patrol, or helped with the rescue. Six of them never came to.

There was no counter-attack. The night was full of bangs and yells, but they all seemed fairly distant, part of the happy uproar of Carnival. No doubt from there the noises at the rail-head had sounded much the same – a few soldiers firing a celebratory fusillade, and letting off an extra-large cracker. Foxe was recovering – feeling restless, even – by the time the patrols came back with transport; two lame donkeys and one sound one, and five decrepit bikes. Some time after midnight they all moved off.

Foxe had been resting in a narrow alley when he heard the next real explosion. All round him, mostly darkened, stood the familiar patched and improvised shanties he had known in Back Town, and the night air had the same stink of stagnant water and excrement and spiced cooking and generalised sweet rots. Ahead and behind the straggle of Khandhars also rested, but Foxe needed the halt more than most because he had volunteered to wheel one of the bikes with a body strapped to it. He was further from collapse than most of the others, and he felt that if he was pushing a bike he couldn't be expected to shoot any more men, but it was a vile form of hearse, needing to be wheeled at a tilt with its bony saddle resting against his hip, which meant that its wheels tried to slither sideways whenever they crossed one of the slimy trickles which veined the shanty area. So he was standing panting in the shadows when he heard four deep bangs that rattled the tin roofs all around and juddered the earth itself. As the last explosion died the hum of aeroplane engines spread gently through the night; no doubt they had been there before, but drowned by the racket of carnival which the bangs now stilled. Four similar explosions, further away, shook the night. A plane roared its engines and came swooping over the roofs, firing a long burst of tracer into the town. Beneath and around these noises Foxe heard people screaming.

'Bombing the road out of town,' said someone.

'But they're bombing the town, not the road,' said Foxe.

'Sure. Can't see the road, and they got to bomb somebody.'

That was another image which continually re-made itself inside Foxe's skull. What was specially horrible was that the planes – there seemed to be two of them – had come nowhere near the Khandhars, but had dropped four more sticks of bombs at random and then spent ten minutes circling around, swooping occasionally to loose off their guns, before droning away. The screaming continued for some time, following the Khandhars into the night as they wound up a steep hill track between rustling groves. They must have managed about another three miles before Plantain let them collapse in the banana plantation.

Drugged with shock and exhaustion Foxe had slept without dreams. They had been woken, groaning, still in the dark, breakfasted on bananas and travelled on, Foxe still obstinately wheeling his corpse-laden bike. Still there seemed to be no pursuit, and they had managed several more miles before the sun rose to show them well away from any kind of cultivation, crossing a sloping plateau of shale and brownish scrub and spiring cactus-like plants. The place had looked to Foxe as though it had been blasted long ago by some appalling spillage of poison which a few weird and unpleasing plants had adapted to endure, perhaps even feeding on the deadly leavings of the accident. There was no real path across this waste, but shelves of the underlying rock jutted through the scree and made for smooth walking, sometimes for several hundred yards at a time, though between shelves Foxe had to lug his bike along, twisting, thorny tracks to reach another stretch of easy going.

They had been crossing this tract for more than a hour when Ginger came back along the file at a weary lope.

'Plantain say to come, Doc. Gimme this bike.'

Foxe had nodded and jogged forward, to find the front of the column halted and Plantain staring ahead.

'Couple women coming, Doc. Better they not know how they seen us. OK?'

'I suppose so,' Foxe had sighed. 'Does it work with women?'

'Why not?' Plantain had said, obviously amused.

'Better you don't come asking Cocoa that kinda joke,' someone had said.

It was amazing how relaxed, even happy, they seemed, despite their losses and exhaustion. Foxe as he walked on ahead felt very different; he seemed to be in the process of being withdrawn, both internally and externally, from any existence he understood, no longer either the observer or the magician of the night before, but somebody quite new, a blank character, waiting to be engraved. *I was reborn on the Mountain.* Suddenly, when the two bright blobs of red and yellow in the distance had acquired the shape of humans walking towards him, Foxe remembered the gardener who had killed the snake outside his laboratory window. He remembered his own feelings at the scene, slightly amused, rather contemptuous, wholly detached. Now he, Foxe, had more in common with that gardener than he had with the man who had watched from behind the doubled glass.

As the women came nearer Foxe had put his hand into his shirt and withdrawn Quentin, who, after a bout of nocturnal fidgets, had been dozing peacefully against Foxe's skin and seemed displeased to greet the morning. The women were close enough now for Foxe to see that they were watching him with some suspicion, and he remembered that he was still wearing uniform, but must otherwise look as though he'd spent the night in a burning building. He smiled and called 'Good morning.' They stood and watched him with their heads tilted a little away – Mother and daughter, plump, dark brown, pocked, unsmiling.

Foxe strolled on, waiting till he was within four feet of them before he spoke again.

'Look at me,' he whispered, holding Quentin up in cupped hands before him. Their faces changed. Perhaps for a moment they thought he was about to make some kind of sexual display; then they looked with sudden amusement at Quentin himself, until they saw the symbol on his back; finally their cheek-muscles stiffened and their glances rose to Foxe's. He blew very gently across the ruffling fur, almost as though he were trying to administer the precise minimum dose of the intangible drug, first at the mother, then at the daughter. The drug took hold at once.

'Turn away from the path,' he said. 'Look at the sky. Hear nothing. See nothing.'

Round they swung, docile cattle. He waved his arm and waited by them while the slow file came along the rock; hooves clopped, bikes rattled, tired lungs grunted and sighed, but nobody said a word to Foxe and nobody met his eye, as if wary of the power latent there. Uncomfortably he swung away and stared in the same direction as the women until the last of the file came limping past; then he

211

turned his captives along the track and told them to wake and walk on without looking back. He stood and watched while their movements eased out of stiffness into the natural buoyant gait of a people used to carrying loads but walking for the moment free. The thought came to him that he would like to have sent a blessing after them, if he'd known how.

No more of that, he thought as he padded to catch up. Not even to save my life. The hindmost man was recognisable from far off, tall and stooped and wearing the rags of a mauve shirt. He carried no weapon, but trailed a branch behind him.

'Still with us?' said Foxe, suddenly cheerful at the sight of him.

'Nowhere to go,' muttered Mr Trotter.

'What's the branch for?'

'Dogs. Bloodhounds. They smell this, they go the other way.'

A month ago Foxe would have wondered whether this was magic or fact. Now the question seemed irrelevant, and in any case Mr Trotter suddenly left him, darting up the scree and tearing a handful of tendrils from a flat-creeping plant that grew there. He handled his find with a piece of rag bound round his palm, and the next time the file wound its way through the scrub between one stretch of rock and the next he spent some minutes weaving these tendrils across the entrance. He studied the effect, made a couple of adjustments to achieve a more natural look, and left it.

'And what's that?' said Foxe.

'Fire-gourd, Colocinthis Urens. Hurts real bad to touch. When it green you can pick it how I do, but when it wither those poison-hairs go hard, burn you through your jacket and pants.'

Mr Trotter spoke with the confidence, the near-arrogance of the expert doing his thing. He seemed less tired than the others and as he loped to catch them up his head quested from side to side for specimens of vegetative ammunition against pursuit.

'Why have they left us alone?' said Foxe. 'We've been going very slowly. I've hardly even seen an aeroplane.'

'Hunting us over toward the Mountain, Denver said.'

'I thought that was where we were going.'

'Look like he taking us west along the ridge.'

He darted off the track to scrape with his bare hands round the root of a twisting, purplish succulent. Foxe left him to it, remembering that somebody even more tired than he was must be struggling ahead with the lurching, corpse-hung bike.

The episode with the two women was the only scene from Foxe's adventures that actually cheered him when it rose in his mind's eye. It came often and always with the same sharpness, unlike, for instance, the apparently more impressive business of burying the dead Khandhars. They had done this that night, in the first fringes of the rain forest that covered the whole ridge of mountain twisting in an irregular S across Main Island. (The Mountain itself — Mount Trotter on maps, but never called by that name – was only the highest of several peaks, thirty miles away south east.) At dusk they dug a row of graves in the soft mould of century-rotted leaves. All night the seven bodies lay in these open graves while watch and watch about the Khandhars knelt beside them and whispered their chant. Two thunderstorms broke in the night, but the Khandhars had made their cemetery under a species of tree with large overlapping leaves which acted like roof-tiles, shedding almost all the rain that fell on them in drumming streams twenty feet from the trunk. At dawn, all chanting together, the Khandhars had tossed earth handful by handful on to their dead friends, then trampled the mounds flat and scattered the spare earth around. A patrol which Foxe had not seen depart returned, carrying in their caps what he took to be more earth, but turned out to be the crawling hearts of four ants' nests, which they placed in holes

213

scooped at the corners of the grave-row and covered with mounds of leaves. The chant quickened, and in a few beats rose to a cracking shout. Then silence. Without a word the Khandhars collected their possessions and went on their way.

They had marched for two more days, crossing two harsh ridges between which lay a strange, wide marsh, dry on the surface but full of patches which were hot to the touch, and whose whole surface quivered with an inner vibration. There was a surprising amount to eat, mostly a cassava-like root which was poisonous raw but became edible after several boilings; also grey-and-brown grubs the size of a man's thumb which lived under rotted bark and tasted like prawns; some savourless bracket fungi; and, once, a drift of incredibly tough-shelled nuts about the size of plums. At last they reached a series of caves that pocked a low cliff which was the inner side of the rim of this dead volcano. The Khandhars seemed to know the place well.

Here there was nothing for Foxe to do. He was like the male of some colonising insect which, in the ritual dance of that one night's violence, had fulfilled its biological role and was thenceforth a drone, tolerated, fed, ignored. Another likeness which troubled him was that of human childbirth, with the Pit as the womb and himself as the seed, penetrating to that inner depth and fertilising the Khandhar egg, causing it to break out in bloody parturition. The idea revolted him but he couldn't keep his mind off it, continually finding fresh details – the smother before the final outburst, the weakness immediately after, his own sense of being re-born.

His solitariness was increased by his refusal to take part in Khandhar rituals, or to have any further truck with their magical practices. These ceremonies occupied most of the time not spent in gathering food from the forest and preparing it for eating, and to the Khandhars seemed as necessary a part of life as breathing. There was little conversation or discussion. If Captain Angiah was right and they were Marxists as well as being magicians, they were unlike any brand Foxe had ever met. In some moods he might even have welcomed the tedium of Marxist indoctrination as a change from the endless chants and dances. Mercifully they didn't try to draw him into those, but left him alone, free to wander endlessly through the mirror-maze of his own self-disgust.

He shifted his seat on the branch, making Quentin twitch into alertness at the movement before returning to his endless grooming.

'Smell of blood still in the fur?' said a voice, so hesitant that Foxe knew it was Cactus before he looked round. She was already filling out towards her natural fatness; most of the starvation-wrinkles had gone, and she looked younger and less troubled than she had in the Pit. She wore a dead man's uniform, much too large for her, with the trouser-ends rolled up to her knees. Her feet were bare.

'I don't know,' said Foxe. 'It may be a real smell, or it may be the memory of a smell, imprinted on his brain, and he'll go on trying to get rid of it as long as he lives.'

She sat down on a branch on the other side of the trunk, one knee drawn up under her chin, looking at Quentin. She had a sack for collecting food, but it seemed to be empty; and the Khandhars usually did their gathering in small groups. Telepathy, thought Foxe. Suppose there were anything in it . . . an image right outside her experience . . .

Deliberately he concentrated on the little cuckoo-clock in Lisa-Anna's room, which would sometimes slip a cog so that the hands whirled round and the bird flew hysterically in and out, striking anything up to a hundred and fifty. Lisa-Anna said it was always a good omen when this happened, and would sit on the edge of her bed with her brown eyes glistening and her fingers over her small mouth as if to hide her smile of pleasure, while she counted the strikes . . .

'Your honey so far,' said Cactus.

'How did you know? Oh, never mind. Did you see anything else?'

Cactus shrugged.

'What her name?'

'Lisa-Anna. She's a singer. An opera singer. Black hair. Brown eyes. Small. Clever. Very serious.'

'Why you leave her, then?'

'She left me. She went off to join a company in Denmark. She isn't a star, but if someone in the chorus has to sing a bit of solo she usually gets that sort of part. Really she didn't leave me just to go and sing; she wanted to get away. I didn't care enough about anything, she thought. She told me that without my work I would be one of the walking dead.'

It seemed easier to tell her than let her unreel threads from the spindle. She looked at him, frowning, but said nothing.

'Perhaps she was right,' said Foxe. 'I haven't got any work. I'm empty.'

'You eat the salt with us.'

'What does that mean?'

'This farmer, he a rich man, he has the power. One night he go to the cemetery where three men just new buried, and he make all the sacrifice and he say all the words, and these three they come out of their graves. So he take them to his farm, working for him, no money, feed like the animals. And his wife one day when he away been making these little cakes and she see these dead men, don' know who they are, feel sorry at them working so hard, give them all a cake. And salt in these cakes. Just soon when they taste this salt, these men remember who they be, remember they be dead. They rush from out that house, tear down that fence, they be so strong. And everybody see them rushing like that do stand out of the path, for fright of tearing to bits, they be so strong. Rush, rush, down that hill, across that forest all back to the cemetery. They dig with their hands, make new those old graves, lie down, go back to death.'

'Do you think it's true?'

'You have eat the salt. In the Pit, in those needles, that is salt.'

'Some of it, certainly – saline solution, at least. You were in that group. But half of you got a stuff called SG 19 – I don't think that does anything to you either. I got a mixture.'

'All salt.'

'Anyway, it doesn't stop me feeling like one of the walking dead!' snapped Foxe. 'The things I've seen and heard – the things I've done myself. I don't want to be myself any more! I don't even want to be human!'

She nodded slowly.

'You need talk with that Lisa-Anna,' she said.

'No good. She doesn't want me. Anyway she's probably got another bloke by now . . .'

He stopped and considered. This was a question his subconscious had always censored. Perhaps she hadn't – Lisa-Anna was not at all promiscuous. She had taken a long time, almost like an old-fashioned courtship, to accept Foxe as her lover. She had shown no resentment of his previous girls, had in fact enjoyed talking about them and had sometimes suggested aspects of their natures that Foxe himself had never noticed. But she herself wanted a relationship which could take root . . . perhaps, Foxe now realised, this was why the courtship had taken so long – Lisa-Anna had doubted whether he was capable of such a relationship. Rightly, too.

'Besides,' he said, 'it's pie in the sky. I don't see how I'm ever going to get off the Islands. I was arrested as a witness to a murder, and now I've done one myself. Several. If I show up in any of the ports . . .'

'Plantain get you a boat. Not just now.'

'Will he? Even then . . . I wonder if they could have me deported back here . . . The Company won't take me back . . . Anyway, Doctor O's quite capable of sending agents after me . . . I'll have to change my name, start from the beginning again . . . I don't even know if I want to do

217

any of that any more . . . I've got nothing to do. Nothing to be. I'm empty.'

'You re-born then.'

'I don't believe any of that! Here!'

Foxe leaned forward and snatched Quentin from his perch. The rat kicked with shock, but Foxe paid no attention, twisting and reaching over towards the girl.

'You hold him,' he ordered. 'He's only a rat. That mark on his back is only the letter Q. That's all. Everything else is rubbish.'

She had flinched from his gesture and anger, but now she held out her hands, palms cupped into a nest. He dropped the rat in.

'Your name is Lucilla Banker,' he said.

She stayed looking down at Quentin, who remained for some seconds in the awkward pose into which he had fallen. His coat was staring a little with fright at his rough treatment. Then his whiskers twitched as he investigated her wrist, and with a sleek flowing movement he darted along her left forearm, stopping to inspect the crook of her elbow with his head cocked, as though he were a well-known connoisseur of elbows who had been asked to pronounce on this specimen. Her right hand drifted across to caress his fur.

'He's all right,' said Foxe, ashamed at having taken his unhappiness out on her in this way. 'He's a bit of a nutter, but he won't hurt you.'

'You wanting a woman? Then you feel better?'

Both sentences were clearly questions, though spoken in a flat, almost bored voice, quite unlike the soft and stumbling tones in which she announced her insights into other people's minds. Foxe shrugged.

'Me?' she said, still caressing Quentin's fur as he slid towards her shoulder.

'I don't know what I want. In any case it's not a very practical idea, is it? I mean, you're such a puritanical lot. The last thing I want is to start any more trouble. What would Plantain say?'

'He say OK. He say we go away from here, live in a village, and he take the others up the Mountain.'

'Do you mean he has said this, or he will say this when you ask him?'

She shrugged.

He stared at her for some time, but she didn't look up. She had come out here to find him – that was obvious – and she wasn't going to say whether it was her idea or part of the group will.

'You're running ahead, my dear,' he said at last. 'Listen, I'm in an emotional mess. When I say I don't know what I want I mean just that, but at least I know I'll only make the mess worse if I get into a sexual relationship just for the sake of taking my mind off my own troubles. I'd end up liking myself even less than I do now. If that's possible.'

Quentin was perched on her shoulder now, sniffing at her collar as if wondering whether that was a good place to explore. She took care not to unbalance him as she slid across the trunk and sat down next to Foxe. There were few opportunities for washing in the forest, and no changes of clothes, so her smell was more than noticeable, though rounder and less assertive than the rancid smell of town poor.

'No need to be scared for me,' she whispered. 'I not a virgin no more.'

Foxe knew that. He had heard the tapes of the torture sessions.

'Long past,' she whispered. 'This how we be living in the villages. My Momma fifteen when I be born.'

Talking with her was tricky. Even your silences were answered.

'What will you do if I say no?' said Foxe.

'Plantain don' want me go up the Mountain with him, case of me getting caught again, but he tell me to choose. I think I choose to go with him, till you say to me my name ain't Cactus no more. You call me my old name, so now I think I come and live in the village with you.'

'I certainly agree with Plantain that you oughtn't to go

219

up the Mountain, but you'd be much better living in a village by yourself. I'd be too conspicuous. Somebody'd be bound to tell the police about me.'

She put her small hand on his thigh. He covered it with his own. She was shivering as if with cold.

'Nobody in the villages go talk with the soldiers – all too scared. And plenty poor white trash living there.'

She took her hand from under his and slid it round his waist, twisting her head at last to look into his eyes. He saw now that her shudders were not of cold, or lust, or even shyness, but of real fear – and no wonder after what the soldiers had done with her. She looked as haggard again as she had in the Pit. Her greyish skin was coarse-pored and her features, apart from her eyes, were too small but also too clumsily moulded to seem neat, and her teeth, though very white, were crowded and irregular – she was infinitely different from the fantasy-girl Foxe had created during the fishing-trip with Dreiser – from any man's fantasy-girl anywhere. But Foxe found himself stirred, emotionally and then physically, by the sudden discovery of her goodness. He wondered for a moment whether it was this, rather than her telepathic gifts, that the Khandhars were so anxious to protect. She was not like Lisa-Anna, earnestly navigating the precise path of virtue all the time; this girl knew it by heart and could walk it blindfold. He found that his own arm, unwilled, had balanced the movement of hers and was round her waist, pulling her close. Quentin's nose came twitching out between the lapels of her jacket, and Foxe lifted him clear and put him down on the tree-trunk. He slackened his arm and kissed her accurately on the forehead.

'There's no hurry,' he said. 'We can think it over. You're scared stiff, aren't you?'

She nodded. Tears began to stream down the sides of her small rubbery nose.

'All right,' he whispered. 'Let's leave it. You don't . . .'

'No, no,' she wept. 'Must begin right off. Tomorrow I be more scared.'

She twisted, levering them both off the branch, and pulled him down to the soft, crackling, insect-swarming leafage of the forest floor.

2

Foxe woke, as he often did, and lay listening to the night. Probably the clatter of big tropical rain-drops on to the palm thatch of the hut had broken into his dream. The bed, which Foxe had acquired three days ago by mending two old radios for Mr Barton, was an undulating and rickety antique but far better than the floor; he had no need to resettle pinched limbs and risk disturbing Lou. Quentin was into a bout of nocturnal activity, threshing around in his tin trunk and banging a lump of raw manioc root against its sides. The night air smelt of people, and rain-damped ashes, and cooking-oil, and (more distantly but strangely insistent, like the subliminal presence of the sea that exists for a mile or two inland from any shore-line) the sap of uprushing tropic plants. Lou's steady breathing had the peaceful quality of very faint music.

Suppose, thought Foxe, that somebody had told me six months ago that I'd now be living with a saint – I'd have laughed, of course. But suppose he'd been able to persuade me that it was true. Then I'd have been filled with a cocktail of boredom and fear – fear of moral pressure, of intrusions of alien standards into my hedged inner being – and boredom with the then totally null notion of goodness itself. I was a sort of civilised ignoramus then, a sophisticated know-nothing. It doesn't matter that it isn't going to last.

The impermanence of the present arrangement was essential to Foxe's happiness, in fact. It would have been mistaken to want it to last for ever. He was having a holiday of the soul, a sabbatical – not very honestly earned. He was not in love with Lou – not in the sense in which he now admitted to himself he was still in love with Lisa-Anna – but he certainly loved her. His feeling for her was something like intense love for a particular place – his grandmother's home, for instance, by the ruined castle on the sluggish Pembrokeshire inlet, where as a boy he had had his own dinghy, his own paths along the shore, his own nooks in the gorsey hillside, his own world recreating itself afresh every school holidays. Lou behaved like all the other women in the village outwardly, chattering and laughing as they threshed dirty clothes in the stream or calling from garden to garden as they hoed, but as far as Foxe could see none of the others were saints – he hadn't fallen into a den of noble savages. Some of them were sulky bitches, some wilfully cruel to animal or child, many permanently half drunk, all fairly stupid. Not that Lou herself was by an academic standard bright; her intelligence was to do with human behaviour, and in that field she seemed able to grasp questions of great subtlety and complexity without putting them through any kind of cerebral processing. When they were alone Foxe did most of the talking, explaining more to himself than her, all he had done with his life, all he had thought, all he had so far refused to think. Lou listened and frowned and smiled, and when she said anything it was usually a question, opening out some central relevance which Foxe had missed.

Thus, between them, they had exorcised Foxe's self-horror. That first scene by the fallen tree had begun it, lying half-naked on the mattress of dead leaves and prickling, crackling twiglets, concentrating his whole will into helping her through her physical terror. From that point he had seemed to begin to walk away from the mirror-maze through which he had been wandering, seeing all the time vile images of nothing but himself; and once he was outside the maze he could also see that it must have existed long before the shocks and slaughters of the Pit – it had always been there, waiting inside him for something like that to open the door and draw him in.

As if in response to the memory of the scene in the forest Lou's breathing changed. She began to shiver. He moved his arm to caress her plump arm but she went on shivering.

'It's all right,' he whispered. 'Nothing to worry about.'

'Bad thing be coming,' she said.

'No. You were only dreaming.'

'Bad thing be coming.'

'Sh. Sh. Come here.'

She twisted and clung to him till the shivers died. The starchy diet of the village had fleshed her out until by European standards she was grossly overweight. (She had contrived, early on, to barter one of the monstrous latticeworks of corsetry which the Island women all seemed to think an essential element of respectability, but Foxe refused to let her wear it.) In bed she seemed almost boneless, her skin slightly oily and flesh very yielding. He kissed her eyelids and found she had been crying.

'Love me?' she asked, hopeful as a child.

'I do love you,' said Foxe, 'but I won't make love to you now. It's not safe for another five days.'

She sighed, accepting his decision but nibbling gently at his collar-bone to compensate. Foxe could never decide whether her improvidence over some things – in this case pregnancy – was a facet of her goodness or part of the cultural stupidity she shared with most of the women in the Islands. She had never said so, but she might really believe that she had no right to deny the possibility of life to a child who would otherwise never be born, and that applied whatever kind of world it would be born into. She certainly talked about herself as though there were no negative dimensions on the axes of her life, so that everything that happened to her, even at the hands of the torturers, was somehow plus, compared with the zero of non-existence. Perhaps, Foxe thought, this was part of what it meant to be a saint – but then perhaps it was only possible to be Lou's kind of saint at a fairly primitive level of society. In any more complex world you would have to

224

use Lisa-Anna's method, considering your every footstep as you made it, because each movement created perturbations in the crowded multi-dimension of lives around you. Not that Lisa-Anna was a saint, of course, but . . .

These musings were interrupted in nature's unsophisticated way by the revolt of flesh against the will's decision. Foxe chuckled and rolled on his back.

'Tell me about your dream,' he said.

'Bad thing be coming,' she answered, not shivering now but speaking in the vague tone she used when picking up a strand of thought from another mind. In theory Foxe had suspended judgement about her telepathy, but in practice he accepted it as genuine.

'I was thinking about the time we first made love,' he said, 'You must have got a bit of that into your dream. You were scared stiff, remember?'

'I was stupid,' she said, giggling as she often did in the act of love and putting out a hand to caress his belly.

'Stop that,' he said, grabbing her plump fingers, 'or I shall have to go and sleep on the floor. Tell me about your dream.'

'Didn' dream,' she said. 'Jus' bad thing be coming.'

'When?'

'Don' know.'

'Tonight? Tomorrow?'

'No.'

This happened several times over the next couple of weeks – the same shivering, and waking, and vague prophecy of trouble. Foxe took it seriously enough to listen to the brief, fanciful news bulletins that interspersed the stream of reggae and calypsoes and Caribbeanised rock on Radio Trotter, while he worked on Mr Barton's truck. Mr Barton was the rich man of the village, which meant that his hut had three rooms and a verandah, and he owned the still and also the large shack where the villagers met with those of two neighbouring settlements for dances – those noisy nights half-way between revivalist meeting and beer-hall stomp when the Islanders with drums and rattles and an old wind-up gramophone summoned out of the forest the dangerous protecting spirits, who would select a human body to inhabit while they joined the carouse.

Foxe refused to join these gatherings from a kind of moral horror, clearly traceable to the night of the escape.

'You scared by your own self,' Lou said, unreproving.

'That's right. You go if you want.'

'Not everybody go. Some people be thinking the Secret Ones got spite against them. Some people just not interested to go.'

So they would lie and listen to the racket and Lou would explain which of the inhuman guests had come – she could tell from the rhythm of the dances and the cries of greeting and general texture of the hubbub. An endless shivery tapping of beer-cans meant that Asimbulu, Lord of Thunder, had housed himself in the body of a man who was now dangling by his knees from a rafter and writhing his body like a gross snake; a sharper tinkling and a cooing undertone to the cries meant that Queen Bridget was twirling round the floor, choosing her lovers for the night; or a quick silence, followed by a rush of yelling and laughter, meant that the Sunday Dwarf had appeared (a man on his knees, like a charade of Toulouse Lautrec) and was shuffling about with a rum bottle in one hand, cracking a litany of obscene jokes about everyone in the hut and trying on people's spectacles three pairs at a time. Lou would never make love on nights when the Sunday Dwarf had been in the village, in however benevolent a mood. On the other hand almost their only quarrel – and it wasn't that, more a patch of shared distress – happened when only Queen Bridget came, on a night in the middle of Lou's unsafe period, and Foxe refused to take advantage of what Lou considered a peculiarly blessed chance.

The village accepted Foxe without question, a piece of white trash – probably a criminal wanted in his own country – who didn't mind mending things. There must

226

have been other men around who could have re-wired Mr Barton's truck, but they'd never felt like trying. Most huts in the village contained at least one broken radio, a few of which only needed a connection mended. And there was a metal wind-pump, jammed for the last three years, or possibly four – the expert chroniclers of apathy disagreed – which Foxe had his eye on. Lou wouldn't let him work in the garden.

'You don' wan' draw notice to you,' she said.

Foxe had his own way over at least supervising the cooking, but despite his care had one mild bout of dysentery.

Quentin throve. He slept most of the day, roamed the hut in the evening and allowed himself to be caught and slipped into the safety of the trunk for the night. At first Foxe had chalked out the Q on his back, but soon the colour began to fade, and then there was a moult until only in odd lights did the sign show through. The villagers attributed no special powers to the rat but the children liked to come and bring him an oddment to eat, and fondle him, and let him explore their clothes while they shrilled with half-squeamish giggles.

Time passed. Lou said that Plantain was on the Mountain, and once the radio mentioned an army exercise in that direction. For more than a week Lou had no premonitions of horror.

'Then, one pouring night, Foxe was woken by shudders so fierce that the whole bed creaked and whined. Lou wouldn't respond to his touch, and seemed to be in a trance, or a fit like epilepsy. Foxe rolled her on to her back and craned over her, gently kissing her quivering cheeks and eyelids. At last she woke with a gasp.

'Bad thing be coming,' she muttered. 'Soon, just soon.'

She dropped back at once into deep sleep, and next morning made no reference to the incident.

Next night there was a dance. It began as usual with rattlings and hootings and clinkings, formless until you were used to them and then turning out to be intricately patterned round three particular scratched old records. This would last till the Secret Ones arrived.

'Nobody coming tonight,' said Lou after a while.

It was rare but not unknown for the villagers to fail to work themselves to a pitch of self-hypnosis which let them believe that they were occupied by the spirits. When it happened, though, they accepted it, resolving themselves into a cheerful song-and-gossip session for a few hours, and then going home with no apparent sense of let-down. Tonight, when Foxe was waiting for them to pack in the summoning ritual, silence fell sharp and sudden. A voice like the creaking of a cricket spoke, too far off for Foxe to hear any words.

'What's up?' he asked.

'Sh.'

Lou pulled him close to her and lay still, shivering. Whatever was happening at the dance-hut lasted less than a minute. The creaky voice stopped. In the silence, far off, one of the night-birds of the forest made its slow clacking rattle, and before that sound had ended the mutterings of talk began, ordinary human voices, speaking a little above a whisper.

'Gone,' sighed Lou, relaxing.

'Who?'

'Sunday Dwarf. Didn' come for the dancing, come for the telling.'

'What's happening now?'

'Everybody going home.'

Most dances ended with a special dwindling uproar, as the visitors from the other villages gathered themselves into drunken convoys and trekked for home, some singing, some trying to complete arguments with the other groups. Tonight they assembled as quietly as a patrol or a raiding party, and in no time were gone along the night-smelling paths. The home village continued its muted buzz, partly still discussion but partly the beginnings of some new activity.

'Is this normal?' said Foxe.

'Never hear it like this. Perhaps he tell a death.'

Lou lay still for a moment, then twisted herself out of bed and began to dress. Foxe lay listening to the rustle and slither of cotton – slip, petticoat, dress, headscarf – no question, even if King Kong had been stomping through the village, of going out in less than that. Her shape blocked the doorway – two or three lights were moving around outside – and was gone. A child had woken somewhere, or been woken, and was crying. The sense of crisis was like fever, a meaningless, pulsing, dry-mouthed tension. Even Quentin was still.

'Dwarf tell everybody must go,' whispered Lou from the doorway.

'What do you mean?'

'He tell two deaths. Two deaths, coming in the morning, just front of the dance-house. Better nobody stay in the village, he say.'

'Oh, nonsense!'

'No, honey – these two deaths – he say a man and a woman – a man and a woman got the power!'

She was gasping the words out rather than whispering, and suddenly Foxe grasped that she was in a stupor of fright. He swung himself off the bed, crossed to the door and put his arms round her. She was shuddering, as she had been in her fit the night before.

'That you, honey,' she sobbed. 'Nobody else here got the power.'

'I haven't either,' said Foxe angrily.

'Get dress. Get dress.'

Foxe let go of her, shrugged and groped for his clothes. If she hadn't been in such a state he would have insisted on their going back to bed. Two people, he thought. Who does she imagine the other one is? Herself, of course. But it was for Foxe that she was shuddering. He tugged at the zip of his trousers, scuffled into his jacket and without thought opened the trunk to take Quentin – no question of leaving him behind. The sleek fur tingled in his hand as he stood in the dark, almost as if he were trying to guess the rat's weight. He sighed, slipped Quentin into his jacket pocket and sat back on the edge of the bed.

'I'm not coming,' he said.

'Oh, honey!'

'I can't. I genuinely believe that this is nonsense. It's real for you but it's nonsense for me. I can't give in to nonsense, even for your sake, darling. These things only work for people who believe they work. I don't.'

He heard her let out a slow breath, a sigh for good times gone and horror come again. Outside the sounds of the village had become the pad and rattle of departure. Cotton rustled as Lou untied her headscarf.

'No,' he said. 'You must go. It isn't nonsense for you, so it might work. But if there's only me here there won't be any women in the village so it can't come true. See? I'll be all right, darling.'

She said nothing. He rose and crossed the hard mud floor to her, turning her gently round so that he could re-knot the headscarf behind her neck. He left his hand on her shoulder while they watched the shadowy groups of villagers, some hunched into nightmare shapes by their bundles, crossing the moonlit strip beyond the door.

'Look, there's Marie-Sainte,' he said. 'She needs somebody to carry Paulie for her. You go with her. Listen, darling, I'll leave a signal for you. Don't let them come back unless there's that blue blanket hanging on the dance-house railing. OK? Off you go.'

He had to give her a slight shove to start her moving.

'Bye, honey,' she whispered, drifting away with a slow inhuman motion, like a ship parting from a quay. He watched her join the group behind which Marie Sainte hobbled, trailing her swollen leg. The shadows altered shape as Lou lifted Paulie to her hip, and then they all vanished together into the blackness under the trees.

Foxe scuffed off his plimsolls and lay on the bed, thinking of the soldier who had run for his gun in the mess-hall of the castle. That man had known it was nonsense too, but he had died all the same.

He woke in daylight. The dawn clatter of parakeets was at its loudest, and the shaggy rectangle of the door was filled with the usual silvery light which looked like mist and wasn't. He was wide awake at once, without a moment's bafflement at his having slept in his clothes, or Lou's absence, or Quentin nosing round the hollow where she had lain with his inquisitive but slightly cynical air, as if he thought Foxe had been a fool to hope to keep her.

Foxe was aware that something had woken him from deep sleep, but apart from the parakeets the village seemed silent. Moving carefully to minimise the clangour of the bed-springs he twisted to his feet and went to the doorway. All was still. He hesitated, full of the silly fear which a child feels who cannot cross a landing on his way to bed because of the shadow of the wardrobe – something meaningless to anyone but that child and real for him. Quentin scuttled on the bed and at the same time Foxe remembered he was barefooted, so he went back for his plimsolls, picked the rat up and slid him into his jacket pocket. This time he strode straight out of the door, as if taking a run at it. The village was empty except for a battered old cat, black as tar, walking along the path with the rigid stalk of a hunter, though Foxe could see no prey. He decided to do one patrol of the huts and if everything was OK eat breakfast and then go and make a start on the wind-pump. He had almost reached the dance-house when Mrs Trotter came out.

She seemed to materialise rather than emerge. At one moment the verandah was empty and the next she was standing, a gaudy slab in a turquoise trouser-suit, at the top of the three steps that led to it. Her glasses glittered, reflecting twice over roofs and treetops and a slice of dawn sky. This was the first time Foxe had seen her silent, but the miracle didn't last.

'You, man, white man,' she called. 'Where everybody gone, then?'

Foxe mimed ignorance, ducking his head away and

cursing himself for not wearing his heavy-brimmed noon hat.

'Foxy!' she cried. 'Hi, Foxy! I come all this way just for seeing you. Ain't you happy?'

'Good morning, ma'am. I hope you're well.'

'Never ill, Foxy. Never ill.'

Foxe stood and stared at her, wholly baffled that she should be here, apparently alone, having, she said, come to look for him.

'Ain't you going to ask me how's my son, the President?' she cooed. Now he could detect a tone of mocking, of toying with him. Perhaps it was she who had somehow sent the Sunday Dwarf to the dance-house, to clear the village of all but him. But how could she know he would stay?

'I hope his Excellency is well,' he said.

'Fine, just fine. Eating his food, bowels going like a factory, only his foot begin to swell a little. What do I give him for that, eh?'

'A mustard plaster?' suggested Foxe.

She nodded and started to rummage through her reticule as if looking for the ingredients then and there. The silence stretched out.

'How did you know I was here?' said Foxe.

She stopped rummaging, and though her head was still bent above the bag he guessed that she was peering at him behind the screening lenses.

'Soldiers,' she said. 'Up towards the Mountain, hunting those stupid Khandhars, they find this fellow hiding in the bushes, pockets full of weeds. They know he been with the Khandhars, like you, Foxy, and they ask him a few questions, don' get to hurt him much before he tells them you here.'

'Was it Mr Trotter?'

'One of those stupid Trodders.'

'He's a very good herbalist. You ought to consult him about your son.'

Her head jerked up, a slight gesture of surprise, as

232

though he'd departed from the script of the dialogue she'd arranged; but she converted the movement to one of decision, of ending the small-talk and getting down to business. She moved to the bottom step of the verandah and pushed her glasses up onto her forehead.

'Come here, Foxy,' she said. 'Come closer.'

He walked towards her until they were less than a yard apart. Although she was standing on the step her face was still lower than his. Her tiny, gleaming eyes stared at him, surrounded by wrinkles so elaborately infolded that the eyes themselves seemed to be set in a special musculature capable of withdrawing them deep inside her skull or projecting them inches beyond her cheeks.

'They saying you got the power, Foxy,' she crooned.

Foxe shrugged, then decided that that was too indefinite a response.

'They say wrong, ma'am,' he said.

'They saying you put your soul through the locks of doors, and you send it round the baddlements, blowing death in the soldiers' faces.'

'Nonsense.'

'Don' you say nonsense at me, Foxy. I got the power. I know all these things. Perhaps you got a little power. But I got a lot. And now I going to have some more, cause of taking your power, Foxy. I put your soul in a little old beer-bottle and keep it on my shelf.'

She leaned slightly forward as she spoke. Her voice, already deep, had become a guttural croak, and her accent had shifted so far into the Island dialect that Foxe wouldn't have understood what she was saying if he hadn't spent the last weeks living with villagers. He started back at her, shocked by his own dislike. Just as he had loved Lou for her goodness, so he hated Mrs Trotter for her badness – not for what she had done to other people, for what she might do to him, but for what she was. Six months ago he would have asserted his civilised invulnerability with a smile or a show of polite interest. Now he watched her fully seriously, waiting for whatever might happen next.

233

They stood like this for at least a minute, face to face and silent. Her lips began to move, muttering breathy invocations; her face changed several times, a series of masks rather than expressions, all unreadable; Foxe faintly sensed a sort of moral energy beaming out of her, aimed at him but making no impact. Suddenly, along with the hatred, an extraordinary freshet of pity seemed to spurt inside him, pity for her, for her power-lust, for her cruelty. His own lips moved involuntarily.

'All that's over now,' he said gently.

At the sound of his voice she stopped muttering and her own face came back to her. Without taking her eyes from his she stepped down to ground-level and he began to move out of her way.

What happened next seemed at the time to be a single convulsion of activity, but he later discovered it to be two quite separate events. Mrs Trotter took her right hand out of her reticule, swung and punched him just above the hip. At the same time she began to dance.

The dance lasted for less than half a step. The swing of her arm seemed to start it and the leap of her body to carry it on, and then it was over and she was falling while the stream of bullets battered into her.

Foxe turned quite slowly to the source of the noise, raising his hands above his head when he saw that the man coming round the corner of the verandah with his gun levelled was Captain Angiah.

Out of the Maze

1

'Happy to see you, Doctor Foxe,' said the Captain with no trace of irony.

'Why . . .?' whispered Foxe, lowering his arms.

The Captain walked past him and stared down at the body.

'One shot woulda been plenty, I guess,' he said, as if ashamed at the extravagance of a whole magazine. But Foxe remembered the stories of Rasputin's death – it was only natural to feel that Mrs Trotter might need more than one bullet.

'Now come this way, please,' said the Captain, like a guide about to conduct his party to the next sight of historical interest. He led Foxe between the huts and down the forest track to where a spick-and-span jeep waited under a timber-tree; he went to its rear, picked up the handset of a transceiver and spoke in a rapid mutter.

'Baby. Baby. Baby. Do you hear me? Over . . . Yeh, but the old chicken's cooked already. Over . . . Sure it's too soon, but she was making to kill the little pig. Over . . . Well, I guess all you can do is hurry along the rest of the dinner. Over . . . Sure. Over and out.'

Foxe listened bewildered while the forest flickered and chirruped round him. Suddenly he was aware of a struggle beginning inside his jacket pocket, as though Quentin, who had either slept or cowered through the whole of these encounters, was now overcome with claustrophobia. When Foxe looked down he saw the faded khaki jerking and twitching, and in the centre of the convulsions a dark spike like a large thorn – it must have been just about where Mrs Trotter had struck him. Alarmed, he eased the

237

thorn free with his right hand and with his left lifted
Quentin from the pocket. The moment his fingers touched
fur he knew that something was badly wrong. There was
a speck of blood on the left shoulder and that paw hung
limp, but the other muscles were unnaturally taut, and
spasms of contraction rippled along them.

'Will you get in please?'

The Captain seemed jittery, and paid no attention to
the fact that Foxe was holding a rat in one hand and a
dart-like thorn in the other; he made a gesture of impatience with his gun, so Foxe climbed into the passenger
seat and was instantly roared back to the centre of the
village. The Captain cut the motor and leaped out.

'You'll have to help here,' he said, bending down by
Mrs Trotter's shoulders and dragging her towards the back
of the jeep. Foxe climbed out, gently settled Quentin and
the thorn on the tramped earth and went round.

'That's not how,' said the Captain. 'Grab her at the
knees . . . Yeh. Up! One, two, three . . . OK, thanks,
doctor.'

'Something's wrong with my rat. I wonder . . .'

The Captain frowned, but before he could speak the
radio gabbled a quacking call-sign. He leaned across the
bloody sprawl of the body and snatched the handset.

'Baby. I hear you. Over.'

As he listened to the quack his expression cleared to
one of strange pleasure. Like the gardener who had killed
the snake his excitement broke out into movement. The
fingers of his free hand snapped as if in rhythm to the
gabble. At last he said, 'Great, that's just great. Yeh, sure,
I'll fetch him along.' He put the handset down and turned
grinning to Foxe with his hand held out to shake.

'Congratulations. Doctor. Now we better be getting
along to town.'

'If you say so. But first please come and look at my rat.'

They moved round the jeep and stood gazing down at
the path, where Quentin was crawling round in circles on

238

his three good legs with his back arched high and his fur staring.

'What's into him?' asked the Captain. 'Something bit him?'

Foxe bent and picked up the thorn.

'Mrs Trotter tried to stick this into me,' he said. 'The rat was in that pocket and she got him instead.'

'Jesus! That must be snake-apple!'

'Uh?'

'I saw her take a swing at you, but I thought I got her before she touched you. Jesus! If she got it into you!'

'Yes, she was off balance already. But what about my rat?'

'Dead. I don't know about rats, but if a man gets stuck with a snake-apple dart, he goes walking round a bit, grinning and walking, but already he's dead. Perhaps he knows where he's going, but he can't stop grinning long enough to tell anybody. Then he drops dead.'

'How long?'

'Ten minutes. Half hour. Varies.'

'I see . . . would you be kind enough to shoot my rat?'

'Sure.'

Foxe turned and walked towards the hut where he had lived with Quentin and Lou. At his third pace a gun made its single sharp note but he didn't falter in his stride. By the time he came back with the blue blanket the Captain was sitting in the driver's seat. Quentin's body was lying motionless on the path. Its head had disappeared completely. Foxe lifted it by the tail and laid it beside Mrs Trotter, then hung the blanket over the rail of the dance-house and climbed into the jeep. The engine growled. They bucketed away.

Two people, thought Foxe. A man and a woman got the power. Mrs Trotter, yes. Quentin? He shook his head, deliberately refusing to adopt a logical attitude to the Sunday Dwarf's prophecy either for or against. It was perfectly possible that Mrs Trotter had arranged for that

239

to happen, intending Lou and Foxe as the victims, and had simply mismanaged things.

'Are you alone?' he asked.

'Sure.'

'Just you and Mrs Trotter? Couldn't you have sent someone? Or brought an escort?'

'Everybody else is too scared to come, Doctor. There's been a lot of crappy stories floating round about what you did in the Castle. But Mrs Trotter, she's not afraid of anybody, and it suits me to bring her up here alone, because my colleagues are scared to begin if she's going to be in the room. They think perhaps she'll smell something.'

The appalling track dipped to a muddy corner, almost a hair-pin. The Captain's sudden bonhomie closed into an ecstasy of concentration as the jeep lurched and slithered under liana-hung branches, with its wheels spewing earth into the rattling leafage. Foxe waited till a simpler stretch let him relax a little.

'You brought her up here to kill her?'

'I guess so. Yeh. I've been telling myself a long time one day I'm going to kill her – long before I joined the Revolution. But I thought perhaps you'd be easier to handle if she helps me to find you first. The Revolution needs you, Doctor.'

Foxe sat silent, not very interested in any of that. His mind was full of Cactus, and what she would feel about Quentin's death. He could see a change coming, heralded by a colonnade of glaring gaps between the shadowed trunks. The track headed for the largest arch. It was like coming out of a cave, out of a primal world, out of Nature's green womb, into the shock of sunlight. By the time Foxe unscrewed his eyes the Captain had his foot well down on the accelerator and the jeep was humming and jolting along a real road, drearily straight and pocked with pot-holes, between a plantation of leprous-looking grapefruit trees and a patchwork of abandoned smallholdings.

With the shock came a change in Foxe's own mind. He had been thinking about Cactus and Quentin with a sad but quiet acceptance, and then between one jolt and the next he seemed to move into a harsh-lit stage, a stage on which he must soon act. The pieces of his world exploded and reshaped themselves, much as they had when he had hooked the skin-diver in Fall Bay. Quentin was only one of the thousands of rats which had died under Foxe's care – and many of those thousands he had killed with his own hands, because he had thought it necessary. He had killed men too, though only one with his own hands, and those deaths now seemed to him as necessary as the deaths of the rats. But there was one death, Ladyblossom, the human Ladyblossom, which had been wholly unnecessary, and now it filled his mind. Facts floated into place and locked there, building an inevitable skeleton. Misty guesses solidified into flesh.

'Is the Prime Minister dead, then?' he asked.

'Yeh. And the President. And three of the Trotter Ministers. They're having a family breakfast, and two of my colleagues dress up like they're waiters, and they get their guns in on a trolley and shoot the lot of them dead.'

'I see. I'm glad it wasn't a bomb. Why does the Revolution need me? Are you going to put me on trial?'

The Captain's head swung round to stare at Foxe, but before he could speak there was a rush of noise, clatter and boom and yelling. Foxe, who had been sitting half sideways, was hurled against the dash, bruising his arm and ribs. He was convinced they had hit something, but they still seemed to be travelling, travelling with hopeless speed towards a mass that towered above them, full of shouting faces, the back of a lorry crowded with workers, shouting with alarm or laughter. It must have swung out of a sideway in the Captain's moment of inattention. He was braking, but the jeep was still rushing in under the tailboard . . . all this in one of those slowed instants, and then the tailboard and the faces seemed to slither away sideways and were gone and the jeep was bouncing over a rough timber bridge into a canefield. The final slither of braking was prolonged by Mrs Trotter's body trundling forwards and nudging the back of Foxe's seat.

Captain Angiah let his breath out but said nothing as he reversed, swung and headed for the bridge; but once there he stopped and sat looking, not at the lorry which was dwindling into dusty distance down the next straight beyond the curve, but at the black and stinking sludge that half-filled the ditch between the road and the canefield. After a while he nodded and reversed the jeep along its tracks until it was again hidden by the tall and whispering canes.

He cut the engine and turned to Foxe. His nostrils as much as his eyes seemed to weigh Foxe up. When he spoke Foxe had half-expected him to revert to the detached, precise English he had used on Hóg's Cay, had used too to supervise the torture of Cactus. (In a way she had been lucky, Foxe realised – almost anyone else on the Islands would have been more receptive of the notion that she had her odd talent.) But he continued to use his version of the Island dialect, nothing like Ladyblossom's slurred singsong, but still somehow claiming kinship with her.

'Yeh, I've been in too much of a rush,' he said. 'You don' know what's been happening, an' we don' know what you're going to say when you get home.'

'Home?'

'Sure. Provided you say the right things.'

'I don't suppose anybody will ask me.'

'That jus' shows you don' know what's been happening. You know the USA got itself a new President this year?'

'Carter? Yes. Of course.'

'You know he started in at once showing the world he's got clean hands, won' have dealings with governments running oppressive regimes?'

'Yes, I remember about that. That was all happening just about when I came to Hog's Cay. It's not the sort of thing I take much interest in, but wasn't there something about South American countries breaking off diplomatic relations because he wouldn't sell them any more arms?'

242

'Sure. Some of them played it angry, some of them came into line. Listen, even the Duvaliers up in Haiti, they started letting a few fellows out of prison – that's what they said. Only guess who's too dumb to see the point? No, he ain't ever dumb . . . but mad. Just mad.'

'He wanted to make people good,' muttered Foxe.

'Yeh. That's bad.'

'You really think so?'

The Captain's impassive mask flickered with surprise at Foxe's tone. He thought for a couple of seconds, then smiled.

'I guess so . . . but it don't concern us any more . . . You were asking what has President Carter and all that to do with you, uh? Listen, when you're running a country like this one, it don't matter much what you do to your own people – it's just a few more niggers in prison. But you mess round with foreigners – educated white foreigners – and you get a lot of questions asked. First off, Doctor O says you're his guest and too busy to talk to people. Then he says you've been captured by communist guerrillas and they're holding you for a hostage . . .'

'I see. The revolution happened now because Doctor Trotter was forcing the Americans to cut off aid, and you want me to tell people that he was a madman and ran an unspeakable regime, but that the leaders of the revolution are honest people doing the best they can for their country, and your letting me go proves it. Then with luck the dollars will start to flow again. That right?'

Captain Angiah looked at him sideways under half-hooded lids. Foxe became aware of how well the ranked canes hid them from the road, and how deep and concealing the mud in the ditch was – no problem hiding a weighted body there. Of course Mrs Trotter's body would be needed to put on show in Independence Square, to prove that she was irrecoverably dead . . .

'What are you going to do about the Khandhars?' he said.

'What are you going to say about them?' asked Captain Angiah.

'You want me to say they're communists, and you need American weapons to fight them?'

'That kind of thing.'

Foxe shook his head, conscious of the Captain watching him.

'They're not any kind of Marxist,' he said.

Some small animal dived with a faint plop into the invisible ditch. The silence seemed to sharpen his other senses, making the sour-sweet reek of the black mud almost overpoweringly insistent.

'I'll do a deal with you,' he said.

'Not much time.'

'Yes, but listen – the Khandhars aren't Marxists, and I'd have thought you'd get just as much milage out of the Carter administration by saying they were a bunch of religious cranks who'd been persecuted by Doctor Trotter.'

'Yeh?'

'I think so. It has the advantage of being true, so you don't have to keep changing the story. Supposing anyone asks me, I propose to tell the truth, but I'm prepared to negotiate about emphasis. In any case, I'd play my own part right down, all of it. But for instance, I'll say I was forced to listen to torture tapes, but I won't say I recognised your voice on any of them. I'll say I was forced to experiment on the prisoners, but I won't make anything of you conducting the negotiations. This isn't just because I'm making a deal, it's because I know Doctor Trotter's style. He cornered me into doing these things, and I expect he cornered you too.'

The Captain grunted uninterpretably.

'OK, the deal's about something else. If you lay off the Khandhars – and by the way you also lay off the village where I've been staying – I'll tell you two things which you need to know. One which you need to know personally, and one which might make a bit of difference to the revolution.'

'You tell me, and then I'll see about making promises.'

'Um. I'll go half way. I'll tell you what it's about. Two related things. Who killed Ladyblossom, and how to stop my Company pulling out of the Islands.'

'Who killed who?'

'Ladyblossom. The woman who was killed in my lab. The caretaker's wife at the laboratories. You must remember – you were holding me as a witness.'

'Yeh? Yeh, I remember – snake-apple. Doesn't matter now, that, compared with the revolution. File closed.'

'It's quite important, and it ties in with the other thing. I suppose that matters.'

'Sure.'

'Is it a deal, then? Mind you, I can't tell you how to make certain the Company won't pull out, but they're planning to go, and I can give you some leverage which might prevent them.'

Captain Angiah sat flicking the steering-wheel with a long forefinger. Foxe wondered whether to push his luck and try and set Mr Trotter as director of a small herbalist hospital. Later, perhaps.

'If we don't go after the Khandhars, what line will they take?' said the Captain suddenly.

'I don't know. All I want is for you to try and negotiate with them. You've got quite a lot in common, I think.'

'With those crazy magicians?'

'You aren't going to be able to abolish any of that sort of thing just by making laws – it's got very deep roots. You told me you'd shot a man for letting a witch get close enough to blow on her palm at him, but that didn't stop any of the soldiers believing in magic, did it? There was only one man in the castle that night who wasn't a believer. If you want to change this country you're going to have to work along with that sort of thing. And at least the Khandhars are honest and serious.'

'Their top fellow's another Trotter.'

245

'Can't be helped. Well?'

'OK – provided I can swing it with the Council.'

'Good. Well, the main reason that my Company came here in the first place was for a combination of tax reasons and security, and the main reason they want to leave is that security has broken down. They think Doctor Trotter was entirely to blame; he started it, certainly, and got hold of documents which allowed him to blackmail the Company to some extent; so naturally when some of our rivals started getting hold of secrets too the Company assumed he was to blame; but in fact the chap who's been selling the secrets is the lab Director, Doctor Dreiser. He also killed Ladyblossom.'

'Crap. He was home with his mother all the time after you come in from your fishing. We have his house bugged.'

'Yes, but . . . hold on – do you remember if he said anything to his Mother about my plans?'

'Sure. That was why we dropped on you so sudden. I was happy when Doctor O started messing you around, because I saw it was going to help the revolution. I brought you in on my own initiative, cause of that.'

'Yes. Doctor Trotter told me that I'd come to Main Island sooner than he'd intended. Mrs Trotter meant to be there to meet me. But the point I wanted to make is that Dreiser knows his house is bugged, so his easiest way of telling you I was making a run for it was to tell his mother.'

'Sure, but I keep telling you he wasn't at the laboratory to kill this woman.'

'He didn't have to be. He didn't mean to kill her. It was just a booby trap. He had three safes in his office, and he wasn't happy about their security, so he'd fixed extra gadgets to them. He showed me one which squirted purple dye over you if you tried to open it without throwing a secret switch, and my guess is he'd fixed one of the others to shoot a dart at anyone who tampered with it.'

'Where'd he get snake-apple? It's not that common?'

'It didn't come from you?'

'Course not.'

'At first I thought it must have, and you'd killed Ladyblossom to have an excuse for arresting me, and you'd used the stuff because I'd accidentally started to get a reputation as a witch. But if it didn't happen like that, it's one of the strongest points against Dreiser. I believe snake-apple plants are heavily guarded these days, but Doctor Trotter told me he'd asked the laboratory to investigate it, and Mrs Trotter said the poison lasts for ages. So there would have been some in the laboratories at some point, and Dreiser would almost certainly have hung onto it – it's exactly his sort of thing. I haven't worked out the details yet – it was the way my rat died that put me onto it. Now the next point is was Ladyblossom working for you?'

'No. Our man there is . . . Forget it.'

'It doesn't matter. She was working for somebody. She had a son in the army called Sonny who she was very fond of, and she hinted she'd been telling him things about my work. And the Khandhars knew about me, and what Professor Galdi was working on from a guard called Sonny. It must have been the same man. Hang on – they said something once about a man at the laboratories who kept all the secrets . . . Anyway, Ladyblossom had been through my papers thoroughly enough to find out which rats were performing specially well. But then I'm afraid I persuaded her that I was a powerful witch, and because of that I think she decided to stop spying on me and started on Dreiser. She found the safes behind the big picture and tried to open one and got shot with the snake-apple dart. She was a very intense believer in magic, and I once told her that Quentin had what she called "the power", because it seemed to be the only way to stop her tampering with the performance of my rats. I think after she felt the dart she was still conscious enough to go up to my lab and get him out of his cage, because she thought that he was the only hope. And that's how she died there.'

'Could be,' said Captain Angiah irritably. 'No way you can prove it and what's it going to do for the revolution?'

'Knowing who killed her, not much. But what's in that safe, do you think? The other safe – the one Dreiser showed me for top security documents – that was only guarded with a harmless dye. What would he keep in one which was guarded with a poison dart? Money, I think, and documents which proved it was he who'd been selling the Company secrets. One of the things he arranged on that fishing trip was to make certain that copies of my report got through to Doctor Trotter. I had to arrive at the airport in time for that. You know, I don't think he's been doing this simply for the cash – I think he felt he wasn't going to be able to leave here until the Company decided to pull out, because until then he'd never be able to persuade his mother to go. So for the past three years he's been systematically trying to incriminate Doctor Trotter in the Company's eyes, and he'd succeeded so well that the Company's been getting ready to go by having completely useless work done here. Now, if I'm right, and if you can get to that safe before Dreiser does, you're going to be able to go to the Company and persuade them that the security-leak has been an internal Company matter. As I say, this won't necessarily make them stay, but it will remove their main reason for pulling out, and there are quite good reasons why they should want to keep a foothold in the Islands. You can offer them whatever advantages are worth your while. My guess is you can get them to hang on long enough to see how the revolution's going to work out. That's all.'

The Captain continued to flick obsessively at the wheel. Foxe sat beside him and listened to the sound, and the whispers of the canefield, and smelt the stink of the ditch. The world had indeed changed since he had left the forest; there it had been dreamlike and magical, only living in the middle of the dream and the magic he had accepted them as ordinary. Now that he was confronted with the real ordinariness of the shabby, negotiating, compromising

248

world he could recognise the strangeness of the dream. He had been on a voyage and was now returning to the place where he belonged, but returning changed. There was no question of retaining any longer the slightest wisp or scent of Lou's goodness and in any case that had no leverage here. Here one had to negotiate and compromise, and accept that the best one could do was only best in the sense that it was less bad than other possibilities.

'I left something out,' he said. 'If I'm right you'll look after Dreiser's mother, won't you?'

'Too late.'

'Rubbish. What better way is there of proving that your revolution is run by civilised and reliable people than by being as considerate as you can to someone in her position?'

'You think so?'

'Yes. And don't forget I've got a lot of emphasis to play with when I tell my story.'

The Captain grunted, started the engine and drove forward between the slashing canes to the bridge. They bounced over timber slats to the road.

'Hang on a moment will you?' said Foxe.

The Captain hesitated, but braked about twenty yards further on and halted alongside the stinking ditch. Foxe climbed out and picked up a stone about the size of his fist, then leaned into the back of the jeep to look for a bit of rag. There was nothing.

'Mind if I nick this?' he said, plucking at the turquoise chiffon scarf that enwrapped Mrs Trotter's thick neck.

'It's yours,' said the Captain, puzzled but affable.

Foxe eased the scarf free and spread it out. There was a little drying blood in one corner. He laid Quentin's body in the middle with the stone beside it, then knotted the scarf by its corners into a tight bundle round the two objects. Without ceremony he tossed the bundle into the ditch and only watched it long enough to make sure it would sink in the black slime.

2

The press conference went very easily. The questions asked were not those which might have forced Foxe to choose between lying and breaking the alliance, but if they had come up he would have told the lie. Yes, he had effectively been kidnapped by the deposed regime. Yes, he had certainly heard hard evidence that the regime had systematically tortured its political opponents. Yes, almost indiscriminate torture. And the break-out? Well, he'd done his best to help, but it wasn't the sort of activity he'd been trained in, and it was difficult to remember much about it because he'd been scared out of his wits. No, no plans to write a book about his experiences. Voodoo? You're thinking of Haiti, but of course there are some vaguely similar beliefs in the Islands – for instance the death-spirit it is called the Sunday Dwarf, which must have some connection with Barón Samedi . . . No, he'd never seen anything you could call an orgy – look, he wasn't an anthropologist, and he'd only been on the Islands a few months. All he could say was that he'd met people who believed strongly enough in that sort of thing to behave as if it worked, even when they themselves were the victims . . . Yes, the Khandhars had been very considerate – in fact it was only when he returned to civilisation that he discovered he was supposed to have been their hostage. No, he had seen and heard nothing to suggest they were Communists; to the best of his knowledge they were primarily a religious sect who were the victims of a personal vendetta by the late Prime Minister, and were not tools of the Kremlin or Dr Castro or even the CIA . . . (*laughter*). And so on and so on.

Water off a duck's back. Foxe felt wholly in control of the occasion. He kept his voice level and subdued, but clear, and felt the tension steadily dropping. Not much of a story here, no real hardship or adventures, no titillatingly unspeakable tortures, except of Islanders. Dull. Dull. Dull. File a few pars, just to tidy the story up, then on to the Chilean death-camps, perhaps, or cannibalism on a stranded weather-station, or a rediscovered species of parrot in a Papuan valley, or bribery in . . .

'You ran that very neatly,' said the young man at Foxe's elbow as the meeting broke up. He wore a pale grey business suit and a quiet tie, and had come to Foxe's room that morning, finding his way as if by magic through the security ring. His official status in the Company was a string of vague general nouns, but his job was trouble-shooting. His name was Hans.

'Anything to avoid a fuss,' said Foxe.

'Exactly. Care for a drink? There's a quiet little bar along here . . .'

The Arab tent and the stuffed camel had gone to join the igloo and the polar bear. Now Mount Fuji covered the far wall and the big black girl behind the bar wore a kimono. Hans ordered pineapple-juice and Foxe Island beer.

'Well, cheers,' said Hans. 'Pity about Dreiser.'

'What happened?'

'Killed himself. Rigged up a most curious apparatus to do it with.'

'I hadn't heard.'

'Why should you? The Revolutionary Council are happy to keep it quiet and so is the Company. He had been selling Company secrets for months.'

'Only months?'

'Nearer two years, actually.'

Foxe nodded. Just after the kidnapping of his mother, of course. He hadn't wanted the money. He hadn't intended to kill Ladyblossom. The whole thing had been

251

a Dreiserism, an intricate method of escape, a monstrous mechanism, all flailing levers and jets of loose steam, to force his mother to go by forcing the Company to go . . .

'Is the Company still planning to pull out?' Foxe asked.

'Too early to say. My guess is they'll give these new people a whirl – they seem very co-operative. You looking for a job here? I'd have thought . . .'

'No – I was just curious. Um . . . Do you happen to know – at one point Doctor Trotter got the Company to ship out some stuff called SG19, which he wanted me to do some tests on . . .'

Hans's all-boys-together laugh cut the sentence short.

'That was in my briefing,' he said. 'I don't know whether you realised it, but by that stage we weren't giving the Doctor a blind thing if we could help it. I'm afraid we wasted your time there. That was just salt, dressed up.'

Foxe nodded again. All salt, Lou had said. He had eaten salt.

'You don't happen to know if the Danish papers have been taking any interest in my adventure?' he said.

'No idea. It's not one of the languages I speak. Denmark, I should think so – fairly pinkish kind of press there.'

Foxe sucked at the sour-clean beer and thought. He didn't know the address, but the opera-house should find her. Telegram? Arriving Flight something stop. Please leave message airport stop. Would like to talk to you stop. Seriously stop?

No, a letter would be fairer, simply saying what had happened, asking for nothing, expecting nothing. But hoping.